Rain, Rain Go Away

<u>Michael Richardson</u>

For Justin

Prologue

2972 AD – New Zion, The Citadel.

Coming down the stairs from the theatre house, Henry stumbled slightly. In celebration of the play's twenty-fifth performance, an outdoor patio and bar were set up on the street. Perhaps it was the glass of wine he had while discussing the play he had just attended with a small group of friends, including Sarah, or maybe it was the second glass he had only half finished. More likely, the stumble was from his nerves getting the better of him, nerves from his desire to tell Sarah how he truly felt, and his hope beyond hope to be with her, someday, maybe today.

Sarah was his co-worker and a fellow educator. She taught English at the same school where Henry held esteem. Being the drama teacher, he was quite a gifted thespian. He had played many roles, finding fantasy always favourable to reality, particularly when fantasizing about Sarah.

Many things were favourable over reality in this day and age. The human race has been on quite a tumultuous path over the past thousand years, give or take. Henry often fixated on history and the plight of humans; acting was in his blood, but history was his passion. He let his mind wander briefly while the others commented on the play, focusing on how he planned to express his feelings for Sarah when they walked home together.

Since the Industrial Revolution, mankind has found even better ways to kill each other. War has remained the cornerstone throughout history, and technological advancement, very little has changed.

Upon reflection on that thought, Henry had to admit one major change in their physiology. It seemed to become most notable a century ago, before the last world war. It appears this one had finally succeeded at being the war to end all wars, mostly because there were almost no people left to fight again. The death toll had been in the billions.

The population had swollen to twenty billion, despite having food synthesizers and other technologies that provided people with all the basic human needs. It proved to be not enough for most people. The war, however, was not fought by countries; those who had antiquated notions disappeared a few hundred years earlier. For a brief time, the world stood united under a single world government. Soon, however, two major factions formed. They started as a movement, then were touted as religions. It was discovered that belonging to one faction or another was not a conscious decision, but rather a genetic one. The distinction between the two groups was as clear as dark and light, left and right, good and evil.

The vast majority of people seemed to be drawn to the darkness and were bent on the destruction of mankind. The few that resisted lived to be honorable, noble, or at least to do the right thing for the right reasons, whatever they were. Those who followed the darkness became more and more radicalized until they launched all-out war on the rest of the world. They even developed and deployed microwave-based weapons, orbiting the planet. One dark day, they had been turned on. People were vaporized where they stood, animal and plant life, until there was almost no shelter from the invisible, deadly storm.

The worst part was that the cities, previously home to millions of people, stood fully intact, but devoid of all signs of life. After the war, the surviving humans faced the new terror posed by the savages. The human gnome had been splintered; those who embraced evil were mutated, their skin turning grey, their teeth more like fangs, and their nails were like claws. They became nearly mindless creatures, attacking out of the need for food or out of boredom. If there were no people around to slaughter, they would even fight amongst themselves, often to the death. They bred like rats, and the females, once old enough, would almost always be pregnant, producing more of the brood, as many as possible, before dying.

The remaining people who followed the light were more akin to humans of the past in appearance, but they were fundamentally different in other ways that mattered. Incapable of performing any evil, violence, stealing, or even cursing something, they could no longer have the thought of committing such an act. It would be enough to cause them to be physically ill and lose consciousness.

They had been forced to construct several massive walled cities to protect themselves, but the walls turned out to be more of a prison. No one dared leave the protection of the Citadel, or the savages would surely have them.

They were free to farm and fornicate, which seemed to be the two most popular pursuits of the people within the great cities. At least the pleasures of the flesh were available to them. It had become almost a necessity. They needed to maintain their numbers. The only way to do that was to procreate.

Defenses were bolstered in the cities, thanks to technology. Auto cannons were placed atop the walls of the different cities. The robots were to police and maintain peace. It didn't stop a deadly virus from wiping out two massive city-states in Mongolia and Australasia. Fortunately, the separation of the Citadel had stopped the spread, but only Europe, Africa, and North America maintained the human population. The suspicion was that the savages had seeded the virus within the affected Citadels, and it was only a matter of time until they found a way into New Zion.

It had taken Henry several seconds to return to the present moment from his musings, only now, realizing Jack had asked him a question to which everyone awaited his answer.

"Sorry – this wine has gone right to my head, I think," he replied, knowing it was a lie but hoping to maintain his social graces.

He did not want to admit that he hadn't been paying attention. The conversation bored him, and he only wanted to start on the walk home. He thought about stealing away with Sarah.

"Well, did you find it was an accurate portrayal?" Jack insisted.

"Of course," Henry answered wryly, prompting Jack and the others to cluck on like the mindless chickens he took them for. Henry stared at Sarah, undressing her with his eyes. He let his imagination run wild.

***   ***   ***

Eventually, the conversation wound down, and the socialites soon saw others they had to talk to about the play. The group dissipated, much to Henry's relief. He and Sarah were left to themselves. He realized she had been standing next to him, her arm resting on his. Her touch was invigorating, and her closeness bolstered his hopes for the walk home.

In his mind, he would profess his love for her as they headed to the park across the street from the theatre. They would kiss and finish walking through the park to Sarah's home, which stood at the opposite end of the park. After, Sarah would invite him in for an evening of carnal pleasure, everything from slow and romantic lovemaking to vigorous and aggressive freaky sex. Sex was, after all, his (and many others) favorite pastime.

Slowly, they strolled arm and arm across the quiet street into the growing shadows of dusk and the shade of the trees in the park. It was a warm and beautiful summer evening. The distant city walls were barely visible, except for the flashing beacons that slowly strobed red. The Citadel was enormous, taking up a good portion of the former state of California.

A prison, perhaps, but truth be told, it was not noticeable, particularly on a night like this. They were in the cultural center of New Zion, a district known for its theatres and museums. Motor vehicles may not have been forbidden here, but it was a rare sight. The evening air carried a faint smell of wildflowers growing in the park and a level of peace that was almost hard to believe. Everything was perfect.

Henry stopped in front of a bench near the pond. They would sit and watch the end of the glorious sunset as it dropped behind the wall, which could just be seen protruding over the horizon.

"Sarah, I wanted," Henry began.

"Hey guys, why'd you take off? Weren't we having fun?" It was Jack, sounding far more inebriated than Henry thought when they left the party only a few minutes ago.

"We just wanted to.. Ah, watch the sunset," Henry replied, deciding not to let it slip that he was hoping for some alone time with the girl of his dreams.

"Oh – what? You guys just gonna fuck here on the bench," Jack yelled, eliciting a response from Henry.

"Now, hold on a minute," Henry insisted and sprang to his feet in protest.

Undeterred by Henry, Jack stumbled closer, stopping as he was nearly eye-to-eye with the drama teacher.

"Or what?" Jack taunted, slurring still.

Henry was too upset to notice, or he would have taken Sarah and fled. He stood his ground, not seeing in the low lighting a slight change in the pigmentation of Jack's skin. The color left the iris of his eyes, leaving only dark, menacing pools.

"I will have you charged, that's what." He stepped back from Jack, looking around. "Where are the patrol bots? There's supposed to be one in this park at all times in case of drowning in the pond," he prattled on nervously. "Oh – there's one – Security!" he yelled, then turned back smugly to face Jack, but the sight that awaited him chilled his blood. The fear took hold when Sarah screamed, dropping her handbag to the ground and covering her cheeks with her hands as the horrific sight unfolded before her.

If they managed to push past the physical discomfort from wanting to commit an evil act, they would be consumed by it. The humans gained a nickname because of this fact, a name they gave themselves. In informal settings, people referred to themselves and their population as "Tickers." Each of them was like a ticking time bomb, just waiting for the right stimulus to go off, and when they did, the damage was unmistakable.

Jack had fully transformed, and he was now no longer human. He was a Savage, the final curse to mankind.

"Security," was all Henry managed to say before the creature tore his throat out, watching with something of a grin as the blood sprayed in all directions and Henry dropped to his knees.

His last thoughts were a mixture of disbelief and disappointment. Why couldn't this happen after he had had Sarah? He slowly slumped to the ground, dead. A pool of blood slowly grew on the ground, spreading out and quickly surrounding Jack's shoes.

The creature slowly turned from Henry's lifeless body, its talons still dripping with Henry's blood. It made eye contact with Sarah and bared its jagged fangs in what might have been a smile. Sarah screamed again, this time attracting the attention of the security droid. Its sensors detect the savage and move at the best speed toward Sarah. Only one thing was certain: it would not reach her in time.

Chapter I

It was so dark in his room that there was no discernible difference between having his eyes open or closed. The only tell was that he was awake was the cold sweat, and his heart was pounding in his chest. His subconscious buried the memory of his dream away faster than he could recall any relevant details. The more he tried, the less sense it seemed to make. Something of a shooting, an explosion, and images of friends he'd never known. It felt like he was reaching for something that was always out of reach.

A glint of light caught his eye from the far side of the room; a reflection he assumed came from his sword. The weapon hung on a rack, directly across from the end of his bed. It was his most prized possession and most useful tool. What concerned him was what had caused the glint of light he had just seen, until after several uncounted seconds that passed in the dark felt more like an eternity, he heard a faint, distant rumble of thunder. Almost at the same time, a dark figure appeared at his door; his eyes were still adjusting to the darkness, and he hadn't noticed.

"Storm coming," The older man said in his grave voice. He confirmed what Quick already knew.

"Yeah," the younger man acknowledged with a grunt. He swung his legs over the side of the bed and silently slipped to the doorway, but not before grabbing his sword. Tonight, the blade would be a valuable tool.

"I'll check it out." Quick had said it more to himself than anything, and without waiting for the old man's response, he dashed to the window and slipped outside, slinging his sheathed sword over his back as he moved. From the second-floor sill, he leaped straight out, catching the peak joist that protruded from the roof, and pulled himself up and over in what was quite a feat of strength and acrobatics, to perch on the top of the house.

The farm was positioned as far away from any city as it could be. For safety, there was no lighting at night, so as not to draw any attention to the fact that anyone lived there. The land was clear and flat, other than the curvature of the Earth. They could see for miles in any direction. The wild grasslands at the edge of their property blended seamlessly with the fields where they grew crops.

As he looked around, Quick could see the light pollution in the sky from the supercity; it looked more like the gathering light of dawn at this distance, but he knew better. From his perch, squatting atop the chimney, he looked for subtle differences in the shadows for signs of movement. Nothing was seen, and for a moment, he allowed himself to think it was nothing. The faint smile he had afforded himself was still taking shape on his lips as the sounds of the first drops of rain reported from the tin roof of the barn; the smile was gone before it had formed.

The smell of the rain was undeniable, carrying

a plethora of scents from all around; the sweet smell of the crops in the field and the few wildflowers that dotted the landscape throughout the acres of sedge grass. The marshland formed the topography of the land outside of their farm. There was also a faint foul smell of death and decay, he knew would overcome all the others before the night was through.

"Damn," he whispered and pulled his sword slowly from its sheath and placed it vertically, the point resting on the roof in front of him. He held his wet stone out and allowed some of the rain to moisten its surface before running it down the blade, and as he did, he saw Rafeo, his oldest and dearest friend, step off the porch back at ground level and look up to his position.

"Friend?" Quick scoffed quietly to himself; in fact, Rafeo was the only other person he had known, or seen for that matter, in years. It had been so long that he had, in fact, lost track of how long it had been. There were some scattered memories from his youth, of others, a city, a family maybe, but they were lost to him now. There had been many other faces, but he had to question if they had been people. Rafeo had found him wandering in the wilds, alone, injured, and without his memory, the old man had taken him in. If he had to be honest with himself, Rafeo was more like a father figure than a friend.

Quick pointed north and slightly east in answer to Rafeo's unspoken question. It was the direction that the storm was blowing from, which would also be the direction the trouble would be coming from. They always came from the storm, as though a force of nature, just like the rain. Rain would renew, but what came with it would only destroy.

The storms were why no one lived in the wilds. Most humans had never gone outside the walls, and no one ever desired to. These things were the way they were from what he could recall of his childhood. But, he had seen for himself the ruins of cities from the age before; buildings and houses rotting away, returning to nature from whence they came.

He had asked Rafeo if it had always been this way. The old man, who was never known to be chatty, replied, "No." His face, however, spoke volumes in pain. Pain over what could only be described as a memory of the times before, but the old man couldn't have been alive long enough to have known.

The world was a different place now. The Savage's forms had mutated skin-like leather armor, and were physically larger. Hands with claws in place of fingers and teeth and jaws like the predators they are now, and it was these Savages that approached with the rains.

Slowly, Quick slid the stone down the length of his blade again, then stood up straight. He looked down at Rafeo and smiled slightly, before realizing he couldn't see it in the darkness. He looked back at his sword, running his eyes down the length of the fifty-eight-inch blade. The polished steel grabbed the rays of the moonlight, throwing its reflection in all directions as Quick spun the blade. Its weight and balance were perfect for him, making the weapon seem alive, and all Quick had to do was guide it to its next target. He completed the next spin of the blade and sheathed the weapon in one seamless motion, slinging it again on his back.

"Hold the house, old man," Quick said playfully. "I'll take the barn," he added, grabbing the zip line pulley hanging from the roof.

"This isn't a game, son," Rafeo warned, as he watched. Quick in the failing moonlight, stepped from the roof and slid towards the barn. The clouds moved quickly to cover the land in their shadow. The pitch was only destroyed for moments at a time by the lightning. Freezing the images in their minds, briefly, like a series of photographs.

"No, it is not," Quick answered quietly, his words growing faint as the distance opened between the house and the barn. Quick dropped from the line at its end, landing in a roll and making it to his feet at a full run in one fluid motion. He grabbed a weapon belt and some light leather armor and slipped them on over his chest and upper legs, then pulled several levers once inside the barn. The levers raised multiple lightning rods from the barn roof and lowered the false floor in two of the stalls. It moved their draught horses and several supplies into a lower level for safekeeping. The lightning rods were attached to several cables that ran out into the fields in all directions, like a spider web. It left a penned-in area of roughly two thousand square feet right next to the barn that Quick would work in.

One flash of lightning, and in the instant, Quick could count dozens of figures in the field around him, perhaps even hundreds. The storm intensified as the shadows approached. Lightning struck the rods, conducting its awesome power through the cables, and nearly instantly, there were half as many shadows in the field around him. The electricity also set a blaze to trenches filled with thatch and diesel fuel, washing the barn and the young man in the light. The remaining shadowy figures in the field all saw him now, and with a series of howls, they moved into attack.

"Damn it, boy," Rafeo cursed as he watched the fire blaze to life. He couldn't leave the house for fear of being electrocuted. He could only watch the fight unfold, which he would do through the scope of his rifle.

Quick, slowly unsheathed his sword and moved it into the low guard position. He waited and listened. One of the figures, a Savage, stepped slowly from the shadows and through the flames into the circle Quick had crafted. The creature of a man moved as if unconcerned with the peril of the flames, as though accepting Quick's challenge. It stood nearly a foot taller than Quick, over seven feet tall. Its form was wider than the young man's. Its skin was gray, yet blackened by dirt, as if it had not been washed clean for some time, if ever, and more akin to the leathery scales of a reptile than to the soft, supple flesh of a human. The Savage's features, hands, and legs were larger than a human of the same size. Their eyes were the opposite of a human's, with white pupils and solei black as pitch. This one's teeth were pointed and sharp, as though intended to be weapons. Quick had come to discover that the teeth, at least, were usually manipulated to a point, filed down by others, and not natural.

Quick had been told that the Savages had been formed, resulting from a pandemic virus that had swept the globe in the wake of the last great war. Those who survived were polarized into two separate groups. The Savages had lost the social graces needed to be in society. They instead lived in packs, like wild dogs rather than humans, and became that which Quick now faced. And in the middle was Quick.

The Savage drew close enough for Quick to hear the rasp of its breath and smell the foul stench from the rags it wore as clothes. They sized each other up. Quick flailed his sword around in a stunning display and finished with a salute. The Savage, in turn, threw its arms back and howled a terrifying scream to intimidate what it clearly did not understand. There was a moment of hesitation, then the Savage broke from his stance and charged towards Quick. The young man steadied himself and prepared to react to the attack. Before Quick could move, the Savage's head burst from its shoulders into a red and gray spray, its body dropping to the ground and sliding through the mud just past Quick. The young man turned back towards the house to see Rafeo mired in a mist of smoke flowing from the barrel of his rifle.

"Were you gonna dance with him, or kill him?" the older man yelled and drew back into the house from the porch.

"Get ready," Rafeo said, even more sardonically than his last statement.

"I was ready," the young man answered,

throwing his arms in the air with disgust.

"You get ready, you old bas-" Before he could finish his thought, several Savages burst through the flames, charging the young man, and almost catching him off guard. Quick had to lunge backward to gain his footing and find enough room to swing his weapon. His sword danced in the darkness. The firelight reflecting from the blade was quickly tinted red from blood. Within seconds, he had bested five more Savages in close quarters.

From behind, he could hear another Savage climbing over the barn roof in a clumsy attempt at a sneak attack. Quick hurled his sword as the creature gained its footing, ready to pounce from the second-story roof of the mud room of the barn. The sword caught the other right between the eyes with enough force to emerge through the other side of its head and lodge the tip into the wall behind him. Quick was proud of this feat, having only recently mastered throwing his weapon. This did, however, leave him without his sword. In his pause, he noticed the reports from Rafeo's rifle becoming more and more frequent. The main body of the attackers was upon him. Quick sprinted towards his sword as several Savages broke from the shadows around him.

He managed to jump up and kick off the mud room wall, and again from the forge chimney that protruded from the barn wall about four feet away. He landed on the roof of the small room as he watched the Savages draw near. With a slight sigh, as if disappointed in himself for having to resort to this, he drew his handgun and fired. With marksmen's accuracy, Quick dropped four more of his attackers.

The noise of the shots had startled a few others who scattered back into the shadows, but only for a moment. The momentary reprieve had given the young man time to retrieve his sword. By then, the Savages had returned and massed around the mud room, clawing at his feet.

Without hesitation, Quick leaped from his perch over the heads of the Savages. He had decided to finish with his pistol and fired while completing a slow sweeping flip in the air. By the time he landed on the ground, the gun was empty, and three more lay dead. He now had enemies in front of him and behind him. His breath was labored but well in control. He could feel every muscle in his body ripple as he readied himself for his next attack. He took in one large breath, then exploded into motion.

His sword landed a mortal wound with every stroke. Not a single motion was wasted on flashy maneuvers, he just got down to business. Before he had exhaled his breath, he had ended another six enemies. He was thankful for the rain, which helped wash some of the blood from his skin and clothes. The handle of the blade was sticky from the blood, and he adjusted his grip for a moment to allow the rain to rinse his hands as well.

"Okay, kid, carve your Z in the wall and get in here. There's a lot more coming. We need to launch," Rafeo yelled out the window. He could tell by the look on Quick's face that he didn't get, or at least didn't understand, the Zorro reference, but the young man did break for the house. He hurdled the fence effortlessly and darted across the distance between the barn and the house almost as quickly as the zip line had carried him earlier. Rafeo could see the storm intensifying, and from his elevated position, now in a makeshift turret built onto the second story of the house, he could see a second wave of the enemy approaching. Though the two men could probably hold them all off shooting from that height, there was a better solution.

Rafeo fired at two Savages that had gotten closer than he liked, as Quick burst through the door to join him on the battlements.

"Z?" he said, confirming Rafeo's earlier suspicions.

"Later!" he answered smugly. In truth, he had hoped the young man would have forgotten by now; after all, there were other things to focus on.

"It's ready," Rafeo grunted, nodding towards a switch on the wall. Quick did not hesitate and threw the switch. Within seconds, a rocket blasted towards the heavens, fired from a port in the roof. As it gained altitude, the wire that remained attached to the ground grew in length very quickly. The Savages had made it to the house by this point, but gave pause to watch the rocket; seemingly mesmerized by the bright shiny things.

It only took seconds before a massive bolt of lightning rode down the path it had provided, thanks to the rocket-propelled cable. The electrical surge raced to the ground, blasting through another series of cables. With more power than the first one, the Savage horde was obliterated before the massive clap of thunder was reported. It was all but over in one fell swoop.

"Now, that's what I call close air support," Rafeo said with a slight giggle. Again, Quick looked at him, puzzled.

"Later," Rafeo dismissed him again. "We have a hell of a mess to clean up first," he explained, then led the young man from the roof.

Chapter II

It was decided that the mess outside would be kept until daylight. Quick wanted to get a chance to clean up and perhaps rest a little before dealing with what awaited them outside their door. When he was done in the shower, he could hear Rafeo snoring. Either a condition of his age or confirmation that Rafeo's nerves were far more accustomed to events like the previous night, or perhaps both, Quick knew that if he could sleep before dawn, it would be a long time coming.

He lay on his bed wearing only his towel, his right hand tucked under his head. In the darkness, he stared at the ceiling, the images from the evening's battle replaying in his mind. What began as a personal review of his performance quickly turned into a parade of the faces of those who had died before his eyes. Rafeo had told him time and again that they were no longer human; he could not convince himself to believe it. Despite everything, he could not help but feel, if not guilt, then remorse for those he had slain.

Soon, the images in his mind turned to other memories and were triggered by his emotions. The faces of the dead soon turned into faces of people, all with a look of fear and hatred upon them, all directed at him. Since Rafeo had found Quick in the wild several years ago, Quick had no memories of his life before that point. Rafeo had been helping him to recall his past; the process, though helpful, had been slow.

The images were similar. Each time, he could see a little more in his mind. The first was of a beautiful, bright city. These were images from his childhood. A mob of people, including those whom he believed to be his parents, was dragging him as a small boy to the city gates. He resisted with all of his efforts, but at such a young age, it proved futile. He could see the gate closing behind him, leaving him to face the wilds alone.

In a flash, his memories moved to a different time. He could see the skyline of an abandoned and dilapidated city, the buildings crumbling, damaged from battles long ago, and rotting from being abandoned over a long time. He is hundreds of feet above the ground, at the edge of the top of a building, and the area feels very familiar to him, like home. The streets below ran with flowing, shallow water; trees and greenery had reclaimed the pavement. A multitude of animals and birds roamed the once bustling urban area.

In the distance, he saw a wall, like a dam or a levee, that held back a large body of water. Many fires from camps and torches dot the area around it, a settlement of some description. His focus was on the levy; in his mind, he was angry, vengeful even, for a reason he could not recall. He had the urge to jump from the building. He stopped when he heard her voice.

He turned to see her.

"Mary?" He breathes her name into the darkness of his room and smiles, though uncertain that he can trust his memory that it was, in fact, her name. He closes his eyes even tighter, fearing the memory will slip away should he open them.

She smiles warmly as she walks to him on the edge of the building. The mere rags she wears hang from her stunning figure in a way that he can imagine her in any gown, fit for any ball. She comes to him and leads him back to their home, little more than a bunker. They stand near the fire and hold each other, the tanned skin of an animal adorning the floor, and soon they lie upon it together, exploring each other's naked form. The light from the fire is so bright, and despite his wish not to, he looks away from the light.

He lay in his bed and opened his eyes. The light from the sun blasting through his window confirms that it is morning and the storm has cleared. He remained motionless for a time, a single tear rolling down his cheek. Before he could wipe it away, the memories faded, fleeting as they always were, more a dream than a memory; all, that is, except for... her. Soon, he forced himself to get up and change out of his towel as it was not only his cheek that was wet.

He remembered his love for her. He wondered if it was a mere fantasy or if it was real. Quick cleaned up and dressed in simple clothes, ready for his daily chores. He had stumbled around in a haze for some time; the lines blurred between reality and his dream, or fantasy. Again, he could see her smile in his mind's eye; she turned to him and spoke in a voice not her own.

"It means Fox." Her face faded to take on its true source; Rafeo was deep into another trivial historical lesson, which he enjoyed, often. "I guess because he proved to be so hard to catch. Zorro was a nobleman who stood up against corruption in his government; he risked his whole existence to help people he didn't even know, and every time he struck, he would carve a Z into a wall so the people would know he had been there." It was Rafeo who spoke. Quick blinked a few times and shook his head to clear his daydream. The moment was over now, for certain, having heard the old man's coarse voice come from his memory of Mary. He had to look around to realize he had not only finished dressing but had wandered down the stairs into the kitchen, poured himself a coffee, and asked Rafeo to explain his comment about the "Z" from the night before.

His head cleared further as the horrible stench from outside caught his attention. Quick looked around, not entirely certain how he had come to be in the kitchen; he certainly did not remember getting a cup of coffee. He stared into the black pool in his cup, as if he expected the answers to break through its surface.

"You okay, kid?" Rafeo asked, noticing the distant look on Quick's face. Quick's gaze darted around the kitchen as though looking for something; by the time his eyes came to rest upon Rafeo, he had forgotten his entire fantasy from the night before. Rafeo noticed a spark, faint though it was, fade from Quick's eyes.

"Yeah, I'm good," the young man finally answered, and with a shrug, drank deeply from his coffee. "You were saying something about Zorro," he said, more to distract Rafeo. He wanted to talk about his dreams less than he wanted to hear about Zorro.

"Just that he was only one man, but he was able to make a profound difference in the world. I believe his example could manifest itself in you," the old man trailed off. He knew Quick didn't want to hear this again. Rafeo was convinced that there was something special about the boy, and indeed there was. Quick did not want to believe it.

Without another word, Quick forced a smile, put his mug down, and walked outside. He didn't feel like cleaning up, but today was not about what he wanted. Smoke hung thick in the air, rising from the still-smoldering corpses scattered around the property. He leered at the scene and then at the barn and thought he would start with something a little easier.

Quick turned his attention to the remains scattered around the house. The one advantage to using electricity as a weapon was that, at the power level of lightning, it turned organic material, the bodies of a few dozen Savages, for example, into little piles of carbon. Quick had to spread the piles over the landscape; the carbon was good for the soil.

Quick was done in less than an hour, the burned bodies had little other choice than to start on the barn. Rafeo had finally readied himself to help with the clean-up.

"Started with the easy stuff, I see," Rafeo

muttered under his breath as he walked past Quick towards the barn. Quick snickered, but not until he knew Rafeo wouldn't see. They always had a playful relationship. Truthfully, Quick thought of the old man as a father or a master to his apprenticeship. It helped that he had no clear memory of his birth parents, but in truth, Rafeo had cared for him, nurtured and trained him, and provided for him since they had met more than five years before. Quick did not know his real age; they had both guessed he was in his mid to late twenties now, but Rafeo had even gone so far as to have chosen a day for his birthday, and they celebrated every year on June 21st.

Quick, in return, had tried to honor Rafeo by being a good apprentice, student, or son. He had learned metallurgy and how to use a forge for blacksmith work. He had learned concepts of agriculture and farming. Also, Rafeo had trained him in different forms of martial arts. Life was not easy, particularly as they had chosen to live outside of the Citadel, and Quick had also learned the appreciation of an honest day's work and having a friend and mentor to share it with.

Rafeo was already working on a large pyre outside of the barn near the edge of their pasture. Quick had raised the draft horses from their safe storage under the barn and hitched them to a work cart. He led the team to the area in which he had slain several of the Savages the night before and brought them to a halt next to the first body. He leapt from the cart and landed near the fallen Savage's head. He caught himself staring down at the creature. This time, he could not help but notice the features that made him look more like a man. He wondered if this one had left a mate or a child to come here last night. If so, would they mourn him when he did not return? A twinge of guilt formed in the pit of his stomach.

"These attacks are becoming more frequent," Rafeo's voice broke an eerie silence.

Quick could not hide being startled; he had been so busy examining the body.

"Sorry, son; guess I should tie a bell around my neck," the old man smiled warmly. Finally, after several seconds of staring, Quick nodded.

"I was about to say the same thing, I thought I was talking to myself," Quick answered, trying to sound casual. He reached under the body's shoulders while Rafeo took the feet and placed the body onto the cart.

"I wonder if that means that there are more of them, or if they know we are here? If they do know, why would they care? And if they do care, why have they not arrived in droves and wiped us out?"

Rafeo looked at him with something of a grin. "I was just thinking the same thing," he said sarcastically.

They continued to work in silence, policing all the bodies onto the cart, then unloaded them onto the pyre that Rafeo had prepared.

"Better light it, son. The smell is bound to attract wildlife." Rafeo had noticed Quick's hesitation as he handed him a small handheld torch.

"I just wish I understood," Quick said, as he

looked once more at the bodies. "They come and they die. Does that make us evil for killing them?" He reached over and set the pyre ablaze.

"Perhaps, if we were seeking them out, one could question our motives, but I believe that evil, in our case, does not apply," Rafeo said, after watching the fire propagate over the fuel and consume the bodies.

"Do you feel evil?" Rafeo asked cautiously. He was uncertain what to expect and had always feared, in the back of his mind, who or what this young man was. Since the day they met, he wondered. But Quick had never been able to shed light on the subject, as he had no memory of anything before they had met.

Rafeo had found him covered in blood and injured. Despite his condition, Quick had drawn his sword and wildly attacked him. Rafeo, able to defend himself, barely, against the young man's rage-fueled attack, until finding himself with the upper hand. He had figured he was about to kill another Savage when the boy spoke. Rafeo knew right away that Quick was not a Savage, but he did not understand what he was, exactly.

"I don't feel evil," Quick answered. "What I do feel is confused and frustrated. I'm tired of not knowing who I am." He looked around and walked back towards the house. Rafeo followed just behind. The young man stopped at the steps up to the porch.

"I am not a killer, but I seem to be good at it," he said, as he gestured back towards the fire. Seeing the conflict in the young man's eyes, Rafeo stopped what he was doing.

"But how did the world get so – wrong?" Quick asked, still mesmerized by the fire. The two men stood watching the fire, forced to back up from the heat it gave off. Rafeo looked at the young man, then looked around the rest of the farm.

"Oh, it isn't so bad -" Rafeo was forced to stop short by the look coming from the young man. As the two stood quietly, as if by intention, the funeral pyre shifted, and a severed leg rolled off the fire. Quick bent down to retrieve it and hesitated for a moment.

"I'm sure this isn't normal behavior, or at least it wasn't meant to be." Quick wiggled the leg to illustrate his point before tossing it back on the fire. He was not looking for reassurance but wanted to know. Rafeo sighed, looking into the young man's face, then drew a deep breath.

"The Guardian – some might refer to him as god, he was responsible for creating the human race – but the Guardian has gone missing from his celestial existence." Rafeo's tone was sarcastic at first. He had been living with this story for nearly twenty-five hundred years; it had become like a bad joke to him, in a way, but for Quick, this was all new. Rafeo understood he should give this story the respect it deserved. He cleared his throat and took another step back from the heat.

"The Quies are a race of immortal beings. They have shed their corporeal form and exist as energy. Despite their power, they are slaves to their duties, each responsible for maintaining the galaxy and perhaps beyond. They like to take what, I guess, could be described as holidays from their nearly emotionless existence and come to Earth as a human. They can experience free will, emotions, and physical stimuli in this form. Originally, humans were created as a punishment, a way to take the Quies and make them mortal once more, a punishment for committing a crime."

"That makes sense, I guess." Quick nodded. He followed along with the story, but was having a hard time. Rafeo was talking about the existence of gods like it were commonplace.

Rafeo read the young man's facial expression and placed a hand on his shoulder, turning them back towards the house. He continued while they walked.

"Anyway, the new humans eventually did what humans do: they multiplied. Before the Guardian knew it, there were millions of us. The Guardian and others of the Quies would come to Earth, take our form, and live amongst us to learn and allow the humans to learn from them. He tried to guide them and teach them right from wrong. While any of the Quies are on earth, they shed their immortal form and become human, their knowledge is transferred into a book."

Rafeo paused in response to an odd look from Quick. "Well, where else would you store knowledge?" Rafeo asked a rhetorical question and waited until he got a nod from Quick before he proceeded.

"I had been chosen as one of the three Magi to bring the Book to the Guardian so that when he was ready, he could absorb the knowledge and return to his rightful place amongst the heavens." Rafeo fell silent, and his face softened. Quick noticed the strain but thought it best not to ask about it.

They lowered themselves onto the deck chairs on the veranda of the farmhouse. Quick was already feeling better, but could see Rafeo's memories were taking him to a memory he didn't want, but the old man cleared his throat again and continued.

"On our journey, one of the three Magi turned on us. He killed Balthazar, dropping his body as if it were nothing." Rafeo trailed off again, his eyes fixed on the horizon. His eyes darted around, almost like he was in R.E.M. sleep. He continued his story, though his voice was raspy, and it seemed like he was talking more to himself than to the present.

"The problem is, a book wants to be read; that is its purpose, isn't it? The book would call to people to read it, but the knowledge within was not intended for a mere mortal–no." Rafeo fell silent.

Quick edged forward in his seat and turned to stare at the old man. He may have felt guilt over killing the savages the night before, but it was quite clear that Rafeo was carrying a far heavier burden. Quick noticed a tear roll down the old man's cheek.

"Anyway, because of my failings, the book did not make it back to the Guardian. He was killed." Rafeo stood and moved to the edge of the porch as though relief from his pain would be found there. "The Guardian was lost; two others took his place at the ascension, and I got this book as a souvenir." Rafeo's voice had grown cold, hard; it was obvious he had resumed his usual gruff demeanor.

"And that is how the world got so wrong," Rafeo finished, turning back to the young man. Quick figured it might be better to nod at this point.

***   ***   ***

Hours had passed, and the fire had burned down to embers. The two had sat at the dinner table for some time, neither one eating heartily. Rafeo had found a small reprieve in a wonderful glass of red wine. He savored it slowly with fresh bread and a little stew, slowly cooked for hours. He wasn't sure what to say to the young man and could finally take it no longer.

"So, we should go to the city?" Rafeo announced suddenly as he stood and leaned on the table with both hands. Quick looked up in surprise. He looked the older man up and down, trying to read his body language, as if expecting a punch line. The great Citadel was over seven days' journey away; they had never been there, at least not that Quick knew of.

"I need to sell some wares, and maybe we can trade for some equipment around here." Rafeo followed up on his earlier statement as casually as he could. Quick sat motionless but looked brighter than Rafeo had seen him in days.

"They also have technology there, very advanced, and that may help you."

"I'm in!" Quick said excitedly as he sprang to his feet.

"Okay, okay," Rafeo raised his arms, cautioning the young man not to get carried away. "We have a lot of work to do to get ready. We should sleep tonight, get up with the sun, pack, and leave by lunch."

"Whatever you need me to do." Quick could barely contain himself.

"Good. You can start by clearing the table," Rafeo suggested, and watched as Quick's expression soured slightly. "I am going to bed. Good night." Rafeo grabbed his glass of wine and disappeared through the doorway towards the stairs, leading to the bedrooms.

"Yes, sir," Quick replied, mockingly saluting behind Rafeo's back before smiling; he was excited to go to the Citadel, hopeful that he could get some answers. He slung his towel over his shoulder and busied himself with his task, the whole time trying to think of what to expect from the days ahead.

Chapter III

They had risen long before the sun; neither Rafeo nor Quick could sleep that night. Quick was far too excited; perhaps this journey would lead to his memories being returned, or at least finding answers to many questions.

Rafeo, however, was nervous. He knew what lay ahead. The trip would be difficult at best; he had made this trip several times before, and each time it had been an adventure, to say the least. Even without encountering any Savages, the world was not a hospitable place. Most of the land had been ravaged by war, and now it was being reclaimed by nature. The absence of man had turned the countryside into a wild place indeed.

There would also be no infrastructure to speak of, and no roads, no shelter, nothing. The only food they would have had was whatever they took with them and what they could hunt or scavenge along the way.

By 10 a.m., the cart was nearly loaded. It was a piece of technology that had survived the collapse of man. Rafeo had found it and restored it after a previous outing

Technology had advanced considerably before

the war. This cart did not have wheels; it used a sort of magnetic levitation or mag-lev propulsion to hover upwards of ten inches off the ground, depending on its load and the settings. The power cells were nearly inexhaustible, a form of micro-fusion perfected over a century ago. It was a good thing, too, as they would not be crossing terrain suited to wheels. The horses would provide a minute amount of thrust to sustain forward momentum, though they did have an engine for propulsion. The engine took a lot of energy. Hence why Rafeo insisted on the horse. Quick believed the old man just liked having the animal around, maybe it reminded him of the good old days.

Rafeo carried his bag over his shoulder and took a very old-looking chest out of the cart. He placed the bag on the bench where they would sit while traveling and put the chest under the seat.

"You almost ready?" Quick asked from the back cargo area of the cart, his anxiety showing. Rafeo paused and looked up at the young man, thankful he did not ask about the chest.

"Yes, I am. Whether you believe it or not, the question is, are you ready for what lies before us?" Rafeo's stare went right through the young man, bringing him down a peg or two. Quick didn't know what to expect from this trip, and they both knew it.

"I'm ready for an adventure," Quick replied, as he calmed himself a little. "I may not know what we are getting into, but I know there is nothing we can't handle together." Quick slung his swords over his shoulder; he preferred to have them there than on his waist belt.

Rafeo continued to stare at Quick, but his expression softened greatly. This young man never failed to impress him.

"Indeed," Rafeo answered with a nod and even a slight smile, then climbed onto the cart and took the reins. "So, we can be off, then." Rafeo looked at the cart; he couldn't tell if anything was missing.

Assuring him they were set, Quick said, "Yeah, let's go." A few seconds later, Rafeo whistled, flicked the reins, and the team lunged into motion, taking up the slack in the rigging and starting without even noticing the cart behind them. They made it across the pasture to the sedge grasslands that lie beyond. The horses trod on unencumbered by the change in terrain.

The ground had given way to shallow marshland, the water barely past the animal's ankles. After several minutes, Quick stood and turned back to watch the farm shrink into the distance. Until now, he had no memory of ever being away from the farm; he hoped he would return someday. Despite everything, at least he had known peace during his time there. He turned back to face the front of the wagon and sank slowly back into his seat. Rafeo took notice but did not say anything.

"So, what's in the chest?" Quick asked after several seconds had passed, a slight grin forming on his face.

"Nothing of your concern for the moment," Rafeo replied sharply. This was to be a long trip, indeed.

They had traveled for hours in the direction of a small mountain range. For the duration of the journey, they talked about many subjects as the trip had been mostly uneventful. The marshland had given way to grassland within a few hours, and a few hours further the landscape resembled more that of a desert than anything else. They had followed a dried riverbed for several kilometers as it had provided easier footing for the horses. There had been no sign of people anywhere, and even wildlife had been scarce. They had seen two large flocks of birds; the first, seagulls, the second, a smaller bird that neither one of them could name.

Quick had been mesmerized by the fluid motion of the second flock. It moved through the air as a single living entity, rippling with the wind at times, almost like a cloud moving through time and space with no clear concern for the state of the world. Quick envied their freedom, but also admired their numbers. The group did not seem to have any inner turmoil or signs of a power struggle, just the outward appearance of a team, every bird working towards a common goal in harmony. It gave him a feeling of hope, somehow.

They had approached the base of the mountain range, which was nothing more than large rolling hills. The only thing that stood out in the topography.

"I'd rather make camp at the top to better see anything coming at us," Rafeo said, interrupting a simple silence that had endured for nearly an hour.

Quick turned his attention from the birds and nodded to Rafeo.

"Might get lucky," he said, turning his eyes skyward again and lifting his eyebrows. "Not a cloud in the sky."

Rafeo grinned. "So far, so good," Quick replied. "We should have a hell of a view from up there as well."

The horses strained only against their weight, and maybe that of the rigging, as they started up the hill. They had been lucky to come across what may have been a roadway at one point. The grade had been evened to make their ascent easier. The cart floated past several derelict vehicles, some left where they had stopped. The other car that had run off the road, all of them having stood motionless for a very long time. Each one had rusted and rotted beyond any trace of color.

Halfway up the hill, the smooth surface was pockmarked by a sizable crater. An explosion of some description must have caused the gridlock; certainly, none of the drivers that day were expecting that day's events as they unfolded. Most of the vehicles contained the remains of their operators, at least the ones closest to the crater. Perhaps the people from the cars further away had been given a chance to flee, but not these.

Quick was observant and feeling on edge, expecting the dead to rise and attack them. He had no memory of anything different, but he knew that what he was seeing was not right.

They had reached the top in silence as the sun reached the horizon. Facing west, they watched a stunning sunset. Rafeo took note of a fuel tanker truck that appeared mostly intact; it would make a good shelter for the night, and even allow them to have a small fire, as the tank would hide nearly all the light from the flames. The horses would find shelter in the back of a cube van parked further up the path. Rafeo doubted they would be this lucky every night.

The sun was nearly gone by the time they were settled for the night. As the darkness grew around them, they could see the lights from the Citadel, a little brighter than from home. The top of its massive walls was now visible on the horizon.

To the south-east was the skyline of a once great city, in the shadows of the ghost town that remained. From their vantage point, they could see a taller building. It was once a display of power and engineering prowess of civilization; they were now a crumbling whisper of days past. Mankind had been forced to abandon their great towers in favor of perhaps a greater engineering marvel, the Citadel. The walled cities did provide sanctuary, but were, despite their grandeur, little more than a prison.

As they looked off the path, they could see dozens more craters, the result of a bombing run long ago. Most of the craters had filled with rainwater, the water having supported some wildlife, perhaps, but had definitely given life to species of algae. This species was phosphorescent in nature, emitting a blue glow that intensified in the growing darkness of the night.

Quick bounded up the side of the cab and then to the top of the tanker to get fourteen feet above the ground for a better look. Rafeo followed the path, to Quick's surprise, and stood next to him. They looked in amazement at the glowing blue pools all around them, and at the fallen city beyond. A few seconds passed, and the silence was pierced by a screech owl that sounded as if from the devil himself. Quick ripped his sword from its sheath and stood ready for battle.

"Easy, son." Rafeo placed his hand on Quick's shoulder and, after getting his attention, pointed laterally away from the truck. In the shadows, several elk gathered near one of the pools; they hesitated only briefly, then dove in and galloped through. When they emerged on the other side, they bore the glowing spores within their fur. And as they pranced past, it was a stunningly beautiful display, the grace of the animals punctuated by a soothing blue glow. They looked more akin to fairies or ghosts than something of this earth.

"I cannot recall ever seeing anything like it," Quick said in a hushed voice, watching the display unfold before him.

"Yeah, but that's not saying much," Rafeo answered playfully; he didn't like to make light of Quick's memory issue, but could not help himself. Quick was so caught up in the visual display that it took him several minutes to respond.

"I will not let even you spoil this moment for me, old man," Quick answered, watching the small herd disappear.

"I'm sorry," Rafeo replied, stifling a laugh.

"You sound like it," Quick replied sarcastically and put his sword away as he walked towards the cab of the truck to make his way down. "That's fine. I'll remember that." Quick didn't want to let him off so easily. He hopped to the ground, then into the tank of the trailer.

Dinner was a simple stew they cooked over a low fire inside the tanker trunk. A rabbit Rafeo had caught earlier served as the centerpiece of the dish. They had added a few potatoes and onions picked from the farm before leaving, perhaps simply, but very comforting. Rafeo also offered a heavy bread to soak up all the broth from the stew. Each of them was full, and soon very tired from the day's travel. The dirty crockery was washed thoroughly in the glowing pools and returned to a sealed box in the wagon, but not before they had rubbed a little of the algae on an area of the floor of the inside of the tank for some faint light; someone might have to get up to relieve themselves in the night. They had little remaining to do, other than to find sleep for the night.

It took neither man any time at all to fall soundly asleep. The day had been long but enjoyable for both. They had covered a respectable distance and were nearly thirty miles closer to their destination. Rafeo figured that only three or four more days like this one, and they would reach the Citadel.

***   ***   ***

Quick's eyes snapped open, his hand already on the grip of his sword. The rain on the outside of the tanker was nearly deafening. He was about to leap from his bunk when he felt Rafeo's hand on his arm to stop him. In the dim light from the algae, Quick could see Rafeo's face in the shadows. The old man only shook his head slightly.

Over the rain pounding on the hull of the tanker. Quick could hear the occasional cry of the Savages that were outside.

"The horses," Quick whispered, though he doubted anything could be heard outside of the tanker over the noise of the rain. In response, Rafeo held out his hand, motioning for Quick to be still.

"They will be fine," Rafeo whispered back. Quick had to read his lips to understand what was being said. He remembered they had put the horses into a cube van and sealed them in. Provided this group wasn't too attentive, they seldom were. They would pass by without incident. Quick threw a blanket over the light source to render the trailer into complete darkness. They had found this tank intact and had managed to get the top hatch closed, effectively sealing them in, as well. The hull did have several small holes throughout its side. Quick got to his feet and peered through one of the holes. A well-timed flash of lightning illuminated a Savage standing just outside the trailer. Quick recoiled, nervous that he had been seen, but the Savage took no notice.

Quick and quietly moved to the next small opening and stared at the truck, which housed the horses. He watched, chanting under his breath "Please don't – please don't – please don't." His only hope was that the horses would not betray their location. For what seemed an eternity, they watched as the Savages slowly proceeded through the camp, not one of them paying any particular attention to the tanker, the cube van, or even their cart.

Quick had counted nearly sixty seconds since he had seen or heard another Savage, and he wanted a better vantage point than the small hole in the tank would afford him. Rafeo had also concluded that the immediate threat had passed and nodded for Quick to go. Quick slipped through the lower drain spout and outside under the trailer without a sound; Rafeo followed right behind.

Once outside, Rafeo headed to the cart while Quick again darted to the top of the trailer, from there. He could see the small horde moving away, down the road. He relaxed ever so slightly and turned to check in on Rafeo. One Savage had fallen behind the group and was just about to stumble upon Rafeo, who had busied himself inspecting their gear and had not noticed the creature's approach from behind. Any sound of struggle, and the rest of the group would be on them again in seconds.

Quick drew his sword as the Savage walked up behind Rafeo. It almost didn't realize it had found something and, luckily, was more curious about Rafeo than anything. Quick threw his blade with perfect aim, catching the Savage through the back, piercing its lungs, taking away its ability to cry out. Rafeo had realized the Savage was there as the blade made contact. He spun to catch the creature, covering its mouth just in case, and helped it quietly to the ground.

Quick turned to see the main group and was relieved to see it had continued in its original heading without notice of what had just happened. He strained his eyes to the rear, down the hill, and could not see any other movement. He leapt to the ground, landing close to his friend.

"Thank you," Rafeo whispered, still not wanting to make a sound. "Getting sloppy, I guess," he added with a shrug. Quick did not respond, wanting to comment on repayment for Rafeo's earlier slight.

"We can't leave this here in case they return tonight," Rafeo warned, gesturing to the corpse lying in front of them.

The solution seemed a bit harsh, but necessary; they decided to weigh the body down and sink it into one of the nearby pools. It was quite the unnerving sight to see the Savage sink through the blue glowing water. It came to rest on the bottom of the pool. Quick stared for a while before Rafeo led him back to their camp.

Chapter IV

Sleep had not come easily, though much to Rafeo's surprise, it must have eventually, he determined, as he rolled over slowly and felt his consciousness claw its way back from the depths of his slumber to realize it was morning. The rays of sunlight streaming through the holes in the truck made this obvious. He could not help but wonder how different his life was now. How did it come to this, sleeping in the back of a rotted-out fuel truck, one among dozens of other vehicles, dead where they stopped decades ago, traveling across a landscape destroyed by war and hatred, with a young man with no memory. And he had lived through it all, cursed to walk the earth until he could finish the mission started centuries ago.

"Quick," he said as he looked to find the young man was no longer in the tanker with him. Slowly, he got to his feet and pulled his clothing on, followed by a layer of leather armor over his chest, upper and lower legs, and forearms, then finally his cloak to hide it all. He knew the boy could take care of himself, but still wanted to know he was all right. There was something special about this boy. He had his suspicions, but it was hard to allow himself to believe.

With some difficulty, Rafeo forced the lower hatch cover open and slid out to crouch under the trailer. He listened intently for the sounds of struggle or rain but could not hear any. After a few more heartbeats, he stood from his concealed place and stepped into the sunlight. It was a beautiful day; the temperature was warm, and he could feel the sun on his face. The only sound that met his ears was the distant chirping of birds. For a moment, he thought that if he closed his eyes, he could imagine he was a boy again, enjoying the summer, perhaps about to go swimming with his brothers. That was a thought that he would have loved to stay in, yet forced his old eyes open only to be greeted by the ugly reality around him.

He was able to find Quick in short order, standing next to one of the crater pools. The young man stood as though he were a soldier at an epitaph, staring into the watery grave they had made the night before. The boy did not move even to acknowledge Rafeo's arrival; several moments passed until finally the young man spoke.

"He doesn't seem all that different from me or you, especially from down there." Quick glanced sideways, finally, to include Rafeo in his thoughts. The water was so clear in the sunlight, they could easily see right to the bottom of the pool. The Savage looked at peace. This was in contrast to what they both knew to be true of these beings. Perhaps, the water played tricks with the image, but what lay at the bottom of the pool looked more human than anything else.

"How did we get like this?" Quick asked after

a long silence; he had become quite mesmerized, staring into the eyes of the dead Savage at the bottom of the pool.

"How do you mean?" Rafeo asked, uncertain whether Quick meant the world in general or something more specific.

"Like this." Quick repeated and held out his hand pointing to their entire surroundings, the abandoned and rotted out vehicles on a barely identifiable road, buildings in the distance that were mere shadows of what they once were, then finally pointing into the pool at a creature you'd have to use your imagination to refer to as human.

"Was it a war, a natural disaster, or a disease?" Quick finished and waited for Rafeo to answer.

Rafeo nodded and looked around. He had the unique perspective of living through every minute of the world's transformation. He thought over the millennia, and Quick could see his expression turn from his normal scowl to a look of pain or regret.

"Well, it wasn't from natural selection, I can tell you that."

"Huh?" Quick tilted his head, trying to fathom what the old man was on about.

"War? Natural disaster? Disease? Yes, indeed, it was." Rafeo turned and walked away from the pool. He stopped in an area that overlooked the valley below.

"Well, which one, Raf?" Quick asked with a slight giggle; he hadn't understood what the old man had meant.

"It was all of those. Well, not all at once at first." Rafeo pulled his robes out of the way and sat down on a rock before he continued.

"Mankind has always had to work at getting along, living together. It seemed their natural state was to be at war with their neighbors." He shook his head solemnly at this.

"At the beginning of the last millennium, the year was 2032, if I recall, the world came together to hold a peace conference. This time, it was political, religious, and social leaders from all over the world. They came to sit together in a huge conference hall to abolish war forever." Rafeo went silent as he ran through his memories again. For a moment, Quick thought he saw the old man's eyes well with tears. However, Rafeo's stone veil was quickly drawn, returning his face to its usual scowl. The scowl that hid the pain that Quick was starting to appreciate, the more they spoke of the past.

"So that failed," Quick said, rather plainly.

"Quite the opposite, actually," Rafeo corrected him, raising a finger and grimacing to emphasize his point. "They did try to interrupt the process, but only a small group of truly brave people joined me to help stop Quintus and Mabus."

"Who the hell is Quintus?" Quick interrupted.

"Right!" Rafeo had to remind himself that Quick had lost his memories, so even if, and it was a strong if, he had learned world history in school as a boy, he had forgotten it now.

"Quintus was a Magi; like me, he had been given immortality until he could deliver the Book of Power to the Guardian on Earth."

Quick had heard this story before about the Book of Power.

"Oh! He was the one who betrayed you?" he asked.

"Correct," Rafeo paused again.

"So where is he now?" Quick, bade him continue.

"He's dead," Rafeo answered flatly.

"I thought you couldn't die?" Quick looked confused once again.

"Not quite," Rafeo fidgeted in his seat, and looked around the countryside to break eye contact with Quick. "A weapon that has been touched by the blood of the mortal Guardian can kill us, and me," he grunted, speaking more to the wind than to his companion. Quick looked surprised; this was all information he had never heard before and had never been brave enough to ask. Quick started to regret asking; this was not easy to hear.

"Quintus had such a weapon. He struck our brother, Balthazar, killed him in battle, and tossed his body into a deep ravine. Balthazar managed to take the weapon with him when he fell, otherwise, I surely would have shared his fate," Rafeo's voice cracked; his emotions still ran high, even after all these years.

"Back to the peace conference," Quick suggested, wanting to give the old man a break.

"Right... yes, of course." Rafeo cleared his throat and slightly sat forward on the rock, rubbing his hands together quickly, as though he was warming them up.

"They tried to blow up the conference, but I, and several other very brave, very dedicated men and women, stopped them. The conference was a massive success, and within five years, the mandates set out at that conference were in place."

"Like what?" Quick was starting to think the old man was kidding him.

"All nuclear arsenals all over the world were dismantled. The standing world armies shrank considerably. Military equipment from every country fell under the control of the United Nations, and that one military force policed the entire world – it was a golden age."

Quick smiled; he liked the sound of that.

"For about one hundred and ten years..." Rafeo continued. "Mabus had moved his operation underground. He had several secret weapons around the world in development, and the production plants were hidden. There were underground training facilities for people who were flocking to his banner. No one had reason to suspect what was going on."

"The United Nations didn't see it coming?"

"No one did; no one could, cause the first wave of attack was from a virus."

Quick recoiled from that news; he feared where the conversation would go next, obviously knowing it would not be good news.

"The disease wiped out thirty-one percent of the world population in six months." Rafeo's voice was darker, louder. "The governments tried to quarantine their citizens, and it did help, eventually. People were afraid to leave their homes, even to get supplies or food, many more died, locked in their homes... locked from the inside."

"The quarantine allowed Mabus and his followers to move more freely; no one was looking for them, as they were all busy trying to survive the plague."

Quick nodded. It all seemed to make perfect sense, a very macabre logic.

"Mabus waged war, though it is hard to call it that. There were no political boundaries or motivations. They would invade an area and wipe out everyone who didn't join them. The only military that could offer resistance was the U.N., but Mabus could strike an area and raze it to ashes before the U.N. could get there."

Rafeo rose from his perch and looked at the rising sun. He wanted to continue their journey, but this was information Quick would need. He led the young man back to their camp, and they started to pack up to leave while he continued his story.

"Soon after, the leaders of what was left of the world committed all their resources to building these massive walled cities."

"The Citadels." Quick interjected.

"Yes. There are nine of them in total, all around the world. They were barely finished in time to survive the "Natural" Disasters. Rafeo made air quotations around the word "Natural, "and said it with disdain.

"They were anything but," he went on to explain. "A series of mega-waves, about two hundred years ago now, all but drained the world's oceans and washed up across every major land mass. The waters have receded now, but I'm pretty sure Australia doesn't exist anymore."

"Australia?" Quick questioned.

"You tell me if giant tidal waves naturally occur at the same time, emanating from several points on the globe?" Rafeo didn't expect an answer from Quick.

"It had to be Mabus, coming into his power," Rafeo explained. Quick nodded; he knew of Mabus and the power he had usurped from the Guardian nearly twenty-six hundred years ago.

"Luckily, the Citadels were able to save millions from certain death." Rafeo stuffed his bedroll into a duffel bag and tossed it onto the wagon. He turned back to find Quick standing, staring off into the distance.

"I'm sorry I asked," he said quietly.

"We should make way," Rafeo said after a while, and placed his hand on Quick's shoulder. Without another word, the two finished and readied the cart. Quick walked to the cube van to get the horses, while Rafeo inspected the load. The team was quickly latched to the cart, and they were underway.

***   ***   ***

They had come upon the remnants of a small town before evening had set in. Each man put a firm grip on their weapon as the image unfolded before them. Mostly overgrown with weeds or covered over by drifting sand, the roads and buildings were still largely discernible. Rafeo slowed their pace and kept a firm hand on the reins. It was broad daylight and not a cloud in the sky, but both feared an ambush. Their eyes were probing every shadow for movement, not relaxing for a second.

They followed what must have been the main street for several minutes before it led them past a building that Rafeo could not mistake for anything else. The church's steeple, still intact, as was the rest of the building. It almost appeared out of time compared to the rest of the dilapidated town. Rafeo slowed the team nearly to a stop as he stared at the church. Quick obviously picked up on Rafeo's mood.

The cart came to an easy stop, and without a word of warning, Rafeo dismounted the cart and walked up the short path towards the church. Quick did not think this was such a great idea, but followed him all the same.

"Uh... Raf?" Quick stammered, as he picked up the pace to keep up with his friend. Rafeo continued without responding.

"Is this a good plan?" Quick tried again. Rafeo put his hands on the door's handle and pulled it open. The door swung open, revealing the inside of the church; ample light streamed through the large windows, most of which were still intact. They could see the Altar near the back of the building.

"Raf, please," Quick tried again, now quite unnerved.

"What?" the old man hesitated without looking at Quick. "It's not like there's anyone in here," he said sternly, then lowered his head slightly. The look on his face changed from something akin to sadness. "Not like there's anyone left to be in here." He stepped into the church, and Quick followed behind him slowly.

"Didn't have you pegged as someone who felt nervous," Rafeo said, slightly under his breath.

"It's not that," Quick answered with a shrug as they stepped over the threshold and into the vestibule of the church. They paused as they passed from the outdoors to the interior of the building, allowing their eyesight to adjust. Quick did not know the significance of the building they were entering, but was willing to follow Rafeo's lead.

"I just don't feel like killing today," Quick finished his thought from earlier. He gestured to the altar at the back of the large building. It was stained black from blood, and the feet of a decomposed corpse could be seen on the ground protruding from the back side of the marble structure. They approached slowly, Rafeo still processing Quick's previous statement. This young man knew no fear.

Quick noticed a note that had fallen to the floor. He picked it up and read it aloud, slowly.

"I have seen the coming of the End. I fear for all and blame myself. I tried my best but was not up to the task. I am sorry, heavenly Father, but the flock is lost, and I am no longer needed. I always served the Quies, but condemned my soul to Mabus. Signed: Jack Taylor."

Quick shivered; the note he had read set an ominous tone. He hadn't noticed Rafeo's mouth on the name before he had read it.

"None of this is familiar to you, is it, boy?" Rafeo asked as he turned to see the look on Quick's face. The boy slowly looked up and shook his head. "Why did this farmer kill himself?" he eventually asked.

"Not a farmer, boy..." Rafeo could not completely stifle his laugh, "...a priest," he explained, regaining his composure. "A man of God, but then that had come to mean something different before the end, didn't it?" he said quietly, and turned to look out the large window at the back. It had grown nearly opaque with dirt. He stepped closer and rubbed a section clean with the sleeve of his cloak. The cleaned area, a large, desolate city, was in view in the background.

Quick had carefully placed the note back on the altar and stepped around the back of the structure. He saw the body, headless, and lying next to a rusted shotgun. When he looked up, he noticed the church's back wall behind the altar had a stain like that on the altar and the floor. He shrugged and walked over to the window next to Rafeo.

Quick winced, his face marked with confusion.

He was amazed at the crumbling monuments of the past that stood before him, once mighty skyscrapers, now a little more than growing piles of rubble.

"What the hell happened here?" he asked, his stomach churning slightly.

"The same thing that happened everywhere," Rafeo answered quietly, with no less sarcasm than usual. He looked at Quick after a moment, fully expecting the look he was getting from the young man.

"Come," he said warmly, after trying to smile to comfort his friend. "We'd best unhitch the team and find them boarding for the night."

"We're staying here?" Quick asked as he turned and followed Rafeo towards the exit. "It's still early."

"Indeed," answered Rafeo. "But this will be neither a short nor an easy conversation," he finished quietly. Rafeo locked his gaze with Quick. The young man had never asked much about the world over the past few years. His existence had been sheltered on the farm, intentionally. Rafeo had not had any success helping the boy with his memory over the past few years. Part of his intention on this trip was to try to shock Quick's mind into recovering. He had always wanted to try it, but fear had always gotten the best of him, until now.

Rafeo smiled warmly, hoping it might help the young man cope with everything that this day might bring, but had little real expectation that his expression would help.

They promptly unhooked the horses from the cart. The church rectory had a garage that would serve as a barn for the night. Rafeo filled a feed bag for each and strapped one to each horse before closing and sealing the door, while Quick stared off towards the big city center. The ruin of it all seemed familiar, like a nightmare, something your mind would create, but you knew it was fake the second you awoke.

They grabbed what they would need for the night and headed back into the church, barring the door. They had both hardly spoken other than the pertinent details for the tasks at hand.

Once somewhat settled in the church, Rafeo started to prepare a meal, another stew, his specialty.

"Where do I begin?" he asked, while stirring some seasoning into the pot. Quick dropped his duffel bag to the floor while looking for a place to set up for the night. That decision no longer mattered, and he rested upon his duffel as if preparing to hear a bedtime story.

"How do you describe the end of the world?" Rafeo said quietly, steeling himself for the task ahead.

"Must have been a hell of a war." Quick figured that Rafeo was stalling.

"Yes, it was, but it was only the one act in the program that had been several hundred years in the making," Rafeo answered off-handedly, looking around the altar area. "It unfolded as if scripted: disease, famine, war, and finally disaster and death. Who knew?" Rafeo was almost flippant.

"Ah ha," he continued, with his eyebrows raised. Rafeo had found a hidden drawer in the pulpit on the right side of the altar and had pulled a bottle from within. "I knew it," he said plainly and pulled the cork out of the neck of the vessel with his teeth and spit it across the room. He sniffed the bottle tentatively, then shrugged and smiled at Quick before taking a long haul from the bottle; he swallowed and coughed immediately. "Sacramental wine – this stuff lasts forever." His comments were met by an unimpressed look from Quick.

"But I digress." He placed the bottle down on the altar and picked up his ladle and stirred the pot on the hot plate, also on the marble altar. "Looking back, I believe it was the first act, or horseman, that was the slow burn. Going back, I guess several hundred years now, at the beginning of the twenty-first century, many world leaders saw the direction the world was heading in and put a solid effort into peace talks, held in a country called Jordan."

"Peace talks?" Quick questioned as he stood; he had a hard time sitting still at the best of times. "Victory defeated us," he said under his breath.

"In point of fact." Rafeo had capitalized on Quick's interjection to take another sip from the bottle. He wiped a wayward drop from his beard and waited to catch Quick's eye, which he did. "...they were attacked twice, at least, by some who wished to see mankind destroyed, but so gallant were the efforts of those who defended the peace envoys that it had inspired people to come together. These defenders gave their last measure of devotion to the cause." Rafeo seemed to trail off, as though in pain. He shrugged it off and reached for the bottle again.

"A last measure of devotion?" Quick asked.

"They fought very bravely, suffered greatly, and finally died for the cause, for love. And the world watched as it happened," Rafeo replied, then drank again.

"So?" Quick shook his head, and gestured in amazing confusion at the scene of destruction out the window.

"Peace, complacency, contentment." Rafeo grew silent in lost thought, handing the bottle to Quick as the young man paced past him. Quick took it, and after smelling it and examining it, carefully took a small sip, despite his better judgment.

"They say, idle hands are the tools of the devil... they were right, as it turns out." Rafeo took the bottle from Quick and poured a little into his stew. "The world's militaries declined, and governments disbanded spy networks. The geopolitical scene became a love fest, but the general population. Well?" He paused to taste the stew and smiled right after.

"That's got it." Rafeo scooped two bowls of the mixture and let them stand to cool slightly before he continued. They watched the steam rise from the bowl and disappear into the darkness above them. Very little light of it, but it managed to make it through the dirty windows to the tall church ceiling.

"Peace brought prosperity, which quickly gave way to a little-known condition that would become the driving force behind it all," Rafeo explained as he handed Quick a bowl. Quick nodded his thanks, then returned to his duffel bag to sit and eat. The stew smelled wonderful, with a slight piercing tang of the wine adding a different element. No matter what he had to make it with, Rafeo could always come up with a good stew.

"Affluence," Rafeo said, with his mouth full; he could read the confusion on Quick's face, so he chewed and swallowed before continuing. "People wanted more and more and more. They believed they were owed the world just because they were born. Boundless desire, which at first was attainable, but soon the pursuit of happiness turned to… something else." Rafeo took another bite and gestured for Quick to eat up. The young man found his appetite leaving him as Rafeo spoke, but they could not afford to waste food, so he forced himself to eat.

"All the while, Mabus used his time wisely, building in the shadows. He used the fact that the world thought him dead to work undetected." Rafeo paused to eat some more.

"He would manipulate and influence. People who started with honest intentions were twisted to his will. He used disease to wipe out nearly a quarter of the world's population. Paranoia and fear infected those who remained, until they turned to their old weapons of mass destruction. Victory ultimately defeated mankind," Rafeo said quietly, as though remembering.

"With no military, the governments had little ability to respond, though I suppose by this point the pandemic was affecting even the governments of the world. The world seemed to start its polarization back then. Those who refused to be caught up by desire tried to return to a simple life; farming, living off the land, many others did not. They started to build walled communities; apartment buildings became bunkers."

"Like the Citadels?" Quick asked anxiously.

"Indeed, just not on the same scale." Rafeo was glad to see that Quick was still following the story.

"People of peace tried to stay together, and the others, well, they just became more and more... Savage." Rafeo nodded and looked around as though not wanting to go on with the story. He took another bite of his stew, avoiding looking at Quick. He took a large gulp of his wine, then moved closer to the window. Rafeo looked out at the setting sun, its reddish hues sunbathing the ruins spread out in crimson color. Though eerie, it did exude beauty.

"When the bombs started going off, it was by no means motivated by political or racial concerns; just a much more basic and simple desire to spread evil, to kill and destroy. And so, they did. Several major cities on every continent were destroyed in this way. The death toll was staggering, and those who had survived faced the horror of further plague and starvation. The Savages tried to ward off the latter by eating each other, which gave way to the plague. Oddly enough." Rafeo had raced through the last part as though the words would have been more harmful had they lingered.

"So scary and gross," Quick answered, putting his bowl down and pacing again. "And yet, how is it that no one saw this coming?" he asked, almost with a tone of accusation, as Rafeo should have been able to warn someone. Rafeo looked at the young man, then lowered his head; obviously, he had picked up on the tone.

"They say the greatest trick the devil ever completed was to convince the world that he didn't exist," he nodded, and drew a deep breath. "Those bombs that went off were nearly undetectable; they weren't dropped from planes or smuggled in the trunk of a car; they were inside people. Not strapped to a person, but inside them, nearly impossible to detect." He made eye contact with Quick, realizing the complexity of the situation. "In all my years, I have learned at least one truth; it is far easier to fool a man than to convince a man that he has been fooled."

The church grew very quiet. Quick had gained a lot of perspective this day. It may not have helped him get his memory back, but from what he was learning, he wasn't sure he wanted his memory back.

"So how did anyone survive?" Quick asked.

"The power of God," Rafeo yelled, his voice dripping with sarcasm as he raised his hands to the ceiling, his voice echoing throughout the building.

"What?" Quick said, almost laughing.

"No, really," Rafeo answered, coming out of his pose and letting his tone return to normal. "The world was at a tipping point. The people who were not on the same path as the Savages were, well, they were gonna lose; it's as simple as that. But then, one day, well, I guess only a hundred and fifty, hundred and sixty years ago, God appeared, and I don't mean in an oil stain on the ground or a mound of ground beef. I mean thunder, lightning and all that great shit." Rafeo waved as though not liking his own story. "He was like a beacon to the scattered remainder of humanity, and they flocked to him in droves. He helped them with technology, allowing them to build the great walls of the Citadels and the automated weapons that adorn their battlements. And all He required in return was their faith." Rafeo listened to his voice fade before he dared look at Quick. "Pretty good deal, huh?" he finished with raised eyebrows, trying to lighten the mood.

"Yeah, I guess, almost too good," Quick answered quietly.

"Keep in mind, the power of faith and hope. Mabus and Constantine can absorb that energy from their followers; they feed on it. That is their power source, if you will. The more humans that the humans believe in them or follow their doctrine, the stronger they become."

"You actually saw him?" Quick asked, his head cocked in skepticism.

"Sure did. The whole world did." Rafeo answered without hesitation. "I've seen his counterpart, too." His words caught Quick off guard.

"The devil?" he asked, dropping his spoon into his bowl.

"He prefers Mabus, actually," Rafeo answered as a matter of fact, a Cheshire cat grin on his face. The smile soon slunk away as he seemed to take notice of a sound, though he tried not to let on that he was aware of it.

"But that conversation may need to wait for another day," he continued, forcing his calm, but slowly reaching into the folds of his robe and getting a firm grip on his pistol.

"What do you mean, it isn't even late?" Quick stood up, unaware of anything afoot until he saw where Rafeo's hand was.

"Because we are not alone," Rafeo answered quietly, his eyes fixed in the direction from which the noise had come.

Quick could feel his skin tighten as his body tensed, his nerves heightened to react to stimuli to help him find the direction the trouble might come. He noticed Rafeo's stare and prepared himself.

Chapter V

For a moment, Quick was unsure whether the old man was just paranoid; after all, there was no sign of rain, not even a cloud in the sky. Then he heard it, softened footfalls, though not entirely silent in the scattered debris on the ground. Something was in the shadows, but he doubted it could be a Savage. A Savage would not have the tact for stealth; it would have been upon them. Quick acted casually and moved back towards the window, for two reasons: to see if there were signs of any movement outside, and to move into a flanking position.

"Did you like the stew?" Rafeo spoke up quietly, exaggerating his tone slightly in the hopes that Quick might catch on, but not wanting whoever was out there to know they were on to them. Quick answered but did not elaborate further than a "Yeah," as he leaned on the windowsill, his eyes darting everywhere searching for movement.

"How many potatoes did you use in there anyway?" Rafeo understood this was a question in code and was relieved to hear that Quick was aware of the situation. He had chosen a very peculiar time to take an interest in Rafeo's cooking.

"Oh, only one or two," Rafeo answered, meaning he had only identified one, possibly two targets.

"Is there any of yours left?" Rafeo asked, wondering if Quick had seen anything outside.

"Only a single bite, but I will finish it," Quick replied, turned for a moment to face the old man and shoot him a reassuring wink. He had seen the silhouette of a lone figure on the roof of a nearby abandoned house, or what was left of it. Rafeo had noticed Quick moving right next to his rifle, leaning against the wall, and had lowered his right hand to rest next to the barrel, ready to grasp the weapon.

"Leftovers are okay, son." Rafeo was attempting to reassure Quick. "You never know when there might be more mouths to feed." Rafeo's words caught Quick off guard. The sound of movement was nearly unmistakable now, but Quick waited patiently and did not grab the rifle; he now knew that Rafeo wanted him to wait.

"Like this, young fella." Quick heard the words; he snatched the rifle and spun, facing Rafeo, who now had his hands in the air. Quick sighted a figure, shorter than Rafeo, perhaps too small to be a Savage. The figure wore a hooded cloak, with its back to Quick, but had Rafeo at the end of a weapon.

"I like stew, smells good," the cloaked figure said, without looking at Quick.

"Not likely." Quick spat, but at the same time, Rafeo spoke over him.

"I would be honored to share my cuisine," Rafeo answered with a smile and gestured for Quick to lower his rifle. "Though I'm not sure there is enough for all your friends."

Quick slowly lowered his weapon and turned to realize several more cloaked characters in the shadows towards the front of the church; the noisy steps had been a diversion, allowing the others to slip silently into a flanking position. Quick didn't want to admit it, but they had both fallen for the ruse, and he was impressed. The fact that the other spoke, proof that he was indeed not a Savage, so Quick found himself curious to see what was happening here. Slowly, he lowered his weapon to the ground, leaving it where it had been to start with.

"It's all right, Quick; we're among friends," Rafeo reassured his young companion, lowering his hands.

"Only one or two potatoes, huh?" Quick said sarcastically to the old man, who could only shrug in response.

Slowly, cautiously, the others from the front of the church moved in on the altar. Quick moved with the same careful pace to stand next to Rafeo. The two groups stood eyeing each other before the other spoke. Quick noted that they all seemed fairly young. Each carried a weapon, something Rafeo had always said, not possible anymore for humans. So complete was the polarization of the human race that should any human ever take up arms, they would either take ill and be rendered unconscious or worse; they could rapidly mutate into a Savage. Quick had never had cause to question the old man's word until now.

"Master Rafeo. I am Gabriel of the Magi," the young man said. The fact that Gabriel already knew

Rafeo's name did not escape Quick's notice. The young Magi appeared quite uncertain about how to respond to Quick. Quick thought he looked familiar, as if they had met before. Due to his memory loss, he had no way to confirm this. He didn't want to create a scene by asking about it; it didn't seem like the right time. He chose to see what else he could learn just by listening. Rafeo reacted with discomfort toward Gabriel for a moment, as if recognizing that he had just been revealed.

"You all must be hungry. Please come and eat." The invitation was taken up quickly by all of them except Gabriel. The others dropped their weapons where they stood and made a beeline for the stew, eating it with their hands. Quick watched, an eyebrow slightly raised in surprise.

"So, this is another of our brethren? I swear he is familiar to me," Gabriel said, staring intently at Quick. Rafeo did not respond. He moved next to Gabriel, placing his hand on the other's shoulder, and led him away from Quick, who, for lack of better ideas, stood and watched the scene unfold around him. His attention was split between the small horde ravenously devouring the stew right out of the pot and following Rafeo with Gabriel.

"I am not exactly sure." Quick thought, he heard Rafeo say as he walked away. Quick had noticed Gabriel bore a similar mark on his neck as Rafeo. Quick had often caught himself staring at the mark whenever Rafeo would go on about one thing or another; it only became relevant now that he had seen another person with so-nearly the same mark. He walked closer to the group who had nearly finished off the stew; he noticed the mark on their necks as well. A small star-shaped purple mark. He walked past, trying to imagine the mark's significance while trying to overhear Rafeo's conversation.

He had walked nearly to the front of the church, deep in thought, before he had realized it. He looked again towards Rafeo and Gabriel, then back towards the front of the church when he came nearly face to face with another cloaked figure. It was a woman; her beauty was mesmerizing even in the shadows, but Quick had a sudden flash of memory. He had seen this girl before. Before he could react, he heard the woman gasp and run out of the church and into the night. Quick followed her, but was not alone; everyone else from inside gave chase.

Quick stopped once outside as he found nothing waiting for him but the night air. After a second, he could hear the distinct sound of guns being readied behind him. He again did not move until he heard Rafeo's voice.

"Are you all right, Quick? What did you see?" Quick had to stop and think about that; there was nowhere for someone to have disappeared to so quickly; no cover. Maybe he hadn't seen anything at all.

"I thought," he hesitated. "I thought I saw someone I knew," Quick answered slowly. Her name had been right at the tip of his tongue, but was escaping him more with every breath. Quick shook his head and turned to face the others; he cocked his head at those who had weapons aimed at him.

"Come now. We should be indoors." Rafeo didn't want anyone to fight. Gabriel nodded, and the others lowered their weapons, then turned to go back into the building.

It was a slow but purposeful march back to the front of the church, each member of the two parties eyeing each other carefully, trying to learn what they could of each other. Quick was, if nothing else, a very observant young man with eyes as sharp as a hawk. He noticed that each member of the other party was young, not one over two decades in age. They were thin, nearly malnourished. As hard as his life may have been on the farm, these "kids" had been through worse. The third thing Quick noticed about the others was that they looked tough, not battle hardened or chiseled like a warrior, but more akin to a callus, weathered from their environment.

"So, what the hell is a Magi?" Quick asked once they were all settled indoors again. They had cleared away the gear. They started a small fire in the middle of the aisle in front of the altar. Quick, Rafeo, Gabriel, and one of the other Magi now sat around the low light of the fire. The other two cloaked figures had taken up sentry positions in the shadows.

Quick was feeling more and more unsettled by the minute. He felt greatly disadvantaged for the first time in a long time, mostly due to his memory loss. Everyone here had intimate knowledge of the world as it was now, and by the sounds of things, as it once was. Quick's oldest memory was meeting Rafeo no more than five years ago, and the old man had been keeping secrets.

Rafeo had promised to help him regain his memories, but now, Quick felt no cause to not trust his oldest friend. None of the Magi seemed violent. Quick would feel more uneasy. Then again, if they were violent, it would make his path clearer.

"Now, they are a secret society, living separately from either race or creed of humans left on earth, small in numbers but determined to restore order to this world," Rafeo explained.

"But only a shadow of our former existence," Gabriel finished with a smile. "Centuries ago, the Magi were the keepers of the Guardian's power and knowledge on Earth, back when Rafeo was a young man."

Quick's first reaction was to giggle at the thought that Gabriel was making light of Rafeo's age, one of Quick's favorite hobbies, until he realized no one else was laughing.

"Centuries ago? How in the name of God is that possible?" he scoffed.

"In the name of God is how, though we know him by another name, He is the Guardian," Rafeo explained and tried unsuccessfully to smile. "I guess it is to be the night for difficult conversations," Rafeo sighed, and slumped slightly where he sat, resigning himself to having to explain all of this as well.

Rafeo stirred the coals, stoking the fire slightly. He placed another chunk of wood, a piece of one of the old pews, onto the fire. They watched the smoke, what little there was, because it was so dry, rise slowly into the blackness of the high ceiling and out into the night through small holes in the roof. The lacquer finish on the wood, although faded, added an interesting odor to the fire.

"A few days from now marks my two thousand five hundred and seventieth year on this earth." Rafeo knew there was no way to ease into this topic. He watched Quick's face curl in confusion, his expression amplified by the long shadows from the fire. "That's two thousand six hundred and one years of living in shame for a failure I cannot seem to rectify, for the life of me." The irony of his last few words was not wasted on himself; Rafeo had chosen them carefully.

"The Guardian," he said with a sense of grandeur. Quick, not sure if it shared an element of sarcasm. "God, whatever he has been called, He has been many things to many people."

Quick was surprised at the casual nature of the conversation. They were discussing God himself, almost as if he were an old friend. Gabriel's lack of surprise told Quick that he had at least heard this story before.

"He was the most powerful, perhaps the oldest of a race of celestial, immortal beings. The true nature of their power is a mystery to us, but suffice it to say, absolute." Rafeo hesitated while he searched for his words.

"From what history records, their power also enslaved them to their tasks of controlling the universe. One may control time, the other, gravity. Yet another would ensure balance in nature, and each one performs that same duty from time immemorial.

Perhaps an eternity performing the same tasks made them stop looking for a different way to do things, but it is a matter that mortal man will never truly understand."

"The Guardian, however, did on one occasion find the will to change his condition and, from how it has been recorded anyway, created man, not so much out of love or some higher purpose but more out of curiosity. Man was made more as an experiment or a dare, maybe, than anything else."

Rafeo paused for a moment to drink from his wine. He looked over to Quick and stared into his eyes. Rafeo could see the questions forming in his mind and decided to take another drink before continuing.

"Simple and mortal, man was given no particularly exceptional gifts, except one, perhaps," Rafeo raised his eyebrows at that moment, perhaps to emphasize an otherwise unimportant fact. "And yet he thrived. The other Immortals soon came to learn of the Guardian's project and wanted to observe. They challenged man. Time and again, through major catastrophic events or simple challenges, one on one; they were impressed with mankind's resilience. Some say it was that quality which caused the others to demand or at least beg for man's destruction."

"And our ONE gift?" Quick asked, referring to what Rafeo had just said.

"Ah, yes, free will," Rafeo smiled, "which can give us hope. Unlike the Quies who are bound to their endless duties, we are free to believe or not; we can choose to be whatever we set our minds to; at least, that used to be the case."

Rafeo paused; he thought he saw Quick forming another question. The young man fidgeted in his seat, even held his finger up slightly as if to interject, but changed his mind, shook his head, and motioned for Rafeo to pass the bottle instead. Even Rafeo had to admit it was the more logical choice for the boy and passed the bottle with a smile.

"Over hundreds of millennia, they did try to wipe us out; there was flooding, fires, volcanoes, war. They were successful several times, but the Guardian would pity the man every time. More often than not, mankind would pull through, overcome the power of the gods, even. The Guardian was impressed; he decided he wanted the chance to walk in our shoes, feel what we feel, live how we live. He relinquished his power, became mortal, and came to be among us, like living in a hamster cage for a day." Rafeo turned to Gabriel, and they laughed boisterously as though it were a punch line. Silence overcame the group as the laughter faded away. Quick wasn't sure, so far, what to make of it all. He certainly wasn't the type to laugh just to fit in. Instead, he sat quietly and stared Rafeo down until he felt it.

"And?" Quick said into the fire, as he looked away from his friend.

"And, it was a golden age for man." The serious, almost painful tone had returned to his voice. "To truly become human, the Guardian would have to shed all of his power; what better place to store all that knowledge than in a book."

Quick had a memory come to him. It was over a year ago, back on the farm. He had finished his chores faster than usual and had bounded into the house. The front room of the house had a fireplace in it and served as a den. Quick had never really spent any time in that room. He found it too warm while the hearth was ablaze, as it usually was. This day, he remembered Rafeo caught by surprise, and he tried to sweep a large book out of sight. Quick hadn't thought anything of it until just now. He remembered seeing the book end up in a chest; the chest he remembered the old man placing under the bench seat of the carriage.

"A book?" Quick said it slowly as he connected the memories.

"The Guardian chose to entrust the book to humans and not risk the others, the Quies, as they are called, stealing his power. There were a few unfortunate instances when the keepers of the Book had read its pages. The power of the Book could not be contained by any mere mortal, but the Book wants to be read. It extends its will to anyone around, whispering and taunting any man to take it up." Rafeo paused for dramatic effect.

"Unfortunate instances?" Quick asked. Whether he believed the story or not, he was at least paying attention.

"There once was an island called Atlantis, one of the early Utopian states of man. The Guardian shared his knowledge and technology freely with mankind. Perhaps it was too much, too soon." Rafeo again stirred the coals with his long stick before continuing. "The entire island's continent was swallowed by the sea, and wiped clean from the earth. All from one human reading one line from the book."

Quick shifted in his seat; he could see pain in Rafeo's eyes. Quick drank again from the bottle and passed it back to the old man. Rafeo nodded and drank deeply from the bottle.

"After that," Rafeo continued after swallowing, "came the birth of the Magi; a race separated from humanity, isolated, trained to handle the book. It was always in threes. Three of their best are chosen, one for his wisdom, one for bravery, and the third for nobility. All three are entrusted to return the book to the Guardian in human form and prepare him to return when his time on Earth is finished. To help them do that, they are given temporary gifts of immortality; no longer are they susceptible to any frailty of the human condition. Only a weapon that has been touched by the blood of the Guardian himself can kill them."

Quick had figured out that Rafeo was a Magi. His thoughts now turned to where the other two of Rafeo's team might be. If they were always three, it meant that a few people were missing from the party. Rafeo could see the gears turning in Quick's mind.

"Time and again, the Guardian would come. It is said that life, mortal life, gave him a whole new experience, the entire gamut of human emotions. The thrill of danger, the rush of physical pleasure, and the pursuit of accomplishing important, meaningful things within a small amount of time before death came for you. These things addicted the Guardian to the human condition, particularly the sex part." Rafeo raised an eyebrow as if to solicit a response from Quick; it did not work, however, and he continued.

"Some of his residual power would remain, enabling the human Guardian to have what would be seen as magic, giving him influence and power. As a bonus, the humans would take note of his existence, spawning a new religion with nearly every visit. Despite the Guardian's attempts to keep a low profile or even discouraging a following, the humans always seemed to want a hero or a savior." Rafeo's voice became slightly hushed, darker even. "The prayers, the faith of the humans, became an incredible power source for the Guardian. The more people believed and prayed to him or offered sacrifices, the stronger he grew. Perhaps this is why the others wanted to annihilate us. But soon the Guardian would be powerful enough not to have to heed the concerns of the others," he chuckled, and looked at Gabriel. "Bloody good for us, that." They both laughed, though they noticed no change in Quick. Rafeo got the feeling the tale was falling on deaf ears. He shrugged slightly and continued his story.

"Countless times he would come, and countless times the Magi would deliver him without a single incident, until it was my turn." Now Rafeo slouched slightly as if the weight of the world was upon him. He drew several deep breaths, as if trying to muster the strength to finish what was to come. His mind seemed to drift, and if what he said was true, he certainly had many years of memories to get caught up in. The fire popped quietly, and the sound filled the hall for several moments. Even Gabriel had a look of desire to help Rafeo finish his story, willing him to go on.

"On my watch, one of the trios killed my other compatriot and stole the book, well, most of it. Fortunately, I managed to reclaim the book before any damage was done. It has changed hands a few times over the millennia, but thankfully, no one has figured out a way to use its power to usurp the Guardian's power. His soul is trapped in mortal form, reincarnated over and over again, with no knowledge of who he is until I could restore him.

It was my failing that has doomed mankind to the fate it now suffers, and my disgrace that has cost me my freedom and consumes me to correct." Even in the long shadows from the fire, Quick noticed a tear run down the old man's cheek. "I have struggled for millennia to restore the Guardian. I have come close, only to fail again." Rafeo gripped the stick he had been using to stoke the fire, as though he would ring his guilt from the staff. "I feel weak and unable to continue, but I am truly unable to die, so what choice do I have?" Though his head hung low, he lifted his eyes to look at Quick again. "I long for sleep, but it never comes."

Quick was disturbed by the performance. His mind raced to process this world-altering news. His first step was to try to figure out if it was believable or not. How could one possibly accept that *not only is "god" real*, but he has visited Earth several times. And now the world is caught up in a plot that would have the power of God possessed by usurpers. If true, why did Rafeo wait until now to tell him?

The story swirled through his mind, dizzying him to say the least. He could feel beads of sweat forming on his forehead as he struggled to his feet to distance himself a bit from the fire. The others stood, as well, but after a hand gesture from Rafeo, no one moved towards the boy. Quick took several deep breaths and stared into the dying light from the fire as it struggled to reach the full height of the church. After several moments, he walked back towards Rafeo, shaking his head in disbelief. Once close enough, he stopped to put his hand on Rafeo's shoulder as if to support himself, and looked into the old man's eyes.

"Raf, why haven't you told me this before?" he asked, still shaking his head slightly.

The old man sighed heavily. "Would you, could you have believed me?" he answered, then nodded to Gabriel, very subtly.

"I'm not sure I do now," Quick answered slowly. "I just don't understand," he shrugged.

Rafeo smiled warmly, then nodded again to Gabriel, this time Quick noticed. Before Quick could turn to see what was happening, the silence was shattered by a rifle blast that struck Rafeo right in the heart. Before Quick's eyes, the old man dropped like a felled tree, his smile still on his lips. Quick dropped next to the old man.

"Raf! NO!" he yelled. His first instinct was to grab his weapons and slay Gabriel where he stood; however, he had laid his weapons where he sat next to the fire, figuring they were safe for the night, and Gabriel still had his weapon. Quick turned and stared at Gabriel; had his eyes been weapons, Gabriel would surely be dead.

"What the hell?" Quick growled as he spat all of his hatred towards Gabriel. Despite having Quick saw at the end of his weapon, he was very frightened.

"Just wait, just wait, you'll see." Gabriel held out his hand, pleading for Quick not to end him where he stood. "He wanted you to see something."

Quick suddenly forgot about Gabriel as he felt Rafeo's hand gently fall on his own as he squatted next to his body. The room fell silent for what felt like an eternity. Blood drained from the lifeless body next to him as Quick's mind raced to process everything.

Although angry, he was more confused. He then recalled Rafeo saying that he could not die. Quick shuddered in disbelief as he felt Rafeo take a breath. He was trying to speak, and Quick leaned down to be closer to the old man, to hear him better.

"Because there is a great distinction to be made between knowing something and believing something," Rafeo said as he sat up and smiled at the boy. "I would hope this display, though shocking, may chase away any lingering doubts." Rafeo smiled wider.

"Now, you know that I did not lie about being immortal; the question is, do you believe the rest of what I told you here tonight?"

Quick stared; he could not hide a shiver as the reality of the situation came to light for him in his mind. "Very convincing, yes," he whispered nervously, and slowly stood. Reaching a handout

Quick moved into help Rafeo to his feet. Once standing, Quick searched his friend for signs of an injury, barely a spot of blood to be found.

"Good god," Quick whispered in astonishment. His search of Rafeo completed, and he finally made eye contact with the old man again.

"Yes," Rafeo spoke quietly, his smile fading ever so slightly. "That is who we are looking for."

Chapter VI

Quick was unable to sleep that night; the hard wooden bench he used as a bed provided little, if any, in terms of comfort. His mind raced as he lay in the dark silence, the peace of the night was only disturbed by the deep breathing, not quite a snore from Rafeo. The coals from the fire offered little light; although the glow was warm and comforting, it was not enough for him to find solace this night. After several hours of frustration, Quick decided to get up; he sat up and swung his legs over the side of the bench. Sitting with his head in his hands for a few moments, he kept going over and over the events from the evening.

The casual conversation of the existence of god, well, gods really, just gave him pause. Every time he closed his eyes, he could see Rafeo being shot, over and over again. He should be dead, but the display was only to prove the power of the Guardian. He couldn't help but feel a sense of doom for the human race if they were, in fact, incapable of defending themselves against a foe they had faced many times; they had no chance, other than their technology.

And what of himself? Perhaps a Magi? One of these few souls who still had their free will? That must be why Rafeo had taken him in all those years ago. Why, then, had the old man never mentioned anything of this before? Maybe it was too hard a subject to bring up. The old man may not have known how to word it, or was afraid of his reaction.

"Hey, pass the butter. Oh, by the way, I'm immortal," Quick muttered to himself quietly in jest, as he got to his feet and slowly, carefully walked towards the large windows on the far side of the church, while imagining Rafeo trying to explain this to him while still at the farm. He had not bothered to grab his shirt or weapon, figuring he was not going far.

He carefully stepped over several young people gathered at the fire that night. He was most careful not to wake anyone, for no other reason than that he was in no mood for company in that moment.

Looking out of the dirty windows, it was hard to miss the glow in the night sky to the west. The Citadel walls could be seen, and the light from the city within reflected off them. Quick figured they had to be about another half day's travel. As he stared into the distance, his mind wandered to what, if any, answers he might find once they were there. Would there be something to trigger his memory, or maybe a doctor to help him? If he did get his memory back, would he like what he finds of himself?

Other than those distant lights, the night was still dark, just like at the farm. He tried to imagine what the city around him must have looked like. All these houses and buildings must have been home to thousands. It must have been full of life, people coming and going at all hours.

Rafeo had shown him images he had called movies on an old computer back on the farm. It was probably the only piece of technology he had ever seen, but Quick could remember fondly watching the images over and over. A glimpse into the past, perhaps how this city had once been, full of lights and life, even fun and adventure. Just the thought of being able to go somewhere and pick out food you wanted, without having to grow it or hunt for it yourself, must have been a magical time.

Quick smiled and made his way to what had been a washroom at one point. He pulled a flashlight from his belt to light the way inside. He stopped and leaned on a sink from which water had not flowed in a century. The mirror over the sink was still intact, though quite dirty and discolored. He rubbed it a little bit with his hand and stared into his eyes; the dark pools stared right back. He questioned who he was and stared as though expecting the reflection to answer his unspoken questions. He studied his face and his upper body. His beard had gotten a little longer and unruly, just like his matted brown hair that now nearly touched his shoulders.

He could make out several scars; one on his face just above his left eye, a small mark he had received recently from the edge of a Savage's blade in a moment of complacency. There was one on his neck and another larger one on his chest, left side measuring at least a foot in length; the origins of either of these were still unknown to him. Nowhere did he find a star-shaped birthmark.

"Who are you?" he asked the mirror, again, still hoping he would get an answer; after all, he did watch Rafeo come back from the dead tonight, and maybe he'd get lucky. But no answers came.

"Thanks anyway," he said, grinning at himself.

There were signs of life emerging from the main hall. Quick gathered himself and slowly walked back towards the altar. As he did, several youngsters could be seen quickly gathering their meager possessions and scurrying away as though the gathering daylight outside brought with it their demise.

Quick looked to Rafeo now, reliving the flash memory of the night before as he rose from slumber, similarly to how he had risen from death. The two exchanged an awkward glance but uttered no words as Quick busied himself with preparing to move camp.

He took a load of supplies, including a rifle and the cooking utensils, out to the wagon. Indeed, the term was contemporary; the term conjured in one's mind an ancient lumbering cart hauled across the ground on wooden wheels. This vehicle was a hybrid electric vehicle, bristling with modern technology that kept the payload and drivetrain sections of the vehicle off the ground. He could also propel it at great speeds when the power cells were fully charged. Quick inspected the power cells and was pleased to find them, in fact, fully charged. He placed a hand on the left rear flank of the Clydesdale that was the power source for the whole apparatus.

"Good boy," he said, as he slid his hand along the animal's body and walked towards the front of the creature. The horse whinnied and nodded slightly; Quick had a carrot he had saved from dinner, and he fed it to the horse. As it chewed on the carrot, Quick surveyed the area. There appeared to be no immediate threat, though the clouds forming in the distance did not go unnoticed.

"A beautiful creature," the voice said of a woman who came out of nowhere. Quick spun and drew his sidearm, coming to rest positioned perfectly to kill the woman he found standing on the other side of the horse. Not only had her approach been obscured from his senses, but from the horse as well, or at least the horse had not reacted to her approach.

To Quick's surprise, he found his eyes locked to the same eyes of the woman he had seen the night before.

"At least, I know I wasn't hallucinating," he said under his breath. They stared at each other for several moments under the neck of the gentle draught horse. The woman smiled pleasantly without words, as though waiting for Quick to break the silence. He stared and squinted at her as if the more he did it, the sooner he would recognize this stranger, but to no avail.

The woman tried to smile but found herself staring back at the man before her. She took in his full six-foot-four-inch frame, his physique similar to Adonis. She noticed the way his clothes appeared. They were hanging from him as though they were the simple layers of a beggar, but still recognized that every piece of the wardrobe was purposeful.

"Thank you," Quick said, followed by an awkward grin. "You meant the horse, of course," he said at the same time as the woman corrected his poor attempt at humor.

"Yes, the horse," she reiterated with a smile. They stared at each other in silence for another minute before Quick could no longer refrain.

"You're the girl from last night," he finished slowly. The girl's demeanor changed only slightly, so little in fact that Quick did not pick up on it.

"Yes," she agreed after an awkward moment. "Last night she repeated, but then faltered.

"You are damned good at hiding; I'll give you that," Quick stammered, without knowing what else to say.

"Oh yes, I learned from the best," the girl said.

"Quick!" Rafeo's voice caught the young man's attention, but for a second, when he turned back to the woman, she was gone. He looked around frantically for a moment, only to confirm what he already knew: that she was no longer there. He questioned if she had been there in the first place or if she had been a figment of his imagination.

"Quick!" again came Rafeo's call.

"What?" he shouted in frustration over the interruption and subsequent loss of the woman.

"We need to get going," Rafeo answered in kind, as he had slipped back into the church and busied himself gathering their stuff.

"The wind is shifting direction," he heard from both Rafeo and the woman's voice, causing Quick to look frantically for the girl. He quickly searched under the horse and through the flat deck of the wagon, before accepting that she was gone. He then looked to the horizon and noted that the gathering storm he had seen in the distance was getting closer; even still, he knew he would risk the storm's presence to find the girl again. As though blaming Rafeo for the reality of the situation, he stared the unwitting man down and leapt from the wagon.

"Okay, Fine. Let's get moving," Quick spat as he dropped to the ground and started towards the church to gather the old man and the rest of their gear.

The pair soon emerged from the church with the last of their equipment.

"Shotgun!" Quick called, as he tossed his bag into the bed of the wagon, racked a round into his rifle, and leapt into the passenger seat, leaving little room for discussion about who was driving the vehicle. Rafeo could sense and understand the young man's discord. He opted not to say anything on the matter for the moment.

Quick sighted in the storm; it had gotten closer. He swept the area for one last glimpse of the woman, an effort that did not go unrewarded. She stood at the base of a tree that had fallen atop a house. She caught his glance, albeit through his rifle scope, then leapt through a nearby window and out of sight.

With a sharp whistle, Rafeo urged their lead into motion and engaged the electric drive; the motion of the vehicle under him caused Quick to lose his balance and his sight of the woman. He caught himself, then spun and dropped into his seat rather abruptly and threw a sideways glance at the driver, a look that went without reaction but not without notice.

As they crested the top of a long, gradual grade in the road, the ground dropped away in front of them, opening to a vast open area of nothing. The huge walls of the city now covered the horizon in its entirety. Not a word had been spoken between the two for nearly an hour, and Quick had finally collected his thoughts.

"Okay, so, to recap." Quick began, and Rafeo straightened up slightly in his seat. "God is real. Well, gods are real; they are highly advanced space aliens who feed on people's prayers. They are the source of mankind and magic? And you're immortal as well."

Temporarily," Rafeo corrected, trying to make the conversation, as outlandish as it was, sound normal.

"Uh-huh, how old are you?"

"Two thousand, five hundred and seventy, give or take a year or two," Rafeo answered casually.

"Temporarily?" Quick answered, as though coming to terms with it all. "Anything else?" he questioned. Rafeo drew in a breath and readied a response, but before he could speak, Quick blurted out another question; Rafeo let him speak.

"So, this wasn't covered; why is the world in such a mess? Why do people have to live in giant walled cities and piss their pants every time it rains? You said something about it was your fault?"

Rafeo was forming his response and twitched in his seat slightly, but again, before he could speak, a single drop of rain struck Quick on his left cheek. The storm had quietly rolled closer than they had noticed. The young man barely had time to raise his rifle as a Savage came flying through the air, its crude blade drawn over its head, ready to strike. Quick sighted it, fired, striking the assailant right in the chest; the force of the impact knocked the attacker off course, and the lifeless body tumbled to a heap at the side of the crude roadway they were on.

The two men leapt to their feet as the vehicle halted, and the horse whinnied nervously as the two scanned the immediate area.

"It'll be on us in minutes." Quick's breath was tight, his voice was sharp.

Rafeo looked to the Citadel, then back to the storm. "We won't make it in time," he said aloud, what they both knew. "Not like this anyway." Quick nodded in understanding, and they both jumped from their seats to the front of the vehicle. Rafeo unhooked the reins and lead from the horse and turned him loose. Quick was fond of the horse and paused, reaching his hand onto the animal's shoulder. Rafeo had already remounted the vehicle and engaged the repulse drives.

"He should be fine. They're after us," Rafeo barked; his tone conveyed his sense of urgency.

Quick patted the horse farewell, and as if the animal understood, it bolted away at a gallop. Quick nodded, then bounded back into the vehicle, which had already started underway. He no sooner planted his feet than he fired twice more from his rifle, dropping two more attackers.

"This bucket better go faster," Quick yelled, as he now had an all too-perfect view of the scene unfolding behind them. The rain started to fall as Quick's eyes scanned the area. The very ground of the valley they were in seemed to move in the gathering darkness; an entire hoard of Savages was upon them.

Quick dropped his rifle in favor of another, an energy weapon. The power cell was not unlimited, but would allow him several hundred shots. The only problem was that he feared he would need more than that, and the nearest replacement energy cell was in the city. He activated the weapon with a shrug as it whirred into life in his hands; a blue glow from the indicator told him the weapon was ready. Quick leaned against the wall of the truck to steady himself as best he could and opened fire at the front line of the horde was right behind them.

At this range, he couldn't miss; every round he fired brought down an enemy. By the dozens, the creature tumbled; luckily, for every dead Savage that dropped, another two or three would stumble over that body. The single rifle was very effective at slowing their inhumanly fast charge. Being bipedal, these creatures, who stood only slightly taller than Quick, could reach speeds of thirty kilometers per hour, nearly matching the speed of their vehicle.

Quick's first volley had opened some ground between them and the horde. He looked around to make sure there was no ambush ahead. The Citadel walls were now a flurry of activity. Searchlights and floodlights flashed into life, lighting up the area for hundreds of meters in all directions around them. This illustrated their plight even more.

"Ahead!" Quick yelled as several figures approached in an ambush on the road in front of them. Rafeo fired from a shotgun with lightning speed and incredible accuracy, clearing the path before Quick could turn. With a shrug, figuring Rafeo didn't need his help, he turned back to the hoard.

Quick fired again, this time with similar results, but it did little more than disrupt the wave momentarily. Judging by the distance they still had to cover, he knew they would be on the two of them before they reached the city. Quick continued to fire; he held them off until the blue glow from the weapon disappeared and the power cell ran dry. He watched as the horde drew closer. He dropped the rifle and reached for his things in the front seat.

"This is gonna be close," Rafeo said, not fully hiding his nervousness as Quick reached for his sword and removed the scabbard.

"This is gonna be messy," Quick answered, not fully hiding his anger.

Quick turned back to the back of the truck as several Savages leapt aboard. He dispatched them easily enough as more jumped aboard. Quick set to work on them, but as he did, the horde behind them became engulfed in a series of explosions.

"Yeah-ha," Rafeo shouted from the front of the vehicle. Quick turned to see the city's defense barrage open fire, bathing the area around them in light and cannon fire. Quick had to handle a few more that managed to make it aboard the vehicle. He could see the open door of the city beckoning them to safety, but they could not let these Savages enter with them.

Another volley came from the city, this time closer than the last. Quick had to raise an arm to shield himself from the heat of the blast.

"They know we're the good guys, right?" he yelled to Rafeo, who didn't answer right away. They were now within a few hundred feet of the opening.

"Right?" Quick yelled a little louder, then turned to face a dozen more of the creatures were upon them. He slashed with surgical precision, wasting no time or effort on form, just dispatching the creatures as efficiently as possible. He felt slightly relieved as he could see the doorway only feet away and only five of the Savages on board, easy odds.

Quick drew his sword back for another blow, but was interrupted as another volley from the city guns, this time trained directly at them, hit home. They exploded just under the back of the vehicle, launching them like a fulcrum, into the air. He saw the blast doors slam shut behind them and managed to slay one last creature as he tumbled through the air. Then everything went black.

Chapter VII

The rear of the vehicle shot into the air from the force of the exploding round right under the rear repulse drive unit. Rafeo was shot forward but stayed in the driver's seat by holding onto the controls for dear life. Rafeo saw several figures fly from the back of the vehicle, not realizing that one of them was Quick. The rear of the vehicle slammed to the ground; the repulse drive unit was destroyed.

The vehicle slid sideways and tipped on its side. It slid for a short distance, then slammed at nearly full speed into a building. Rafeo's injuries were not life-ending; he knew he'd have to play up because it would raise too many questions if he walked away from the wreck without a scratch.

His main concern was Quick. He dropped to the ground and searched frantically for the boy before the crowd could gather. Much to his disappointment, Rafeo found the young man's body in the wreckage, he knew he had to act fast so as not to give away his secret. He pulled and stashed from his belt, a small stash of gold, frankincense, and myrrh. He placed them next to the young man and quickly spoke the word "resurrectio a Latin key phrase for the spell. The three ingredients vaporized, the resulting gases floated over, then into the young man's body. Moments later, Rafeo was relieved to see

Quick breathe again. Quick was still unconscious, but he was alive. Finally, several people came to his aid, and Rafeo allowed them to assist him with walking, though he did not need the help.

"Master Rafeo." One of his helpers recognized him. Before he could acknowledge the man, several security robots showed up on the scene. The security bots were big lumbering figures concealing weapons, so as not to panic the humans that were present. One of the bots found a Savage that was still alive and blasted it to dust with a weapon, causing many of the people present to lose consciousness for a moment. The robots continued to walk around the scene uninterrupted.

"Found another," the mechanical voice reported as it held another figure aloft by its foot.

"Wait," Rafeo ordered, as he recognized Quick in the clutches of the machine. "He's not one of them." Rafeo continued as he marched towards the robot unassisted, his arms waving frantically.

"Termination halted," the robot answered. "Identity unconfirmed," it continued, then turned from Rafeo as if he weren't there. "Taking subject for processing," was the last thing Rafeo heard from the machine as it walked away. Rafeo could not go after Quick, as the crowd was reassembling around him.

***   ***   ***

Quick awoke slowly in a dark, cold room. He was in pain throughout most of his upper body and had a pounding headache. He tried to remember how he got there, but the last thing he remembered was "flying through the air." He grunted out loud as if expecting a response. When none came, he attempted to sit up but couldn't move his feet. He wanted to rub his head next, but discovered his arms were chained.

"What the hell?" he muttered. As if on cue, the bed he was on began to retract into the wall, and the chains on his wrist were pulled upwards, forcing Quick into a standing position. The exertion, in his condition, caused him to lose consciousness again, and he fell limp, held upright only by his bindings.

***   ***   ***

Quick awoke later with a start to find himself in the same room, still chained to the wall in a standing position. He noticed quickly that his clothes had been removed, and, in their place, he had what could only be described as a poncho draped over his neck, barely covering him.

He was also not alone. There was a young woman in the room with him. She was red-haired, almost a foot shorter than he, and no bigger around the waist than his left leg. She was quite attractive, but for obvious reasons, he tried to ignore that fact. The woman crossed the room to him and dropped to her knees at his feet. Quick nervously looked down, giving away the fact that he was awake, but it did not affect her.

The woman worked on cleaning and dressing a wound on his upper right leg near his hip. She had brushed the hanging poncho aside, out of the way of her work, twice with no success. Without a word, she stood and tucked the lower portion of the poncho over Quick's shoulder.

"Hi," Quick said nervously as she did, but the woman did not say a word. She dropped back down and set to work, pausing only for a moment to notice his growing manhood, and glanced up at him with a smile.

He tried to relax, wincing once as she applied bandages to the wound. The woman finished with the dressing and, without a word, took his phallus into her mouth and began to pleasure him.

"I. Oh god." Quick stammered, uncertain if he should object to the treatment. A full-blown conversation erupted in his mind between his conscience and his desire, the latter winning, of course, as he struggled against his bindings. But unsuccessfully, while the woman continued.

"I'm Quick," he blurted out finally, and nervously after several minutes. The woman stopped only for a second to respond.

"Doesn't seem like it," she said and continued her task.

"Well, this is... awkward," Quick said, resigning himself to ride this out.

"I can't imagine anything more awkward, really," he continued as he closed his eyes, only to have them dart open again as the door at the other end of the room swung open. Rafeo entered alone and stopped short in the shadows as the scene unraveled before him.

"Wrong again," Quick whispered more to

himself, continuing his thought from earlier. The girl remained unaffected by the old man's presence.

"Quick!" Rafeo shouted.

"She would disagree, apparently," was all the young man could muster to say in a rather squeaky voice.

"What the hell are you doing?" Rafeo barked at the young man.

"Me?" Quick answered and sarcastically shook his restraints.

Rafeo was uncertain what to do next; he took two paces forward as if to intervene, then turned as though to leave the room.

"Owe – hey. What was that?" Quick had felt a sharp pain in the back of his leg. It felt as though the girl had dug her nails into his flesh at the moment of climax. Rafeo lingered through another awkward moment by the door. In that time, he heard some grunting from Quick, followed by a short giggle from the girl.

Rafeo turned back to see the woman stand and lower his poncho; she kissed him on the cheek. The look on Quick's face was absolute bewilderment and a hint of desire to know her name at least. The Girl then turned and walked past Rafeo, who was now speechless. She paused at the door, turned back to wink at Quick, and let out a rather loud burp. Quick offered only an incredibly awkward smile in response.

Rafeo watched the entire exchange, still in shock.

Several minutes passed; the two men stood in awkward silence, trying to find a way to ignore the elephant in the room. Finally, Quick coughed nervously, waiting for what was to come.

"I suppose it would be somewhat pointless to ask how you were feeling," Rafeo did not attempt to hide his sarcasm in the slightest.

Quick smiled like a Cheshire cat and cleared his throat before he returned to reality.

"I'm just as much in shock as you - what the hell was that all about?" Quick yelled, but his voice was choked. "I thought these people couldn't commit any sins!" Quick spat.

"Awkward, maybe, but sex is not a sin boy, just a natural part of life," Rafeo said, with a small grin poking through; then his face returned to its normal scowl. "I wish I could un-see that, but here we are." Rafeo was still in the moment.

"Okay, okay, never mind. How 'bout you get me out of these bloody chains?" Quick allowed the momentary euphoria to pass, outraged by his current predicament.

"About that." Rafeo began but was cut off by the door opening and the room lights coming up. A party of five people entered the room, each carrying a clipboard.

"How does it speak?" The first man was dressed either as a doctor or, from what Quick knew of the society, possibly a priest. The rest of the party was more of the same, except for a woman at the back. When Quick saw her, he had a flash of images in his head, none of which made sense. They felt like memories, and she was in them, though he was at least fairly certain she was the woman he had seen the night before at the Magi camp. He shook it off for the moment, as he was too angry to concentrate on that.

"Because I'm not a dog or a monkey, I'm a man, that's how!" Quick shouted.

The group froze in their tracks and scribbled notes on their pads.

"Do something!" Quick grunted at Rafeo.

The group retreated from the room, leaving Quick in his chains and only the light that crept through the window. Rafeo accompanied the others, attempting to get some answers, presumably to secure Quick's freedom. He waved quickly and nodded to Quick, trying to comfort the young man on his way out the door.

"Damn!" Quick whispered as the room fell silent. "For a minute there, I thought they were gonna let her have a turn while they took notes," he said sarcastically to the shadows, examining his restraints, just in case he had to free himself.

***   ***   ***

As darkness fell, Quick could see out of the window. He could tell he was in a tall building that overlooked a large area filled with much shorter buildings. Judging by the lights from each building, he imagined they were houses.

It had been hours since he had seen Rafeo

leave with the others, and no response from anyone. He felt his strength had returned, and he pulled at his restraints, still with no effect. He wished the other girl would come back to help pass the time. He giggled at the thought, but the smirk on his face soon faded as he heard the raindrops starting to fall against the window.

Surely there was nothing to worry about here. The city walls were impenetrable, and they bristled with automated weapons. He allowed himself to relax until he saw the lightning, a sight which he had only seen once or twice before. This meant something big was afoot.

"Raf!" he yelled while pulling against his restraints again. The storm intensity grew while he struggled.

"Raf!" he tried again, then froze in place. Outside, atop a water tower a good distance away, stood a man cloaked in black, his eyes glowed red. The lightning appeared from the figure's hand, exploding onto houses below. The figure then turned and seemed to stare directly at Quick. There was a flash of light and an explosion, and Quick fell unconscious again.

***   ***   ***

Rafeo stood over him, shaking him, trying to wake the young man. Quick sat up and looked around, trying to gain perspective on the moment, then jumped to his feet. The blast had ripped a hole in the wall and, more importantly, released Quick from his bonds.

"They are getting in." Rafeo gestured to the wall where they could see dozens upon dozens of Savages pouring into the city through a gate that one of the earlier lightning strikes had blasted out of position. He handed Quick his pants, his sword, and a pistol. The young man jumped and slipped into his trousers, leaving the poncho to cover his upper body. He landed on his trousers in one fluid motion as he walked to the newly formed opening in the wall of his cell.

A handful of the large security droids had stemmed the flow of attackers through the gate by blocking their path and using their weapons to keep them at bay. The auto-cannons at the top of the wall were dormant, leaving the Savages that had entered the city free to pillage, almost unchallenged, as they were too fast for the cumbersome droids. The lights all over the city were flickering; the lightning controlled by the cloaked figure must have overloaded the electrical system for this entire section of the city.

Quick pointed at the cloaked figure. "He took out the defenses."

"Mabus," Rafeo explained.

"I don't care what his fucking name is." Quick scoffed.

"You get the defenses back up; I'll handle the rest!" Quick was all business now, and leapt from the hole in the wall, performing a series of parlor stunts, bouncing from window ledge to balcony to land on one of the neighbouring building roofs. From there, it was almost a level surface to get to the water tower and Mabus. He sprinted away as soon as his feet were under him.

Quick had at least a kilometer, as the crow flies, across the rooftops, getting closer to his target. As he sprinted and jumped across the open space between buildings, he could see a pack of Savages running along the street below. They would swarm and attack any person who had not yet made it indoors. He hoped his main quarry would wait, but had to deal with the immediate threat below.

Quick drew his sword and dropped from the rooftop to the street below, landing directly onto one of the Savages, driving his blade through the enemy's body, using it to slow his descent or at least absorb some of the impact of his fall. The two Savages that were behind him were caught so completely off-guard watching their compatriot be butchered, that they ran straight into Quick's blade before they realized what hit them. Quick chased down the rest of the pack and, while attacking them from behind, dispatched them all one by one without being discovered.

A series of wall kicks got him back to the rooftops, again, and he focused on Mabus. Quick could feel his hands were sticky on the hilt of his sword from the blood of those he had slain. He could feel his heart pounding in his chest, not from exertion, but rather from rage. Quick was angry by the cowardice of the attacks; no fair fight here, other than his. The people in this city were unable to defend themselves. The lack of honor Mabus incited emotions from Quick that he was not accustomed to.

He ran toward the water tower, covering the distance at a speed greater than he was used to. Quick drew his pistol and fired until the gun was empty. Every round found its mark, and every round seemed to pass through Mabus without causing the slightest amount of damage. In response, Mabus turned to him and, with the wave of his hand, directed a mighty blast of lightning from the heavens to Quick's position.

More by luck than anything else, the charge mostly missed Quick. The energy impact caused an explosion on the rooftop right next to him, sending him flying to the next roof, landing on his side, and sliding into a chimney. Quick grabbed the chimney to keep himself from falling off the roof.

He found his feet as fast as he could and propelled towards Mabus again, stopping after two strides. Noticing another large group of Savages closing in on a group of citizens, huddled in fear on a neighboring roof. He was torn about where his duty lay. Of course, he would save the people, but wanted nothing more than to rip Mabus apart, preferably by hand. From the corner of his eye, Quick could see the marker lights on the century cannons come on; Rafeo must have been successful in his mission. The cannons could handle Mabus once their boot sequence was completed; the people on the roof did not have the luxury of time.

***   ***   ***

Rafeo ran as best he could from Quick's cell, down the corridor to a dispatch station at the first conjunction. The observation team had been in

Quick's cell earlier and was there along with two computer operators; they were all having a heated, panicked discussion amongst themselves.

"I don't know why they aren't working, but I can tell you they are not," a computer technician shouted.

"Tell me the containment protocols are still in place. I don't want that prisoner getting out," the lead doctor screamed.

"Well, it's too late for that; he is out, and you'd best be thankful he is," Rafeo bellowed over the fray to get their attention. "We have bigger issues; I can assure you," he continued. "Where is the automated defense control center?" he asked. The only answer he had was seven stunned faces staring back at him. He raised his hands, shaking in frustration.

"This city is under attack; the walls are breached, and the defense cannons are down! Now, if you all want to die, please keep staring at me like that!" Rafeo was screaming now. It took a few seconds for his words to sink into the group's collective consciousness, and as it did, several of them fainted, but the woman from the group stepped forward, finally.

"Follow me," she said quietly but confidently, and took off down the hall at a running pace. Rafeo followed her as best he could. He slung his rifle over his shoulder as he gave chase.

Rafeo was relieved to learn the control center was in the same building as they reached the stairwell, and the woman paused for him to catch up.

"Top floor," she panted. "My name's Mary, by the way."

"Rafeo," he answered quickly.

"I know," Mary answered as she darted up the stairs. "Everyone knows who you are," Mary continued casually as she accelerated away from Rafeo. He raised an eyebrow at her last statement, then gave chase once again.

They reached the top of the stairs and burst into the control center. Every person inside fell to the ground and took cover, not knowing who or what had just broken into the room.

"We're here to help," Rafeo explained. Several heads slowly rose from cover before realizing it was Rafeo and came out of hiding. They all stood as if waiting for instruction. Rafeo stared back at them, his frustration quickly getting the better of him.

"What do we do, people?" he yelled, and they all clumsily returned to their workstations. There was a flurry of activity and the sound of multiple keystrokes from many different keyboards until one of the groups came forward; he looked at Mary and Rafeo.

"The defenses are down, but we are not sure why." The young man threw a nervous glance towards the window.

"That thing out there seems to be the source of the lightning. I think the lightning is shorting out the system."

Rafeo slowly walked to the window. He was

just in time to see Quick fire a hopeless volley at Mabus, and then a huge lightning bolt appeared to strike him down. Rafeo could feel the hair on the back of his neck stand up; he was angry now.

"Are there any weapons in here?" he asked. The young man who had spoken to him earlier nodded and led Rafeo to a cabinet marked PROTOTYPES. He unlocked the cabinet and had to slip away, dizzy from the ordeal and fearing that he might pass out. Mary was able to stand next to Rafeo, gesturing for him to take up the one weapon that lay before him.

"Is that a neuro-interface in the handle?" she asked. The young man shook his head nervously in agreement but was unable to speak. The fact that Mary was okay was not lost on Rafeo, but he did not mention it at the time.

Instead, he walked right over to the window, picked up a nearby chair, and threw it through the glass, bringing the activity in the room to a halt. He held the weapon in his hand and shrugged as if waiting for further instructions.

"It's a nanite-based weapon; the neurotransmitter in the handle reads the tactical situation through your mind, then the nanites produce the type of projectile that you feel would best suit the situation. There may be a half-second delay as the munitions are produced. It can also change configuration to form swords and other melee weapons," one of the others in the room explained nervously. Rafeo looked down at the weapon in his hand; he was impressed.

"At least that's the working theory," the voice continued. "It was designed and simulated, but no one could test it."

Rafeo's expression now turned skeptical. Rather than debate, he chose to aim and fire at Mabus. Faster than a half second later, several explosive rounds burst from the barrel, screaming towards their target. The rounds impacted the top of the water tower, resulting in an explosion that opened a hole, dropping Mabus into the water and out of sight. Moments later, the defense cannons came online en masse and opened fire on the water tower, vaporizing most of the structure and the water within. Rafeo knew they were not lucky enough to have killed Mabus, but perhaps had convinced him to withdraw. Moments later, a bolt of lightning erupted from the remains of the water tower, streaking towards the sky. Mabus had fled.

***   ***   ***

Quick bounded towards the people on the rooftop. As he jumped from the edge of the neighboring building, the light from a massive explosion erupted behind him, from the direction where Mabus had been. He paid it no mind as he had other things to occupy his attention.

Luckily, the bright light of the explosion obstructed Quick from the Savage's view, like a fighter plane hiding in the sun. Quick was able to use the light from the explosion to his advantage, as it was at his back, he could see just fine, his enemies, not much. he was able to count eight enemies on the rooftop and had his sword at the ready before he landed, wasting no time to go on the offensive.

Quick, cut down two of them almost effortlessly as he landed on the rooftop, as it turns out, the rest of them would prove more of a challenge. Quick dodged two separate overhead blows from the two lead attackers. Getting low and inside the Savages, he drove his sword upward and caught one in the neck, then spun to the left and slashed the blade out of the neck of the first Savage. His blade swooped down and across the torso of the second, splitting the Savage open.

Quick then leapt backwards to the left using his mass and speed to knock three of the Savages into each other, causing them to stumble backward at the same time. Hethen drove his sword back into the lead Savage's gut. The attackers fell, the middle one being stabbed unwittingly by the Savage at the rear, dropping the two dead weights onto the third. Quick's momentum carried him past the pile of bodies, and with a small jump, landed him on the raised edge of another roof. A second, more powerful leap launched him over the heads of the remaining three Savages. He slashed at them frantically, landing before they turned to face him. They all dropped, dead from their injuries.

The last remaining Savage was pinned under the other two lifeless bodies near the edge of the roof, and it was frantically trying to free itself as Quick slowly and purposely approached. As he walked over, he noticed the citizens huddled in a group in the other corner of the rooftop. There they were, all of them, crying and screaming in horror. Quick could hear them, but it did not register as he was steadfast in his intentions.

He paused, standing over the last Savage, its human-looking hand stretched out as its only defense. Quick looked into its yellow but otherwise human-looking eyes. He saw how the red blood from those who had fallen on him contrasted against its gray skin. He waited, examining the creature as if waiting for it or daring it to speak; he wanted the creature to plead. Quick tilted his head as if to say something himself, but instead drove the tip of his sword straight through the other's head. He paused there and twisted the blade to be sure of the kill.

He slowly turned to face the people he had saved, though as his anger subsided and the adrenaline waned, he felt a twinge of guilt over what he had just done. The people on the roof now stretched out their arms in defense, just as the Savage had done moments before. Quick dropped his sword, calming the people only slightly. He realized as he stared at them, confused by their gestures, that one had been injured. He stepped closer to the injured person, a young boy, maybe ten to twelve years old. He had been hit on the head, by the looks of it, and was bleeding. As Quick moved closer, the people shrank away in fear, as though they did not want Quick to touch the boy.

"No, please," a woman, possibly the boy's mother, whispered as Quick leaned closer to the boy. Quick turned his head to face her, staring her down but unable to speak. What a sight he was; the right half of his face blackened and burned from the blast, his blood dripping from his ear and neck, the other half of his face splashed red with the blood of his fallen enemies. The woman fell silent as he stared at her.

Quick then scooped the boy into his arms and walked towards a staircase that was a fire escape, which led from the roof down to the street. The street was a chaotic scene. Public announcement speakers were blaring instructions and signaling the "all clear." People were rushing out of their houses, some to aid in the clean-up and rescue, most just in a panic to find out what had happened, and all were in a state of shock. Through it all, none paid much, if any, attention to Quick or the boy in his arms.

Quick walked in a nearly catatonic state back towards the tall building where he had been held earlier. He made it there unchallenged and stumbled into the lobby. Once inside, he looked around; although many people were there, none came to his aid. Quick screamed at the top of his lungs, easily drowning out the noise from other people.

"I need some help here!"

Finally, someone he had thought was a doctor took the boy from him; still, no one came to his aid. He wandered until he found the stairwell and climbed back to the level he had started on. Once in the hallway, many ran past him, some screaming, others trying to help, and getting annoyed that Quick was in their way.

He was able to navigate back to his cell and made his way into the dark. Tears now streaming down his face, he had never been in such a battle, and it had taken its toll.

Not to say that Quick had never faced as many foes before, but he had never had an audience while doing it. He felt guilty for having terrified the people he was trying to help.

He walked to the back wall and bent down to pick up his bindings. One was gone, destroyed in Mabus' opening volley, the other had opened. Quick clasped the one cuff around his right, blood-soaked and burned wrist. Within seconds, he collapsed, falling nearly to the ground but held somewhat upright by his shackle. He succumbed to his injuries, welcoming the darkness and the silence.

Chapter VIII

Rafeo stayed in the control room to assist where he could. He monitored the remains of the water tower for quite some time before daring to look away. He knew the explosion had not been enough to finish Mabus, but figured they may have thwarted his efforts for the time being.

He had safely tucked the prototype weapon into his jacket, figuring it would come in handy at some point in the future, and since there was no one else in the city, except perhaps for Quick, who could use it, what was the harm?

He was given a city communication ear implant that would allow him to participate in control room functions without being in the room. His reputation always seemed to precede him, but this time, he would gladly take advantage of that fact. He took a second implant for Quick, knowing full well, the boy would not object

Rafeo busied himself directing rescue teams throughout the city, using the implant and the video feed from cameras throughout the city. A small group of section chiefs and directors huddled around Rafeo as they all worked together to do what they could to assist anyone who needed help and, sadly, to collect the bodies of those who had been killed. Droids unceremoniously collecting the bodies of the fallen Savages.

"That's at least twenty-two of them by my count," Rafeo said, oddly proud of Quick's handy work. "How many innocent lives would have been lost if not for that boy," he said under his breath, not wanting to remind anyone of the events any more than he needed to.

Rafeo felt a warm, soft hand on his wrist; the hand tightened slowly when he did not react instantly.

"My Savior." There came a shocked whisper; it turned out to be Mary's hand on Rafeo's wrist. She pointed at the monitor in front of her. The two of them shared a pained look of confusion for a fleeting moment, then quit the control room without a word.

***   ***   ***

The pair quietly rushed into Quick's room and froze just past the threshold; the image before them was difficult to see. Quick lay slumped against the wall, shackled in place in a puddle of his blood.

"My boy." Rafeo rushed to the young man's side and tried to help him up. Quick was, luckily, unconscious.

"Mary, a stretcher! Hurry," he whispered to Mary, who sped out from the room like a scared rabbit. Rafeo turned back to Quick, placed a hand on the chain, and closed the other into a fist against his chest. He closed his eyes and spoke in a voice and language not his own. His eyes took on a slight glow, and he pulled the remaining chain from the wall, freeing Quick to slump to the floor.

"What the hell was that?" Quick wheezed as he came to rest on the ground. Rafeo squatted next to him, checking his injuries.

"Never mind that right now, my son. Are you okay?" Rafeo was beside himself. "Who put you in here?" Rafeo asked as Mary returned with a medical gurney and two medical people to help. They rushed in and picked up Quick, placing him on the gurney.

"Who? Tell me, who?!" Rafeo pleaded as Quick came to rest on the stretcher.

"I did," Quick answered in a whisper, and his arm, which Rafeo was holding, went limp as he passed out again.

Mary and the others rushed the gurney out of the room, leaving Rafeo to deal with what he had just heard. He felt such sympathy for the young man and wanted to help.

***   ***   ***

Within five days, Quick had almost recovered completely, physically, anyway. The doctors had employed nanites, similar to the ones used in the weapon, to repair Quick's burns, his damaged inner ear, and the flesh wounds from his slide across the rooftop. He could sit up, eat, and drink, but as of yet, had not spoken. Rafeo had not left his side since he was rolled into the recovery room, and Mary had never been too far away from Rafeo. They were there, at the ready, but no one pressured the young man to speak; they were just there for when he was ready.

Quick sat slumped on his bed, his head on his chest, then looked up to make eye contact with Rafeo. Still, neither spoke. After a moment, Quick turned away from Rafeo and dropped his legs over the side of the bed; he struggled to his feet and again put his chin down to his chest.

"What is wrong with me?" His voice cracked under the strain of his emotions, and his shoulders shook as he sobbed. Rafeo didn't hesitate but rushed around the bed to grab him. He hugged the young man and let him cry, then took his head in his hands.

"Not a damned thing," he said, as he forced eye contact which he held until he saw Quick's eyes dart to the doorway.

"I'm sorry," Mary said sheepishly, and turned around to leave the room. Quick's voice, clearer than before, stopped her.

"You can stay, please," Quick pleaded. Mary stopped and turned slowly.

"I feel peaceful when you are here," Quick said, hesitantly. Mary slowly looked up and smiled, making both men feel suddenly better.

"Ah, right. Quick. You didn't make it to the introductions the first time around. This is.."

"Mary," Quick finished Rafeo's sentence. Both of the others looked at him in astonishment.

"I must have heard it over the past few days," Quick explained with a shrug, wiping his eyes. "Two, three days, how long has it been?" Quick asked, trying to change the subject.

"Five, actually," Rafeo answered slowly.

"I need some air; can we go for a walk?" Quick asked.

"Sure, I mean, can you?" Rafeo asked.

"I feel stronger. Okay, I mean," Quick replied.

"Well, why not? This is your first time in the great city, and so far, you probably haven't seen the best parts."

"I sure as hell hope not." Quick attempted humor and got an honest chuckle from the other two.

"A tour, then." Mary offered her arm; Quick joined her, and they slowly walked from the room.

***   ***   ***

The sun shone brightly, forcing Quick's eyes closed as they headed out of the medical building. They had exited to the east, into a park-like area. The late morning sun was warm and welcoming. It was high enough in the sky not to cast any shadows from the city walls. The walls fell into the background, and for a moment, Quick forgot about the world's plight and its people. He forgot about the violence from the last attack, Mabus, and everything else. He enjoyed the sun's warmth, the fresh smell of the air, and the feeling of Mary's soft skin in his hands.

They walked down the cobblestone path, which led through a shrubbery and even over a small footbridge spanning a small pond. From the bridge, a view of the city around them was possible. The tower, medical, and control buildings sat atop a hill and stood out in the skyline, perhaps to make it easier to navigate. The walls of the city faded into the distance. The city was huge; from what Mary explained as they walked, it was over 380,000 square kilometers, stretching to nearly one thousand kilometers on the north/south axis by 380 kilometers east to west.

"Larger than the state of Montana," Rafeo said aloud, taking a moment to realize that no one else may know what the State of Montana was. He continued anyway, remembering back when the city was built.

"It spans from what was once Portland, Oregon, west to Moscow, Washington, then south to Boise, Idaho, and back east to Redding, California. The walls are 60 feet high and 20 feet wide at the top, spanning 35 feet wide at their base." Rafeo looked to his companions, only to see a look of confusion from them, having no idea what any of those places even were that he had mentioned. He waved his hand in the air, gesturing for the two of them to ignore him. With a smile, they continued on their tour.

Mary went on to explain that the Citadel was home to over 50 million people. It housed farmland, industrial parks, and housing for all. There were several other cities across the two great oceans, and although it sounded like a lot of people, the nine cities represented the total remainder of the human race. That last statement took some time for Quick to process. They walked silently for some time, exiting the park and strolling onto a quiet residential street. As they walked, the smell from a local shop caught his attention.

"Is that?" Quick asked and motioned to go inside. The shop was a bakery, and the smell of fresh bread, unmistakable.

Mary knew Quick would enjoy the experience and wanted to show off the wonders of the city, not the least of which was the craftsmanship of the local bakers and artisans who had been able to develop their craft within the safety of the Citadel.

They walked into the shop, and Quick closed his eyes and breathed in the wondrous smells in the air. Mary took a loaf of bread from the shelf, smiling at the shopkeeper, and broke a piece for Quick. Quick hadn't noticed the nervous look from the baker, who was only placated once he recognized Rafeo. Quick took the bread and ate it. The last time he had had bread, it took him nearly a week to collect and prepare the ingredients. It had been so much trouble that it almost tainted the experience of the finished product; here it was just on a shelf, and it was marvelous.

They turned down the next aisle, following the look and color of fresh muffins. Quick did not notice the young boy standing in the aisle at first, but within a second or two, he recognized the woman standing behind the boy. She had been on the rooftop the night of the attack; he had taken her injured boy from her.

Quick froze in place, staring at the woman. This time, his look was much different from the last time he had made eye contact with her. The woman still had the look of fear in her eyes, but there was something else. He could feel his eyes welling up. He wanted to leave, to disappear, or to apologize, but any words he could form in his mind seemed hollow. He swallowed roughly in an attempt to keep his composure.

Before anyone could speak, the young boy ran down the aisle, grabbed Quick around the waist, and hugged him tight. Now the woman's cheeks were wet with tears, as were everyone else's. Quick stared at the woman, who mouthed the words "Thank you." Quick had to think about it before realizing he had taken the boy to medical help, possibly even saving his life. He also thought of what could have become of them all on that rooftop had he not acted.

He squatted to one knee in front of the boy and hugged him back.

***   ***   ***

They had left the bakery, walking back through the park towards the tower. Once on the bridge, Quick stopped and sat on the railing to rest, and Mary joined him. He started eating a muffin the boy's mother had given him.

"So, you were telling me about this Mabus," Quick said with his mouth full. Rafeo took a moment to compose his thoughts and propped himself up on the railing across from where Quick and Mary sat.

"I told you of the Guardian and my failing," Rafeo started. Quick nodded.

"Our three-man journey to meet the Guardian brought us to the land of the Britons near a place of power known as the Standing Stones. Along the journey, one of my compatriots, Quintus, killed my friend Balthazar, and attempted to kill me and take the Book of Power, yes?" he tested for understanding. Both Quick and Mary nodded. The fact that Mary was following along with the story was not lost on Quick.

"Part of the process of restoring the Guardian is performing the ascension. It requires a place of natural power like the Standing Stones; what you now know as the Stonehenge, for example. It becomes a conduit for the power required to open a doorway to the heavens. There's an incantation, and the Guardian is intended to stand in the light of ascension with the Book of Power, and he returns to his immortal, omnipotent plane of existence."

"Yes, of course," Quick blurted out sarcastically, unable to help himself; the casual delivery of the story was surprising to him. Rafeo had been looking away to the distance as if focusing on a picture tangible only to him, but had turned back to face Quick, taken aback by the young man's comment.

"Please continue," Quick said sheepishly.

"When I had arrived at the Standing Stones," Rafeo continued, his eyes focusing elsewhere again as he did. "The scene was absolute chaos. I was alone and injured, having been left for dead by Quintus."

"A battle raged between an army of Saxon invaders commanded by Mabus, and the Britons led by the house of Constantine. I made my way through the fray, desperately searching for the human Guardian or Quintus, or the Book. And it all came to me at once: Quintus had already summoned the light of ascension. While that was going on, I watched in horror as a Saxon soldier decapitated the Guardian in the heat of battle. And even before Quintus could reach the ascension, as I'm sure was his plan, the two faction leaders, Mabus and Constantine, were locked in combat. They tumbled into the light and disappeared in a concussive blast that knocked to the ground every single man for miles."

The group sat silently and stared at each other for a moment while the words fell silent around them, like a leaf on the wind settling on the surface of the pond below them.

"Where there had been one, there were now two..." Rafeo continued quietly, the sound of defeat heavy in his voice, as if the event had happened yesterday rather than twenty-six hundred years ago. "Two men, Constantine and Mabus, ended up absorbing the power of the one, The Guardian. The two men would become like gods, but what of the Guardian?" Rafeo paused for feedback but was met by a look of bewilderment. "He was now trapped in a mortal existence, to live one life, only to die, as mortals do. Luckily, he would be reincarnated time and time again, unaware each time of who he is. I only hope I can find him and restore him to his true form."

"No small task," Christian added with a troubled look upon his face, realizing the immensity of the task ahead of Rafeo.

"As luck would have it, and only by luck, they require the Book of Power to fully become the Guardian. Without it, they were able to become..." Rafeo struggled for the words, "...something else," he finally settled on.

"Those who had witnessed the event returned to their homelands and told the tale to those who would listen. The prayers of the mortals now flooded from their hearts and minds to those they elevated to heroes, then legends, then gods, and fed the power of the new deities. The dichotomy of those two, the evil and malice of Mabus and the righteousness and piety of Constantine, would become the curse of the human race. I have sat by helplessly and watched a history unfold that was never meant to be.

Humans and Savages have a common ancestry, but are now very different, even at the genetic level. Their Lords and Masters had caused it in pursuit of more power from their followers." Rafeo's voice had gone hoarse as he ended his story. He lowered his head in shame and left the trio in silence. The silence was only interrupted by the wind softly brushing the trees around them until the long shadows from the walls to the west crept up on them.

"We'd best get you back to your bed," Mary said, finally standing up, reaching her hand out for Quick and then doing the same to Rafeo. The party stood in silence and walked somberly back up the path to the tower. They reached Quick's room, and he lay himself down and pulled his blankets up, feeling comfortable after the strain from the day's activities.

He had more healing ahead of him. Rafeo fell into the chair next to Quick's bed, as he had for the past five days, and Mary sat on the foot of the bed. After several more moments of silence, Quick turned to Rafeo with a puzzled look on his face.

"And what is my part in all of this?" he asked

slowly. Rafeo did not have an answer. He had always assumed Quick was a Magi, and it had been fate that he had found him that day, after the Savages had thrown him off a cliff and left him for dead. He was an ally, a friend who would help him set things right, but up until this moment, he had never really given it any thought.

Rafeo had never noticed the telltale sign of the Magi anywhere on Quick's body, and he was not ready to put any of that into words.

"Time will tell," Rafeo answered eventually.

Chapter IX

The next morning, Quick awoke in his medical suite. He was alone in his room for the first time in days. Slowly, he lowered his feet over the side of the bed and carefully stood up. He was pleasantly surprised to feel none of the pain he had grown accustomed to over the past few days. His mind raced as he still digested the news from Rafeo the day before.

He stretched, bending at the waist and rolling his shoulders. He flexed every muscle from his neck down, and when happy with the results, he flowed through his tai-chi forms, using each to stretch him and strengthen him to the utmost. He was so involved in his exercises that he had not noticed Mary enter the room along with a young girl.

The pair kept quiet at the doorway while they watched the shirtless man contort and stretch in front of them. Moments later, Quick had noted their presence and stopped short, turning to face the two newcomers in the room.

"Hi!" Quick yelped.

"The best part was when you flexed your big muscles," the young girl blurted out.

"Oh, yeah," Quick answered, as he scrambled

to put his shirt on. He smiled at Mary but looked back at the little girl. The girl stared off into the corner of the room as if looking into outer space.

"Sorry," Mary said as she tucked a wisp of her hair behind her ear. She smiled warmly at him and then looked down at the girl.

"I wanted you to meet my daughter," she explained, and put both hands on the girl's shoulders as she moved to stand directly behind the girl. "Charlette," Mary said her name, and the girl seemed to rejoin the conversation. At least she appeared to.

"We call her Charlie, though," Mary went on, and as she did, Charlette looked up at Quick.

"Your name is Quick?" she asked, staring into his chest.

Quick smiled and took a big breath. "Yes, that's right," he said with a smile, before looking back at Mary.

"The best part is that it's easy to remember, not like Balthazar or something crazy like that. That's hard to say, Balthazar." she repeated, while spitting slightly as her tongue struggled with the *th* in Balthazar. Mary smiled, as did Quick. No one recognized the odd name Charlette had referenced.

"Yeah, it's easier to say, too."

"This is my daughter," Mary said again, now nervously strumming her fingers on her daughter's shoulders. "We thought we'd check on you, and if you were up for it, we'd show you around the Citadel some more."

"Yeah," Charlette agreed with a big smile.

Quick looked around shyly before making eye contact with Mary. "How could I say no?" he said, smiling. Quick sat back on the bed and put his socks and shoes on, after which he was ready to go. He noticed his sword sitting on the chair in the corner of the room behind the ladies. He picked up his bathrobe and threw it to cover the weapon before either of his guests realized it was there. Both turned to see the robe hanging off the chair, but only Mary recognized what was under it.

"Are you sure?" she asked, fully prepared for Quick to change his mind and insist upon bringing it.

Instead, he nodded. "Yeah, I'm sure," he said. Forcing a smile. "I hope there's more bread on this tour." Now he was forcing to change of the subject.

"Yeah, bread," Charlette yelled, and grabbed Quick by the hand, leading him out of the room and into the hall. They left the tower, making small talk as they walked. Their first stop was the bakery, where they picked out a muffin each for breakfast. Mary also insisted that Quick try a warm brown drink she called coffee. It was bitter at first, until she added some sugar.

They made their way back outside and walked while they ate their breakfast. They headed towards the end of the street, which opened up into what turned out to be farmland. Charlie was the first to finish her muffin and threw her napkin on the ground. Mary stopped and picked it up without a word.

"The best part of my muffin was the strawberries," Charlette reported, while staring at Quick, then turned without another word and resumed walking. Quick was at a loss for how to act; he had never interacted with a child before.

Quick forced a polite smile, but he knew he was out of his element. Mary had picked up on that and tried to continue their conversation from where they had been interrupted. She was describing the farming process. Quick was more comfortable with this than the technology of the rest of the Citadel. He was amazed to see people working the fields, figuring they would use robots for that, as well.

Quick had lived on a small farm with Rafeo for the past several years out in the wilds. It had been a rewarding but tough life.

"I've always felt at peace working the land. There is something very special about reaping what you've sown," Quick explained to Mary. "I suppose that's why there are no robots for this," he pointed at the fields.

"I never thought of it," Mary explained. She smiled, then looked around nervously. Charlette was nowhere to be seen. Quick realized it right away, too.

"Charlie," he yelled; there was no answer.

"She won't answer," Mary explained. At that moment, they heard a horse whinny from around the corner of the barn they had wandered towards. Both picked up the pace to a jog, then a run. Rounding the corner, they found Charlie standing in the middle of the paddock with a stallion standing up on its hindquarters. Mary stopped at the fence and yelled for Charlette with no reaction from the girl.

Quick hurdled the fence in a single effort, landed, and sprinted over to Charlette, placing himself between the girl and the animal, his arms spread wide, yelling for the horse to back off. He scooped Charlette up onto his back and held her with one arm while still gesturing to the horse with the other. He backed away from the horse slowly, until he approached the fence and passed Charlette over to her mother, then hopped the fence again. Quick squatted down on one knee to look the girl in the eye.

"That was really dangerous," he told her, but the girl only gave him a blank stare in response, until she finally blurted out, "The best part was the piggy-back ride," then fell silent again.

"Are you kidding?" Quick whispered in disbelief, then stood up next to Mary again.

"She was born like that," Mary tried to explain. "The doctors call it autism, but the priests say it is an abomination." Mary began to tear up a little before she went on.

"I was found six and a half months pregnant, wandering around out in the wastes just outside the north wall, almost eight years ago. I also have no memory of anything from before the medical droids picked me up and brought me into the city."

They walked quietly along, making sure to keep Charlette in front of them and in sight. Quick had taken her arm. He had developed an instant bond with Mary since the first time he had seen her;

something he'd never known was possible.

"Even with all our advanced technology, there's nothing they can do to restore my memories or to change Charlie, though I'm glad for that."

"Glad?" Quick was embarrassed as soon as he said it. He didn't want to make it sound as though he didn't like the little girl.

"Yeah, I know it sounds weird, but her mind works in such a cool way; she's so different from me, and it forces me to see this crazy world differently."

They walked on a bit; Quick had to admit she was right. Charlette was, indeed, an interesting girl.

In the distance, they could hear bells sounding, calling people into the church for worship. Quick was curious, but Mary seemed not to want to go. She soon gave in to him, and they walked towards the church.

They took a seat at the back of the building. Quick had never been to a religious ceremony; not one he could remember, anyway. As the event progressed, he realized he had heard a different rendition of the proceedings from Rafeo over the years. And most of what was said contradicted the revelations Rafeo had recently made. The priest approached the pulpit and removed his headgear. He pulled a large book out from a drawer and placed it on the shelf to read from. He read a few short passages and then proceeded to define what he had just read, in his own words. The priests' musings were, in Quick's opinion, inaccurate and seemingly self-serving. He wanted to say something but didn't want to invite attention upon himself and the ladies.

"The best part was when the bald man lied," Charlette blurted out quite loudly. A gasp ran through the congregation. The comment drew the priest from the altar and down the aisle in search of who had said such a thing. As the priest approached, Mary stood and ushered Charlette out of the pew towards the exit of the church without a word. It took Quick a few seconds to realize what was going on. The priest stood, blocking the pew, and grabbed Mary by the arm.

"How dare you?" the priest bellowed, causing everyone present to turn and face the rear of the church. "You, who brings this abomination amongst us!" The priest gestured towards the child. Mary didn't hesitate but slapped the priest across the face. The priest stumbled backwards. Quick was impressed that she was able to strike someone without succumbing.

The priest regained his composure and moved as though to hit her back, but Quick stood up from his pew, placing himself directly in the priest's path. A hush fell over the crowd.

"The Savage Slayer." The whispers spread throughout the congregation. The priest froze in his tracks. Quick did nothing but stare at the man. He held the priest's gaze until, out of fear, the priest retreated towards the altar. Quick followed very slowly, leaving Mary and Charlette at the back of the church, the crowd following Quick with their collective gaze.

"And what were you about to do?" Quick asked

as he pointed to the priest. This frightened the man further, and he began to pray.

"Constantine. I beseech thee. Come to my aid."

Quick scoffed. "Oh yeah, this should be good." He crossed his arms as if waiting and looked to the roof of the church after several seconds of nothing happening; Quick continued with his sermon.

"Oh, Constantine," he said in a truly mocking tone. "If he was gonna help you, where was he the other night when you all really needed him?" Quick's voice filled the entire hall. "That was me that saved you – not your absentee landlord." He made eye contact with the young boy and his mother from the rooftop; they looked scared again. Quick instantly stopped in his tracks and turned to leave, not wanting to hurt anyone.

In a flash of light, a figure appeared before him in the center aisle of the church. The congregation all fell to the floor, most of them unconscious. Quick tilted his head to the side.

"Let me guess," he said quietly and steadied himself, not knowing what to expect.

"Not as absent as you would have liked, I imagine," the glowing figure said coyly.

Quick looked past the man for a moment when he noticed Mary and Charlette were still standing. He didn't want to provoke a situation that might lead to anyone being hurt, especially if Constantine had powers like Mabus.

"Constantine," Quick said, trying to relax.

"Indeed!" Constantine agreed. "I figured I owed you one from the other night." Constantine reached out for Quick and pulled him into his aura.

His surroundings faded from view, and soon Quick found himself in total darkness. Flashes of light and images broke the darkness randomly, until he realized the flashes were his eyes blinking, opening into a different world or, as it turned out, a different time. He could see a young boy that he immediately recognized as himself surrounded by a crowd; moreover, and an angry mob. With his next blink, he was the young man.

"But what of Constantine?" Quick thought to himself, but the moment was fleeting. He stumbled ahead as the mob shoved him, yelling and screaming at him.

"I remember," he muttered aloud. The comment had not been intended for anyone to hear. In that moment, he realized that Constantine was, in fact, giving him his lost memories back through this process. At the moment, it seemed he was reliving the past.

"You had best remember - blasphemer! Monster!" A priest amid the crowd yelled over the top of the others.

"Is this what Constantine meant by 'he owed me one from the other night?'" Quick thought, as he put his hands up to shield his face from the hands of the crowd as they shoved him through the streets. He recognized the Citadel around him. Then he saw their faces: a woman, crying, reaching out for him as if to help him, a face he suddenly knew as his mother. She called for him by name.

"Christian." It had seemed so alien at first, but to hear her say it, it felt right; it felt like, no, it was his name, Christian.

The other was a man trying to prevent his mother from getting to him, and in turn, she was spitting at him. The man he knew as his father.

He realized that he was being shown his memories. It began to return to him. This day was less than a week after his sixteenth birthday. The day had started as any other; he had gone to class, but midway through the day, he had gotten into an argument with a classmate. Usually, all he had to do to win an argument was raise his voice and wait for the other party to get dizzy, weak, or even pass out. This affliction never seemed to affect him, for some reason, and he had become accustomed to getting his way.

This time, however, the young man he argued with became angry, hostile, and then violently slammed Christian to the ground over a simple trade of their lunches. The young man then turned on a female classmate. Christian had never seen a human turn Savage, but he had heard of it. The idea was drilled into their heads every day at school and church.

"Do not give in to anger or hate as the Savage awaits." This saying was repeated ad nauseam. Humans ran the risk of turning into a creature possessed if they allowed themselves to become too angry. Usually, a genetic precondition causes people who get angry to pass out, but if not, this was the possible result.

The girl instantly passed out from being exposed to the yelling, leaving her easy prey for the fledgling Savage. Christian, who was unaffected by it all for some reason, grabbed a knife from his lunch bag and stabbed his Savage classmate through the skull, killing him. A priest, the one leading the mob he now faced, had entered the room, not having witnessed any part of the rest of the exchange, just in time to see Christian kill his classmate.

Despite Christian's objections, the priest passed judgment on the spot, banishing the boy from the Citadel in the name of Constantine himself and for the safety of his flock.

It took no time for a massive crowd to assemble and ensure his ejection from the walled city. In hindsight, Christian wondered why no one in the crowd had mutated into a Savage, as there was plenty of anger and hatred around that day. He could see it in their eyes, especially in the eyes of both his parents. Even his mother, though she begged to save him, could see the disgust in her eyes. The faces of his parents were now burned into his mind, and the faces of the others in the crowd became indistinguishable from each other in contrast.

They reached the gate of the city, and the mob paused for a moment. Christian pleaded with them, to no avail.

"Mother? Father?" he begged, but they turned their backs to him and walked away, leaving the mob to their business. They picked the young man up and physically tossed him from the gate and into the wilds. The ground sloped away from the walls, acting like a slide, and Christian tumbled for a distance before coming to a stop on the hard-packed stone surface. But by the time he got to his feet and turned around, he was met by the image of the closed gate.

He had never seen images of the world outside the city walls. Stories were told of packs of Savages that roamed the wilds, killing and even eating anyone who dared enter their domain. The sun was still high in the afternoon sky, and Christian felt some comfort from the light, but he knew it would be dark eventually, and without shelter, he was sure he would end up a Savage's meal.

He stood upon a surface that looked like it could have been a road at one time. It was overgrown with weeds and shrubs, though the forest along its edges had not yet engulfed its surface. He took one last look behind him, for lack of a better idea, in hopes they might let him re-enter the city. The gate remained closed, and with that, he began to nervously make his way north along the road, passing an old, rusted sign barely legible. It read: I-5.

Chapter X

The first few days on his own, Christian wandered through the world for the first time. A combination of wonder at the sights that he beheld and fear of the unknown was his motivation for exploration, or lack thereof. He was fortunate not to encounter another living creature at that time. He did not sleep the first night, having not found shelter. He climbed atop a large derelict vehicle and lay on its top, seeing the night sky for the first time. Within the walls of the Citadel, the light pollution from the artificial lights blocked out everything in the night sky, except the moon. The experience had been an emotional one.

The moon was nearly full, providing enough light to cast shadows. The stars of the Milky Way were thick and resembled a careless painter's brush on a black canvas. His heart raced from fear, making it hard to calm himself to sleep. He was hungry, cold, and alone. Christian was happy to be wearing two shirts under a sweater. His shoes were nearly new, as were his multi-pocketed cargo pants that he preferred to any other trousers.

Christian decided to go through his pockets and take stock of anything he had with him. In his left leg pocket, he was delighted to find a granola bar he had pulled from his lunch the day before to have as a snack later. He inhaled the meal and was happy to have had it.

Next, he found his folded carving knife in his right pocket. It wasn't much, but he was happy to have found a weapon either for hunting or self-defence. He had grown up in the farming district, and right now, he was thankful his parents had not been in some office or another department. He knew how to start a fire without a match or a lighter. He knew how to make knots, not that he had a rope or use of it at the moment. He was physically fit from working the land. He was used to being on his feet for hours at a time.

The night was quiet, except for the occasional rustling from the trees that could have been from a small animal or something worse. Whenever he heard it, he would freeze in place, hold his breath, and wait for something horrible, which, thankfully, never came.

At the first light of day, he quietly climbed down to the road, knife in hand, and resumed his travel to somewhere else. As he crested a hill an hour or so later, he could see buildings grouped a few kilometers away. He had no idea if he should be happy or worried about this, but, if nothing else, it might provide shelter or even food, and he continued towards them.

Christian saw no movement of any kind as he approached the first building, which turned out to be a house. He had found a small town, but by the condition of the structures, he was quite certain that no one had lived here for some time. As he approached the first house, he readied his knife and carefully entered. He recognized the appliances enough to know he was in a kitchen. Excitedly, he searched the cupboards and refrigerator for food, only to find anything of the like had been emptied from here long ago. The shelves were covered in dust as thick as sand.

He decided that food was his immediate concern and quit the first house to continue his search in the next one. A similar scene played out in this one, as well as the next five. The sixth house, however, held a different story.

Christian entered the front door and stopped short as he tripped over something. As he looked closer, he realized he had tripped over a bone; several. From his count, there were three skulls in the pile: two smaller than the third. Maybe they died of disease, or starvation, or worse. But at the bottom of the pile, something glinted slightly, catching his eye.

Christian was a little disturbed, having never encountered a human skeleton before. He kicked the bones aside with his foot to expose what had caught his eye; it was a pistol.

His excitement overcame his fear very quickly, and he reached through the bone pile to claim his prize. He knew little about weapons, having only ever researched them in the historical archives when he figured no one would find him. He didn't know it yet, but the rust in the barrel from years of neglect had rendered this weapon useless in its current state, but it made Christian feel better to hold it.

He now continued his search for food. The fridge in this house had a lock on it; Christian frantically looked around for something to help him open it. He went down a set of stairs into the basement and discovered a workbench and hanging from it, a hammer. Christian grabbed the hammer and bounded back up the stairs. His excitement had allowed him to move around without checking to ensure he was alone. He paused for a moment when he returned to the main floor to rely on his ears. The silence reassured him he was alone in the house, and he set upon his task to open the fridge.

He swung the hammer multiple times before finally breaking the latch from the side of the fridge, leaving the lock intact. The result was all that concerned him, however, and he slowly opened the fridge. A funny smell met him first, but nothing offensive enough to halt his search.

He found several unspoiled bottles of water and packages of shiny material marked M.R.E. (freeze-dried beef steak). The other packages all read M.R.E. but had other titles. He read the other lettering on the package to discover that inside was a meal that only needed water added to it.

Christian wept from excitement; this was the first bit of good luck in nearly a day and a half. He opened a bottle of water and guzzled half of its contents, after it passed a smell test. He had been parched. His thirst abated, Christian ripped open the package labeled "ham omelette gave it a Christian smell test, and with a shrug poured some water into the pouch. He stirred it with his finger into something of a paste and poured it into his mouth.

The texture was very foreign, nearly enough for him to spit it out, but his hunger forced him to endure. The flavor was not entirely bad, and he managed to swallow and keep it down.

Without thinking, he ripped open another package, this one marked "Granola and repeated the same as before. This one was much better, he had to admit. Once he swallowed the last bit and wiped his mouth, it occurred to him that he had probably just eaten two days' worth of rations. This food had not been easy to come by, and how long would it take him to find more?

He carefully closed the fridge, blocking the food from his sight and the urge to eat more along with it. He looked out the window and noticed the setting sun. Maybe he could make this a place to stay, at least for now. It had food, water, and even a roof over his head. He just wanted to find a room he could turn into a bunker, and maybe he would be able to sleep tonight.

The gathering dark was exacerbated by rain clouds rolling in. Christian was happy to at least be out of the rain tonight. He had gathered all his supplies into one of the rooms on the second level of the house. A bookshelf was used to cover the window as it no longer offered light. The door to the room was closed, and he had piled a large amount of debris inside the room in front of the door, barring the entrance, although he did not look forward to digging his way out the next morning.

Before barricading himself in, he had completed a more thorough search of the house, finding an ammunition box complete with bullets, a cleaning kit, and even an instruction manual. Christian had built a small fire in the corner of the room inside the fireplace, its existence being the major deciding factor on choosing this room for the night.

He read through the gun manual, it occurred to him that he had not tested his new weapon, and from what he had read, he had his doubts that it was functional. With a shrug, he closed his eyes and pointed the gun at the far end of the room and pulled the trigger; the only feedback from the gun was a 'click'.

Christian put the gun down and continued to read; as he did, he could hear the rain falling outside and on the roof. It brought a smile to his face; he loved the rain growing up in the Citadel. Tonight, however, the smile was fleeting. Along with the sound of the falling water drops, he could make out growling. Something was outside.

He quickly doused the fire, blackening his room. The sounds of more than one creature were now evident. Christian crept to the window and carefully shoved the heavy bookcase over an inch or so, exposing a sliver of area he might look. At first, there was nothing, then on the far side of the street that ran past the house, he saw it. A two-legged man-like creature, but it did not move like a man, more demonic in its purpose, sniffing at the wind as though on the trail of something.

Christian stared, praying that it had not been lured here by the smell of his fire. As he continued to watch, another Savage walked across the roof of the house's first floor, right in front of his window. Christian was frozen in fear; somehow, mostly through luck, the Savage did not see him nor realize he was just inches away. Christian noticed the long, unruly, dangerous-looking fingernails on the creature's hands; its body was barely covered, and by only animal pelts. It carried a rather ominous-looking hatchet or axe. It paused in front of him to smell its surroundings, then, after what felt like an eternity, it lumbered off.

Christian dared not breathe, his eyes darting in every direction, his ears straining to hear footfalls in the house, which, he was relieved, never came. He stayed by the window for the next twenty minutes or so, watching and waiting. He figured this night would be his end.

To his surprise, within the time he spent by the window, the rain ended, and with it faded any other sounds of anything or anyone anywhere near him. Rather than re-ignite the fire and risk luring more of those things to him, Christian instead curled up on a pile of blankets he had found and moved together. The smell of the blankets was unpleasant and strong, but it was the most comfortable he had been in two days. Eventually, he managed to fall asleep.

***   ***   ***

The next morning, when he awoke, Christian lay motionless for several minutes, intently listening for evidence of any other living things nearby. Once finally satisfied, he reached for his gun for reassurance before remembering his test fire from the night before. He got up and forced the bookshelf aside, allowing light to enter the room.

He flipped through the gun manual until he got to a section called TROUBLESHOOTING. He smirked at the irony of the title, then proceeded to take the gun apart as he read through each section. It took several hours to disassemble the weapon, oil it, clean it, and get it back together until he was ready to test it again.

Christian moved the bookshelf further aside to allow him to exit through the window. He felt it easier than digging out the door blockade, and safer than going through the house and possibly coming across one of those things from last night.

He stood on the roof and studied the area around him for some time before feeling convinced that he was alone. He climbed down to the ground, his senses on overdrive, straining for sounds or sights of danger. He walked to the house across the street, aimed the gun at the front door, and pulled the trigger. There was a tremendous crack, and the weapon kicked, almost leaping out of his hand. Instantly, there was a ringing in his ears that would block out any other sounds, and it took a few moments to begin to clear. The round had found its mark, struck the doorknob of the front door, and blown the door open.

Christian was terrified that the noise would attract unwanted attention. Without a second's hesitation, he bounded across the street, up onto the roof, and into the window from whence he had come.

Once inside, he shoved the bookcase back in front of the window, then froze and listened. The sound of his heart pounding was the only thing he could hear. With a giant grin, he looked slowly down at the gun in his hand. He brought the weapon up to meet his gaze and nodded with approval.

He had enough food for several days and enough bullets to load the gun two times over; not a bad bit of luck, he thought. However, he felt unsafe in this area after last night, and feared those things would be back. He collected as much water and food into a bundle as it would fit, shoved the pistol into the waist of his pants, and resigned himself to the fact that he would have to move on further down the road. He could find a new place to call home, but this was not it.

As he headed north again, heading down the same highway as before, Christian saw a faded sign that read "Thanks for visiting Salmon Creek, see ya real soon," he said with little care other than to scoff; he doubted he would ever set foot in this town again.

The highway followed a river as it wandered north. The journey was long, and he walked for days without really knowing where he was trying to get to. The road took him to towns like Castle Rock, Chehalis, Olympia, and Tacoma. He would search through houses and buildings along the way, finding what supplies he could, never really finding a place to stay.

Over the days and weeks that followed, his confidence grew. He was able to figure out a pattern correlating the arrival of Savages with the rain; there was never one without the other. This helped him to decide when it was safe to venture off the road to explore and when it was time to seek shelter.

After Tacoma, Christian realized he was traveling around a lake to his left as he traveled north. One clear night, he had finished scavenging within sight of the water; he couldn't help himself and wandered down towards the shore. He dipped a foot into the water, and the temperature was crisp, a touch on the cold side but inviting. Weeks on the road had left him less than fresh. He stripped down and quietly submerged himself. He stretched out, floating on his back while staring at the sky as he had on the first night from atop the vehicle. The difference was that, at the moment, he had no reason to be frightened or anxious. He had food and protection in his gear and felt ready to handle whatever came next.

Christian missed some of his friends, or at least the idea of them. It would be nice to have someone to share this adventure with, but other than that, he was comfortable. If he was honest, he felt free for the first time in his life. His thoughts drifted to his parents, then quickly to his last image of them. His parents, like the other citizens, were terrified of him, or more so, of what they thought he was turning into. He had never seen such a horrified look from his parents, and it had been directed at him. He had to shake the memory away and, in that moment, he hoped never to see the Citadel again.

He finished up in the water, settled into a house he had scouted earlier, and prepared for the night. He lay on the roof of the house, staring at the sky again. He felt at ease, maybe a little too much so, and drifted off to sleep.

Christian bolted upright from a dead sleep only seconds before he felt the water drops hit his cheek; it was raining. He crept into the window of the house he was using as silently as possible. There were no sounds of Savages that he could hear, but he knew they were around.

His stuff was on the floor near the closet. He picked up his knife and his pistol from his belongings and covered the rest with a blanket. He tucked the pistol into the waist of his pants, hoping not to have to use it, as the noise would certainly attract more Savages. He readied the blade in his hand, crawled into the closet, and closed the door.

It seemed like a very light rain, and he hoped that meant a small group of Savages. Maybe they were just a scouting party or trying to get home, wherever that was. He hoped they would pass him by without incident, as they had many times in the past. He could hear the raindrops fall slowly on the old pie plate he had set on the window ledge two feet away, an early warning system he had discovered by accident and used ever since. His pulse slowed as he figured it would soon be over, and then, the floor creaked near the door of the room.

Christian froze. The hair on the back of his neck stood on end; he forced himself to take a long, deep breath and readied himself. He visualized what he would do, or at least what he would want to do. He would try to lunge upward from a crouched position, using the strength in his legs to add to his power, and drive his blade into where he figured the Savage's lungs would be. He figured if the creature were unable to breathe, it would die, but also it would not be able to scream in pain or cry for help.

He could hear footsteps slowly approach the closet. The tell-tale sniffing came next; did it have his scent? he wondered. Christian listened carefully and could not hear a second creature. If he had to strike, he certainly didn't want to have to face more than one of them at a time.

He was still rehearsing his attack strategy in his mind when the closet door swung open. Just as it had been in his mind's eye, Christian leapt up, driving his blade right into the creature's midsection. He could feel the Savage's body tense and then go limp almost instantly, and then the dead weight dropped on him. The only sound was the two of them landing on the floor as softly as Christian could make it happen. There had been some noise, but Christian had to admit, not much. He lay slumped against the wall, the weight of his dead quarry pressing on top of him, the creature's eyes still open, staring him in the eye. Christian was not even thinking of moving just yet as he listened intently to sense the presence, if any, of another Savage. There was not another sound to be heard, apart from the soft tapping of the rain on the window ledge.

Christian was nearly overwhelmed, both horrified by what he had just done, and at the same time, he had to admit he was impressed. He was only sixteen years old, not old enough, according to the rules of polite society, to drink alcohol or vote. But today, he had killed a creature that had haunted his nightmares, and those of many of his childhood friends, for years. It was not something he had hoped to never have to do, but now done, Christian's confidence soared to new heights. He knew he was capable of it, and now he was not as afraid to act as he had been. According to the teachings of the church, such actions should have turned him into the very thing he had just slain.

The shock wore off quickly, and the reality of what he had done set in. Christian did not feel guilty, but was terrified of the possibility that these things could tell when another of their kind was dead. He waited for what felt like an eternity, staring at the corpse and listening to his heart racing. He waited for a sound that never came. Eventually, Christian got to his feet and moved quickly away from the dead creature in the closet. He looked intensely at the pie plate on the window ledge; not a sound from it or a splash to be seen.

"It's over," Christian said to the darkness, letting out the breath he didn't realize he was holding.

A Savage suddenly appeared in front of him at the window, and scrambled to come through, knocking the pie plate down. It had caught Christian completely by surprise, as though it was something he'd done a hundred times before, he drew his weapon and fired a single round, catching the creature right between the eyes, killing it instantly.

Without hesitating or waiting for a cause, Christian abandoned his other belongings. He bounded through the window, across the roof, and dropped to the ground. With all the speed he could muster, he sprinted from the house, and back to the lake, unaware if he was being pursued. He ran to the pier he had seen earlier and straight to the end. He stopped, the gun at the ready, anticipating a fight, still, no rain, which he took as a good sign.

The light of dawn was beginning to creep into the world around him; it illuminated not a single enemy. He thought back to his earlier thoughts of the light rain.

"Maybe it was just the two of them," he panted, still sighting down the pier, looking for a target that was not there.

Christian stayed where he was until the sun was well above the horizon. Eventually, he was convinced it was safe, as there was not a cloud in the sky. He breathed in the morning air and allowed himself to relax. He lowered his weapon and slowly began to head back towards the house.

"Maybe I can grab my stuff," he said aloud, again. He reflected on what had happened that night. He had killed not one, but two Savages, and one with little more than a carving knife. He couldn't hide the smirk he wore, his pride overcoming him slightly.

As he retraced his steps back towards the house, he realized his shirt was wet. He looked down to see a large blood stain. He ripped the shirt off in panic to search for the wound. He was relieved to find there was no wound to find, though he continued to braille-check himself in disbelief. He tucked his gun back into his trousers so that he could put the shirt back on when he smelled it. The blood carried a powerful scent; one he feared may draw the creatures to him. He still had only the clothes he had left the Citadel wearing, and wasn't too happy about it, but decided to leave this shirt there. He carried on back to the house, exposed from the waist up.

Once back through the window, he could smell the same odor as on his shirt. He wasted no time getting the rest of his clothes on, gathering his things, and leaving the house, never to return.

Chapter XI

Christian continued his careful but determined trek north, along what must have been a large highway, known as I-5 according to the occasional sign or fragment that he could identify. After his experience a few nights ago, he realized his heart didn't explode in his chest with every stray noise. He hadn't seen a drop of rain or a single sign of any Savage since he had killed the two the other night. He was by no means getting cocky, but was far more confident in his choices than he had been the first night after being cast out of the Citadel.

Along his way, he passed several towns and cities, now all of them ghost towns, heavily into the process of being reclaimed by nature. Where roads once lay were long, level fields of grass; the tarmac was only visible in small patches. Tall buildings resembled oddly shaped trees or hanging gardens. Many houses had been burned; the ones that weren't were in poor repair and overgrown with greenery.

Every town he had dared to explore bore the same signs of struggle, conflict, or battle. He had found many military barricades and bunkers. Whatever had happened here, the now derelict and destroyed military equipment was at one time the last line of defense. More often than not, they gave up little, if anything at all, along the lines of useful supplies.

As he walked, Christian thought back to the night of his banishment. They looked upon him as though he were evil incarnate; the hatred was palpable. It pained him to think of his parents.

"Who needs them?" he scoffed aloud and kicked at the dirt beneath his feet. Yesterday, he had passed a town; from what he could tell, it was a place called Tacoma. He had paused, looking from the highway; he had seen evidence of buildings burning. He hadn't wanted to wander off the roadway, but a bigger city could mean the possibility of supplies and also more danger.

Christian had to run from a pack of feral dogs. Perhaps once domesticated, these animals had reverted to the wild once more. They seemed hungry, and he did not want to be on the menu; the dogs had given chase. In a field, surrounded by a fence, he could see large colorful tubes winding through the air like snakes, big enough around for a grown man to stand upright in. The towers looked as though they would prove too difficult for the dogs to climb. He leapt the fence and headed into the facility. He dashed up the ladder to the top of the tower and was relieved to see his theory had proved correct. After several hours of barking and pacing, the dogs had not given up, however. Christian tried to conceal his presence inside one of the tubes; this did not work, either. He attempted to exit the tube in hopes of finding another way to the ground, but his grip failed, and he slid down the tube; it was covered with moss and slime.

He picked up tremendous speed as he slid closer and closer to the ground. It was almost fun, were it not for his fear of where he would come out, what he would land in, and, most of all, would the dogs have followed him down there?

He emerged back into the daylight; the scenery around him was blurred by the speed he was traveling. He could see at the end of the tube what looked like a ramp, and when he hit it, he went flying through the air, landing in a pit filled with stagnant rainwater. The water slowed him to a stop with a splash. He was thankful for the soft landing, but not so much for the green slime that he was covered in.

Christian immediately dashed from the water, over another section of dilapidated fence, and into what remained of the building. He eventually found a room completely intact and ran inside; the noise of the pursuing dogs grew louder. He swung the door shut and barricaded himself inside.

Safe for the moment, Christian took some time to try to make sense of his surroundings. On the walls were multi-colored images, many faded almost to the point of being unidentifiable unless under scrutiny. Images of people smiling, splashing each other in clear water under sunny skies. Others were riding a tractor tire through the colorful tubes outside. Some images were of people riding small cars over what looked like monorail train tracks. This place had at one time been some sort of entertainment park, something he had never heard of.

He searched for what turned into hours. Through the images, remembering the fleeting moments of fun he had felt as he fell down the tube outside. He tried to imagine a world where such a thing could be enjoyed by children, no fear of attack from Savages, and no armed auto cannons in sight. He could not believe such a thing had ever existed, yet here he stood. Whatever tragedy or conflict had befallen the world, he was certain this place had been abandoned long before the end.

He found a pile of folded pictures that turned out to be maps. The laminated coatings had protected them from fading or dissolving. He recognized I-5 on the lines on the map and quickly figured it was a map of where he was. There was another map exactly like this affixed to the countertop next to him. He re-folded the map in his hand, put it in his pants' pocket, and examined the map on the countertop.

As he studied it, Christian noticed markings scratched into the surface from someone writing on it, the ink having faded into the midst of time. They had circled the word *"Seattle,"* over a section of the map that looked different from the rest. It must have been a city nearby.

"Outpost Lima Charlie," was also etched into the laminate. It was the southern section of the city, just south of the river. He pulled his map back out of his pocket and poked a tiny hole in it with his knife as close to the same place as Outpost Lima Charlie had been indicated on the other. He had a feeling that this would be a place worth looking into. He also noticed that *"Last Chance,"* had also been scratched into the second map right next to Lima Charlie.

He folded his map and placed it in his pocket again, then went about continuing his search around the room. He noticed a cabinet with what looked like cloth sticking out of it and moved in for a closer look. He pulled a shirt out of the cabinet; it looked like it might once have had writing on it, but it had long been faded. He was relieved and elated to find the shirt fit him perfectly. He found others, as well, and put as many on as he could, shoving others into his bindle, figuring it best to stock up.

The scratching at the door had stopped; Christian hadn't noticed how long ago. The light coming through the windows was dimming considerably, and night would be upon him soon. He figured this place was as good as any to stay until tomorrow. He set up a bed using any spare shirts he could find, surprising himself at how comfortable he was. He lay in bed, not risking a fire, and straining to study his new map as long as the failing light would allow. He wondered if the people had made it to Outpost Lima Charlie, and if they might still be there. Maybe, just maybe, there were people he could meet up with, be friends with, maybe even live with. He wasn't sure why, but Outpost Lima Charlie was now his goal, his destination. He drifted off to sleep, daring to dream of what could be, and dreamed of a second chance.

***   ***   ***

Christian rose with the dawn and was happy to be surrounded by silence; the dogs must have given up in the night, and there was no evidence of any other unwanted guests. He cautiously disassembled his barricade and made his way outside into the fresh morning air. He was quickly on the road again, this time at a jog, hoping to put some distance between himself and the dogs, if they were still around.

Several hours later, as his path curved to the right, he could see a bridge ahead; his immediate concern was whether or not it was still intact. His second concern was the clouds he saw forming in the distance behind him, indicating, if the pattern held, that he would soon have another pack of creatures to evade. He quickened his pace again to a jog, having had to slow earlier from exhaustion. His food supply was low, and all this foot travel was taking its toll.

Minutes later, the rain caught up with him, sooner than he had hoped. He ran towards the bridge, thinking maybe, if nothing else, he could take shelter under the structure. A noise from behind him told him he would not be so lucky - a noise he knew only too well, a Savage. His legs and lungs burned as he met the incline to the bridge, not wanting to stop or even slow to see exactly what, or more importantly, how many were behind him.

Without warning, the surface he ran on dropped away, and Christian slid to a stop at the edge of the former roadway. The bridge had collapsed, exposing the river below. He peered over the edge; the drop was not very high. He attempted to gather his thoughts and look for alternatives to jumping. As he frantically searched for a route across, he reached for his gun and turned to see how close his pursuers were, and whether he might be able to fight his way out of this.

A Savage, who had been closer than he realized, tackled him, but instead of landing him on the ground, the impact took both of them over the edge. The impact had also knocked his gun and his bindle from his grasp. He struggled in the fall to get into a position to defend himself from his attacker. The fall felt like it took forever before they hit the water, but could not have been more than fifty, maybe sixty feet, he figured.

They hit the water, and the impact was enough to knock the wind out of him. The fact that his gun had splashed into the drink away from his control was not lost on Christian. He struggled to the surface, nearly out of air, and as he broke through the surface, he immediately prepared for the attack, but none came. A few seconds after he filled his lungs with much-needed breath, he saw his bindle pop through the surface of the water; the plastic bag he had wrapped around the package in case of rain had held enough air in it to give the bindle buoyancy.

The Savage followed the bindle to the surface seconds later, but not as a vicious enemy but as a helpless, panic-stricken victim. It was obvious that the creature could not swim. Christian, however, was quite comfortable in the water. For the moment, he focused on collecting his bindle. He watched the Savage struggle to keep its head above water. As Christian took hold of the staff of his bindle, he watched the Savage's head dip below the surface. Christian turned back to the bridge and was surprised to see at least four more of the creatures holding position at the edge of the bridge. The Savages dared not follow him into the water. After several seconds, they turned and retreated the way they had come. Christian assumed that they hoped to find a route along the banks and continue their pursuit.

The Savage in the water surfaced again. Christian could hear it choke as it sucked water and air into its lungs. He had to admit he felt no guilt as he watched the creature suffer and eventually lose his battle with the river and drown. Christian swam against the current briefly to put some distance between himself and the corpse, but then decided he would allow the current to carry him for a time. He could float and rest his legs, at least, as the water seemed to be still heading roughly north in the direction of Lima Charlie Outpost.

***   ***   ***

A few hours later, in the gathering darkness, Christian noticed a fork in the river ahead. He had also noticed the rain had dissipated; obviously, the water was too much of a threat to the Savages to pursue him; a valuable lesson, indeed.

The fork in the river tweaked his memory from the map. As he floated under another dilapidated bridge, he stuck to the right fork and eyed the shoreline of the island that the water had cut in front of him. Lima Charlie had been on an island. Perhaps, the outpost had been put there intentionally, as they had likely known of the Savage's fear of water. The island was an empty, wide-open space on the side closest to him, with tall structures visible on the far side. Some metal structures lay in a crumpled pile close to the shore, spread apart by a few hundred feet; perhaps they had once been guard towers. Christian didn't care about the nature of their origin; he was too excited to have found Lima Charlie.

He was able to climb to land via one of the crumbled structures. As he made his way to his feet, he slowly scanned the entire area. It was flat and level, mostly tarmac, with little vegetation. He could see from one edge to the other, from north to south. Only on the northwest side of the island could he make out any kind of structure. Derelict vehicles also pocked the surface of the area, as well as a few rusty metal boxes that had to have been forty feet long. Right near the center of the island, he could make out a structure that looked to be intact.

He walked, dripping from head to toe, but not cold in the slightest. Christian's heart skipped a beat when he recognized the letters L and C on the side of the building. His pace hastened in anticipation.

He carefully walked around the entire structure, taking note of the fact that there was only one entrance. The building was windowless and built of a similar-looking material to that of the walls of the Citadel. They were thick and stained from years of dirt and weathered from facing the elements, but still intact.

Near the door on either side, sat what he considered to be some type of military vehicles; no wheels or supporting equipment on the ground. To his surprise, as he walked closer to the door, a faint light appeared as though a section of wall about the size of a golf ball was glowing. Before he was done examining the source of the light, the door hissed and slowly opened upward into the wall. It met with some resistance from corrosion in its path of travel, but the door did reach its full opening height and stopped. The glowing light shut off, and a light inside the small room, now exposed through the open door, lit his path, and Christian could see nothing and no one waiting inside.

With a shrug, Christian figured he hadn't come all this way for nothing, and sauntered through the opening. Once over the threshold, the door slowly lowered itself into its closed position, sealing with a hissing sound. He now found himself in a ten foot by ten-foot room with only a single light in the ceiling at its center. Christian looked around for what he should do next.

The structure was bigger than the room he now stood in, but there was no sign of a door, or a switch, or anything. He was beginning to feel trapped when a series of red beams flashed from the two walls on either side of him. They swept over him up and down for several seconds before stopping, and as they disappeared, another hissing sound indicated an opening door similar to the last. As it opened, several lights came on behind the door, illuminating a much larger space.

"Zero pathogens detected; non-Savage subject, clear to enter," a digitized voice could be heard over a crackling speaker, followed by "Welcome," as the door came to a full open stop. Christian realized he had dropped his bindle and pulled out his knife, the only weapon he had on him. From the doorway, he darted his eyes to every corner of the exposed space in front of him. There was no movement, and no other sounds, except for a low rumble in the background. Christian cautiously entered the room, his senses fully alert, his eyes still darting everywhere. He was relieved not to face an immediate threat, but was sad to find he was still alone.

Several computer monitors blinked to life, catching his attention. He walked towards them, then stopped, going back for his bindle, placing it on the ground next to the computer screens.

"Welcome to Lima Charlie Outpost. You are safe," the first screen read.

"Broadcast signal tower malfunction; unable to send signal," he read on the second screen.

The computer station was built into the wall; three computer screens in a pyramid configuration with a keyboard and a pair of gloves resting on a molded shelf.

"Inquiry?" was displayed on the third and top screen. Christian stood and stared at the third screen for a time, then turned his attention to the rest of the room. He was more interested in the possibility of food, right now, than anything else. He looked around closely, finding many cots spread out end to end, twenty-five in all, and a cabinet at the end of each cot. In the corner, he noticed a staircase heading up.

I may not be alone, Christian immediately thought to himself. He moved towards the staircase, passing one of the cabinets that was open; it contained, among other things, a rack of plasma rifles. Christian paused to grab the weapon and fumbled to arm it before heading to the stairs.

Better safe than sorry, he thought. As he approached the stairs, the next level lit up as the lights came on. Since they were motion-activated, he figured he was alone, or whatever was up there could stay very still. He cautiously ascended to the second level, only to find more cots and more loneliness. The far wall, where the computer was on the lower level, housed more cabinets of a different design, and no other stairs were to be found.

With a grimace, Christian slung the rifle over his shoulder and walked to the far side of the room. He swung open the first cabinet and stood in awe, unable to stop a tear from rolling down his cheek. He was greeted by hundreds of bags of freeze-dried food, labelled M.R.E., similar to the ones he had found earlier in his travels.

Christian frantically opened the other cabinets; all of them contained the same shining packages. He ripped into two packages marked "Granola." He knew he liked them. He poured them carelessly into his mouth at first, spilling some on the ground. He swallowed and smiled, elated to have food going into his stomach. Christian choked, as he had been a bit over-zealous with the portion size.

"Water," he said aloud as he managed to clear his throat. As if on command, a faucet appeared from the wall, and the top of the cabinet beneath it rolled away, exposing a sink. Water poured into the sink. Christian approached and put his hand into the stream; it was cold at least. He moved his hand to his nose; it passed his next test. With a raised eyebrow, he bent down and allowed the water to flow into his mouth. He swished it around as though he knew what contaminated water would taste like. After several seconds, Christian swallowed. He waited for a moment, and having survived that long, decided the water was safe, he then drank heavily from the faucet. He stood straight again and belched loudly, so loudly in fact that he startled himself. He laughed heartily, the first time in the many days since before he was thrown from the Citadel.

"Home," he said aloud to no one, and nodded, still chuckling. He did have to admit that he felt more at home here than he ever had in the Citadel. Here, he was in charge of his destiny, and with the supplies he now had, he knew he would be okay. He pushed aside any lingering doubts, standing taller as he drew a large breath and exhaled slowly. He had felt nothing but fear and anxiety, but maybe here he could not only survive but, maybe, even do a little better. Christian felt that living a great life would be his best revenge on those who had exiled him.

"Now I have some inquiries." He said aloud again, remembering the computer station downstairs. He closed the food cabinets he had opened and headed back downstairs.

Chapter XII

Christian had returned to the ground level of the outpost and made his way back to the computer station. He wasn't sure where to begin, and decided to request information on the bunker, how its systems worked, and the like. The computer buffered for a moment, then displayed on its screen.

"For faster interaction, please use biometric exchange devices." Christian read the line three times and was no closer to understanding it. In the Citadel, he had grown up on a farm. Though aided by modern equipment, he had to admit that computer work was not a daily thing for him. Even at school, when computer interaction was required, it was all done through holographic projection; the computer appeared as an avatar, and asked it questions to perform tasks; it was like having a friend who knew everything.

He remembered moving gloves from the keyboard earlier and wondered if that had something to do with it. He reached for the gloves he had set aside, and as he picked them up, a pair of glasses dropped to the ground. As they landed on the ground, he noticed a flash of light across the lenses. Christian picked up the glasses and studied them for a moment; they appeared to be intact, and with a shrug, he put them on. As he did, images began to drop over his surroundings, with small descriptions of everything he turned his gaze to. Through the end of the earpieces, sound was transmitted into his skull bone and then into his ear canal, and he could hear a voice.

"I am Charlie, your virtual assistant. Please ask of me whatever you require. If you need a tutorial, say – tutorial." The voice stopped, and Christian looked around the room, not entirely sure what was going on, and with a raised eyebrow, he said, "Tutorial?" not hiding his confused tone.

Charlie explained how Christian was hearing his voice. Charlie then cycled through several augmented reality visual aids that he was capable of using, x-ray vision, infrared for night vision, and heat signature detection. It pointed out that the station was powered by a cold fusion reactor that was found twenty feet beneath the structure. As Charlie spoke, it produced a wire overlay of the structure, showing the electrical systems inside the walls. As Christian turned his gaze to the floor, he could see a virtual representation of the reactor and the ladder that led from the southwest corner of the structure, which provided access to the unit should the need arise.

"So that's why there's power here," Christian said, then thought about it for a moment. "What is the projected life span of the reactor?" he asked.

"Another five hundred years," Charlie answered without hesitation.

"What is the current food supply?" Christian was testing the system now.

There are nine hundred and ninety-eight freeze-dried Meals Ready to Eat rations available. As the sole occupant of the facility, if you were to consume three meals a day, the supply would last you three hundred and thirty-two point six days. As no rescue signal has been transmitted due to system failure, if you are to make this a permanent residence, an alternate food source will be required. Would you like me to bring up tutorials on farming techniques?" Charlie prompted. Christian smirked; he was happy to have someone or something to talk to. He figured the one thing he may not need help with was how to plant crops.

"No, not right now," he answered, and thought for a moment. "What about weapons?" he asked.

"The structure has a limited cache of weapons in a locker located here." As Charlie spoke, the cabinet in question was illuminated through the display goggles. "But humans may experience discomfort or even pain through the use of violence or weaponry," Charlie explained.

"Yeah, yeah. I know the story. Anything sinful could be painful," Christian recited the line from his childhood.

"There is also a small transport scout on the upper deck." Christian looked up to see the image of the transport's outline appear in the X-ray imaging setting.

"Cool – my very own speeder bike," he whispered, secretly. He wanted to run up there and take it out right now. He had seen similar ones back in the Citadel and always wanted to try one.

"And a personal tri-glide repulse transport in the closet indicated," Charlie continued. It illuminated two other locations in the heads-up display. Christian crossed the floor and opened the closet; the repulse board dropped down and rested eight inches off the floor. Christian tentatively stepped onto the board. It compensated for his jittery movements, as he was a bit shaky.

"The craft will compensate for the rider until you have grown accustomed to it. The craft is capable of traveling at speeds of up to twenty-five kilometers per hour and an altitude of twelve feet. It has a range of eight hundred kilometers or thirty-two hours before needing to be returned to the docking station to recharge for one hour."

"Hmm." Christian was impressed. He was excited to try it out, but wasn't sure if it was day or night outside, or if it was raining or clear.

"Agh, why are there no windows in here?" he muttered.

"Window mode," Charlie answered, and the view in the glasses was changed to display the view outside the facility as though the walls were not even there.

"You are seeing imagery from cameras positioned three hundred and sixty degrees around the building. For safety and structural integrity, no windows were installed during the facility's construction.

"Okay!" Christian was again impressed. "Do these glasses work outside the facility?" Christian now thought how handy these would be if he were to be out in the wilds searching for supplies.

"If you take the mobile unit with you." The mobile unit's location was highlighted in the display. "It will link with the central processor and sensors will provide ninety-five percent functionality when not in the facility for a range of up to twenty-six kilometers; after that, the functionality drops to seventy five percent, losing the descriptive overlay, but access to the database, infrared, and navigation functions will remain."

"Slacker!" Christian answered sarcastically. He then turned back to the weapons cabinet that he had not checked out. He walked over to pick up the rifle he had found earlier. Then he walked to the weapon cache.

"Warning," Charlie started, but Christian cut him off.

"I'll be fine, Charlie," he said as he opened the cabinet. Inside were two rifles, similar to the one he carried, and six handguns.

"Ooh!" Christian exclaimed as he placed his rifle into the empty slot, trading it for one of the smaller units.

"Two-hundred-watt plasma discharge, capable of firing three round bursts per second or single fire. Each weapon can fire six hundred rounds before needing to recharge. Discharge power is adjustable from non-lethal, to max discharge, which is sufficient to vaporize a human-sized life form," Charlie explained while highlighting other details visually in the goggles, like the laser sight, adjustable discharge power from stun to lethal, and the integrated tactical light.

Christian studied the weapon for another few seconds. Afterward, he put it back in the charging bay. He looked around the cabinet, and with the help of the goggles, identified a holster for the gun and portable charging modules. He then turned back to the outside wall, noticing it was dark outside.

"No wonder I'm so tired. Been a long day," Christian muttered, and turned to one of the cots that Charlie was now highlighting in the display.

"That's it," Christian said, as he crossed the room and flopped down on the first cot he came to. It was the most comfortable thing he had lain on in some time.

"Charlie – what day is it?" Christian asked, realizing he had no idea how long it had taken him to get here from the Citadel.

"The date, according to the Julian Calendar, is May nineteenth, 2963," Charlie explained. Christian was quite sure it had been early April, right around the eleventh, when he had been thrown from the gates of his home. He had wandered the wilds for over a month and survived, and finally found a place he felt comfortable in.

He was safe for the moment, had food, shelter, and weapons, not to mention a comfortable bed. He kicked his shoes off and squirmed under the covers on the cot. As he did, his thoughts drifted to how he had managed to survive, why he was able to kill those

Savages, and handle weapons without succumbing to the curse he had been told his whole life. According to the teachings of his parents and teachers, he should have become a mindless Savage by now for giving in to evil. But obviously, he was different, or he had been lied to.

"What happened to the world?" Christian asked. He could feel his drowsiness becoming worse, now that he was lying down, but he had so many questions, and for the first time in his life, it seemed he had unrestricted access to the truth.

Images of the early twenty-first-century news reports began to pop up in his glasses as Charlie answered his question.

"Events believed to have been set in motion hundreds of years earlier came to a head in the early twenty-first century. The emergence of what was labeled a terrorist group, which seemed to operate outside of the need for funding and bereft of any political motivations other than their own agenda, threatened to disrupt what would become a critical global peace treaty."

As the images flashed on the lenses in front of him, Christian felt as though his consciousness was pulled from his body, and he had slipped into the past. The story and the images, though this was his first time hearing them, felt so familiar.

"Were it not for the actions of a group led by a man believed to be of a race known as the Magi, and suspected to still be alive to this day, the peace initiative would have failed. His name is Rafeo."

The images turned from bombings and crime scene photos to those of a man who looked familiar to Christian.

"Rafeo," Christian repeated. The man was a priest who was known throughout the Citadel; Christian had never spoken to the man but had attended at least one of his lectures that he could remember.

"The other participants," Charlie continued, cycling images in Christian's display as he did. "Gabriel Frost, Sam Carter, and Christian Perditus, the latter losing his life in the final struggle to bring the terrorists down and save the peace conference. The group was led by one known only as Mabus."

"Wait!" Christian yelled as he leapt from the bed, his heart pounding.

"Detecting elevated stress levels," Charlie began, but was cut off.

"Shut up about that, go back to that other guy – Christian," he panted. The image turned to a stock photo of an older man, perhaps in his early forties; other smaller images appeared of the same man from a coroner's report to the side. Christian stared at the pictures and staggered through the outpost towards the washroom. He burst through the door, nearly falling over but catching himself on the sink. He pulled the glasses off and ran the water, splashing some in his face, then stared into the mirror. He slowly looked down at the glasses. He knew what he had seen, but had to see it again, just to be sure.

Christian slowly put the glasses up to his face.

The Augmented reality showed the picture of the man from the past superimposed over the face he saw in the mirror. Though the photo was that of an older man, Christian recognized it instantly; it was his face. As the reality sank in, he felt his knees weaken and had to steady himself with one arm on the edge of the sink again.

"Curious," Charlie said to cut the silence, startling Christian slightly. "The DNA on file from the man in the image has a seventy-nine-point nine, eight percent match to yours."

"Yes, thank you," Christian snapped, having already made that assumption before Charlie had said anything. Charlie had confirmed what he knew in his heart. Somehow, he had been there; he had participated in the events that had shaped the present world in the horrible state that it was in.

The images on his glasses faded away before Charlie spoke again. "The strain is too great on your physiology. I'm afraid I must insist that you lie down and take a moment to recover before we continue." Charlie's voice was quieter than before, but somehow more authoritative.

Christian stared into the mirror for several seconds before turning the water taps off and acquiescing to Charlie's orders. Christian shuffled back across the room and dropped into his bed. He panted, out of breath from the strain. His mind raced, trying to make sense of it all.

"Your DNA sequence does not match that of modern humans," Charlie continued softly.

"Perhaps that would explain why you can handle weapons."

"Or kill," Christian finished Charlie's sentence. He understood, but could not believe or understand why. The science was right in front of him, not to mention the picture. There was no denying it.

"Please, continue," Christian spoke quietly.

"Mabus." Charlie brought up a poor-quality image of the figure of a man in a full-length cloak. "The only image available from the period. He was the leader of a cult; its followers were zealots to the last. Mabus was believed to possess magic powers, claims that were dismissed at the time, but recent occurrences made that difficult to dispel."

Images of a man, again cloaked in black and surrounded by a mist, floating in the air. He rose from the ground to reveal a horde of thousands of Savages hidden in his shadow. He gained altitude and, with the wave of his hand, commanded lightning to strike at multiple targets while the Savages burst from their ranks, flooding into a city. The lightning destroyed military vehicles while the Savages ripped people apart.

"The fall of New York, October 2874," Charlie explained.

The room fell silent. The display turned dark as Christian's vitals had spiked. It was a lot to take in. He dropped a leg over the side of the bed and put a foot on the floor in an attempt to stop the room from spinning.

"Focus on breathing," Charlie suggested, as

Christian tried to resist vomiting. After a few minutes, some semblance of rationality returned. "But you said there was a peace treaty. How, how did it come to this?" Christian wept, tears streaming down his cheeks.

"Indeed, the sacrifice of the team and the momentum gained by the initiative led by Constantine. He convinced the world leaders to abandon the military weapons development and to scale back the deployment of troops and machines across all borders of the world." Pictures from the time began to scroll across the glasses once again.

"World leaders, political leaders, and religious leaders were all unified in a singular goal of renouncing evil. The cult had nearly brought them to the brink of destruction and served as a common enemy. People soon found a way to share with their neighbors, both locally and globally, and for a time, it was. It can only be described as a golden age.

"Generation after generation forgot what it was to wage war, or even commit a crime. All the while, guided by the house of Constantine, which would in short order, spawn a new religion. One that would be accepted globally and unify the human race in a way never seen before in the history of man." Charlie finished.

"Yeah, until it led to their destruction in 2874, I guess," Christian connected the dots in his head. "Victory had defeated them," he said in a whisper.

"You're quick," Charlie answered.

"What did you say?" Christian sat up again, the

impulses in his eyes read by the glasses scrolled through all the pictures and came to rest on the picture of Christian Perditus. He felt a twinge of guilt as he raised himself to a seated position on the edge of the bed.

"Yeah! Call me that from now on," Christian said, nodding his head, as though using an assumed name would somehow separate him from the past. Not only did he wish to forget his life in the Citadel, especially his eviction, but after seeing his likeness through the augmented reality glasses, he wanted nothing to do with his old name until he could come to terms with what it all meant. It would take time, and for now at least, he didn't want this machine reminding him of it every time they communicated.

"Call you what, sir? I do not understand your instructions." Charlie replied.

"Quick." He paused for a moment to look at the picture one more time before taking the glasses off. "Call me Quick."

"Of course," Charlie answered quietly, "Quick, it is, sir."

***   ***   ***

For days after his first night inside Outpost Lima Charlie, Christian, now Quick did barely anything. He would spend hours in bed, getting up only to eat or use the restroom. If Charlie questioned him, he would use the excuse that he was feeling sick. Charlie could, of course, read his vital signs and knew differently, but allowed the young man some time.

Christian would pore through the historical

175

documents, photos, and video files for the last hundred years or so, trying to learn whatever he could.

On the fourth day, Charlie could read a change in Christian's body language and demeanor, and figured now would be a good time to try to ease him into action.

"Perhaps an inspection of the facilities' vehicles would be in order, Quick," the computer prompted. Christian sat up in his bed, and for the first time in days, he wore a smile on his face.

"Oh, yeah," he answered, then peeled his clothes off down to his jockey shorts and headed towards the showers.

"You can't see me in here, right?" Christian yelled as he turned the water on in the shower.

"Well, technically, Quick, I can't really see you anywhere, but I do have sensors in the shower room as well," Charlie answered. "But if it makes you feel any better, I can disable them while you are in the shower."

"Kinda creepy, but whatever. Yeah, I'd like that," Christian answered, as he stepped into the water and yelled, as the water had not quite gotten to the preferred temperature.

"I could have warned you of that if my sensors weren't disabled," Charlie said, causing Christian to jump again.

He didn't like the idea of someone watching him shower, but Charlie wasn't exactly a someone, more of a something.

"K- whatever," he said, as he plunged his head into the warm water stream.

***   ***   ***

After the shower, Christian stared into the mirror for long enough to lose track of time. The image of the other Christian's face superimposed over his haunted his memory. He wiped away the condensation that had accumulated on the mirror from his shower and examined his face carefully, noting how it had changed since he had last had time to look. It had only been thirty-eight days since his unplanned departure from the Citadel, but the strain of the journey had taken its toll. His brown hair was, though clean now, longer and a matted mess compared to the high and tight appearance he had maintained before. Even his young face produced a stubbled surface, which added to the aging effect.

He stepped back to take in a wider view of himself. His six-foot-two-inch frame was even leaner than he was used to. His muscles protruded through his thin skin to give him a chiseled appearance, though he was sure that malnutrition had contributed to that. He was also happy to notice there was no sign of scars or injury. Even to his own eyes, his reflection did look a little unrecognizable.

"I have produced clothing that will fit you, if you are ready," Charlie's voice came from the main room, his speakers and sensors still not active in the bathroom.

"Clean clothes?" Christian thought to himself;

it was something he had figured he would never wear again. With that as a motivator, he shook off his self-inspection and darted from the bathroom. He saw the clothes set aside on a counter near the computer terminal.

"I can recycle any unwanted garments to produce new ones if you wish," Charlie prompted, and a chute opened up a little further down the counter. Christian grabbed his bindle and headed straight for the chute. He stopped before throwing his one t-shirt into the recycler. He looked at the shirt, noting various stains, including blood from the Savages he had killed. It didn't feel right to wear anything else, shrugging he pulled it over his head.

"Surely you want that cleaned!" Charlie rebutted, but then rescinded. I guess not."

Christian put the BDU trousers on and clasped the belt. Then a light military style tunic before a tactical vest over his weathered t-shirt. He admired the clothing as he dressed, but was most impressed to find a new pair of boots. He placed them on his feet, pleased to find they were a perfect fit and had self-lacing.

"So, about that speeder bike," Christian asked, with a grin; he didn't try to hide his excitement.

Charlie led Christian to a ladder/tunnel, which led to a hatch that opened to the roof. Once through the hatch, he was greeted by a beautiful early morning. The sun hangs low, near the horizon, and not a cloud in the sky, which was always a welcome sight.

The sun glimmered from the dew that still rested on the synthetic cloth tarp that covered the scout bike under it. Christian loosened the tie-downs and slowly pulled the tarp back to expose his prize, like a kid on Christmas day.

"Scout vehicle HD-357c2," Charlie's voice carried through a small speech dot Christian had secured to the base of his skull, just behind his ear, the sound traveled through his skull bone and jaw, directly to his oral cavity, similar to how the glasses work. He would be able to converse with Charlie at all times. He had brought the portable computer module with him in case he needed help.

"Sweet," Christian whispered, then slowly straddled the vehicle. He slid into the saddle with ease, as though it had been made for him, as he reached for the controls. He slid his fingers over several buttons on the dash, directly in front of the seat. The steering controls came away from the body like handlebars on a bike, rising toward him. As he reached for them, he brought his feet from the ground to the floorboards that sat near the ground. He was in a near-seated position with his hands in front of him on the controls. He eyed the start button, but hesitated.

"Awaiting your command, Quick," Charlie said in a level tone.

Christian flipped the thumb switch, and with a low-pitched growl, the repulse drive came to life, lifting the vehicle slightly off its moorings. He feathered the throttle to hear the engine's hum turn to a rumble. He engaged the drive that Charlie had illuminated in his augmented reality glasses, but Christian knew where the switch was without the prompt. He then turned the vehicle to face the far end of the island and the open water of Puget Sound.

Christian cracked the throttle, and like a beast, the vehicle leapt from the rooftop and blasted towards the horizon, lowering to five feet from the ground. Christian didn't even try to stifle his cheers of excitement as he felt the rush of acceleration. He watched the heads-up display in his glasses as the speedometer reading blurred through numbers until he eased the throttle, and the numbers slowed and leveled, the speed settling around 220 KPH with plenty of throttle to go.

In a flash, the scout was out over the water, lowering to only two feet off the surface of the fairly still water. Christian buried the throttle and was pleased to notice the rooster tail of water that had sprouted behind him; his speed was over 400 KPH in seconds.

Christian indulged his inner child for several minutes, blasting around the bay, cornering at near breakneck speed, gaining altitude, then dropping back to the deck, even firing the onboard plasma cannon before slowing and settling into a cruising speed of just over 120 KPH. As he looked across the bike, every switch's function was illustrated by Charlie through the AR glasses, Christian felt like he had been riding one of these vehicles all his life.

He turned back towards the outpost, skirting around the banks of a city, and at that one time, it was home to millions of people.

"Charlie, what can you tell me about this place?" Christian asked, while he slowed to look into the city, half expecting to recognize some of the things Charlie described.

Charlie spoke of Seattle's early history, being founded in 1851, and of the Space Needle and a popular music scene in the late twentieth century. The city had been an epicenter for the beginning of religious terrorism in the early twenty-first century. The cultists had planned and carried out several horrendous bombings that had splintered a country and eventually humanity itself.

"Historical figures interred here include rock legend Jimi Hendrix, FBI Agent Gabriel Frost, Martial Arts legend Bruce Lee, and his son, Brandon Lee," Charlie was finished as they approached Lima Charlie outpost.

"Who's that last one, Lee?" Christian asked. He wasn't sure of the meaning of martial arts and why they were noteworthy in Charlie's trip down memory lane.

He carefully lowered the HD-357c2 onto its moorings and cut the power, working on covering the vehicle while Charlie explained.

"Bruce Lee was the founder of Jeet Kune Do, and he was a philosopher turned movie star from the mid-twentieth century," Charlie explained.

"What's a movie star?" Christian asked as he opened the roof hatch and lowered himself down the ladder back into the outpost. He intended to have something to eat and continue his history lesson, but something about Bruce Lee caught his attention.

"Observe the monitor on the south wall," Charlie explained as Christian opened a freeze-dried meal and poured some of the contents into his mouth. The whole south wall came to life as a projection screen, and video clips of Bruce Lee fighting and demonstrating Jeet Kune Do flashed to life. Christian was instantly mesmerized by the movements of the man on the screen. He watched for hours while he slowly ate his meal and begged Charlie to show him more and more videos of martial arts.

"I gotta learn how to do that," Christian whispered in a hushed awe while he watched.

Chapter XIII

Rafeo glanced up from his computer. He was handling their resupply business at the Citadel, checking an inventory list from a friendly outfitter he was longtime friends with. He considered what he needed and eyed an old scout cruiser, hoping to persuade the shopkeeper to part with it. Rafeo knew Quick would love it.

But something was wrong; he didn't know what yet, apart from a feeling he had. It had been hours since he had left Quick, Mary, and Charlotte to go on their walking tour of this section of the Citadel. Rafeo put the computer display down on the shop counter and motioned to his friend that he would be right back; the shopkeeper smiled and watched as Rafeo picked up his walking stick and walked out of the store.

"Everything okay, Raf?" the shopkeeper asked, but got no reply.

Rafeo looked around him; he heard the bells from several churches sounding, calling the faithful to prayer. Rafeo didn't think anything of it, but kept his head facing the sky as if the bells or something else from above would explain his feelings. He walked in the direction where he had seen Quick last.

For reasons he still did not know, he felt his pace quicken. Rafeo wasn't even sure if it involved his friend, but he wanted to know the young man was safe, either way.

Rafeo was nearly at a jog as he rounded a bend in the road that led past a farm. In the distance, he could see another church, this one had a definite glow to it.

Brilliant white light poured from every window of the building, and just as Rafeo saw it, he noticed a leaf in the wind that had slowly blown past him a moment earlier. He looked around, confused, his gaze meeting a bird in mid-flight yet nearly frozen in place. The animal's wings moved too slowly to sustain flight, yet it did not fall from the sky. Time was being slowed down, yet it did not affect him. There was a powerful force at work, and the church seemed to be its epicenter.

Rafeo was certain that Quick was somehow involved, and he pressed forward, having to struggle against the phenomenon, similar to a powerful wind. He pumped the muscles in his legs, begging him to propel him faster, making sure the boy was alright.

Rafeo had made it to the doors of the church and threw them open. The light from within was nearly blinding, but somehow his eyes adjusted, perhaps in the same way that he was able to adjust to the slowing of time. He looked into the church to see Quick and Mary in the center aisle. Mary's child, Charlotte, stood just behind them. They, and the entire congregation, stood frozen in place. Constantine proved to be the source of the light. A deity floated a few feet from the ground and maybe ten feet away from Quick. From his hands came the beams of brilliant light directed at Quick and Mary.

Constantine looked up, not having expected anyone to be moving, much less poised to interfere.

"I mean them no harm; you must not interfere," the voice boomed through the air, stopping Rafeo in his tracks. The old man gripped his walking stick like a weapon and continued forward.

***   ***   ***

Weeks turned to months; in what felt like the blink of an eye, it was the middle of August. Christian had passed the days tending the garden he had planted. He welcomed help from Charlie in the matter, but he had years of experience already. He went out hunting small game around the island and fished, having found great luck with both towards the North End of the island.

He had explored the island in detail, not finding much more information. One such ocean-going vehicle was once moored next to the island, its mooring lines having rotted and allowed the vessel to drift freely in the harbor. Eventually, it lodged itself under the remains of the bridge that had connected the island to the mainland at one point. Another such ship had sunk a few hundred feet from the northern tip of the island, was partially capsized, exposing a large hole in its hull that appeared to have been caused by an explosion.

Christian's other main pursuit was studying and practicing any type of martial arts that Charlie was capable of teaching from his memory archives. Through the Augmented Reality glasses, Charlie was able to provide the forms and verbal instructions to be a formidable sansei. Christian had come along rapidly, devoting four to five hours a day to rigorous training. He would train outdoors if the weather permitted; otherwise, he would use the space he had cleared within the outpost. He would drill his forms, often while watching what Charlie called movies, as entertainment and incentive.

Often, in the evening, he would spend hours atop the remains of a gantry crane, staring into the sunset or studying the city across the river for signs of another person. It was mostly from a sense of curiosity or security, rather than loneliness, that prompted his evening meditation. If Christian was honest with himself, he had never been happier than the time he had spent at the Outpost. His curiosity begged him to explore the fallen city, but he did not believe he was ready yet to leave the sanctuary of the island or the outpost, though that time was coming.

Another month passed; most of his crops neared harvest. Charlie had assured him that the flash freeze unit in the outpost would help preserve the vegetables over the winter, and should anything spoil, the bio-recycling unit would be able to convert the rotten organic material into something nutritious and edible.

Now, with little to do in the garden, Christian had more time to train, more time to stare, and more time to wonder what he might find in the city. He was coming back from a jog around the island as the sun moved slowly across the morning sky. Everything on the island was the same as it was the day before, and the day before that. Christian slowed to a walking pace and wiped his brow with the back of his hand.

"Today's the day," Christian said to himself with a nod. He bounded into the outpost and right into the shower. He didn't linger in the water as he usually did, and when he dressed in full gear, including his belt and vest, Charlie questioned him.

"Are you changing your itinerary today, Quick," Charlie asked.

"Think I'm gonna go explore the far shore today. The hover board will work over the water?" Christian asked.

"It should," Charlie answered after a short pause.

"Are you sure about that?" Christian asked tentatively. He walked to the weapon's chest, pulled out a plasma pistol, checked it, and holstered it.

"I'll be careful," Christian continued, bouncing his eyebrows as he slid the weapon into its holster.

"Careful is good, extra careful is better," Charlie noted. Christian heard the tone in the AI's voice and paused, then reached for a rifle and slung it over his shoulder.

"Extra careful, it is," Christian said with a shrug, then crossed the room and pressed the release command for the hover board. The unit slid down the wall from a vertical resting position to being horizontally inches from the floor, ready for a passenger.

Christian pulled the portable interface from his pocket and directed the hover unit to the exit with a gesture across the screen with his finger. He placed the Augmented Reality glasses on and walked towards the exit himself. Once there, he waited, then looked up at the security camera as though looking at Charlie, gesturing for the computer to open the door. A few seconds later, the exit opened, and Christian walked out next to the hoverboard. Once the board had come to a stop, he carefully stepped up onto the floating surface. Not having used the board very much, Christian shakily guided the vehicle slowly towards the shore and out over the water.

Once he reached the other side, Christian stepped off the board, glad to be on solid ground again. He took the rifle off his shoulder and held it at the ready, placing the portable computer into a slot clamped to the gun rail so he could use it like a heads-up display. He clicked the *"Hold"* button for the hover board to remain where it was. Christian looked around without moving anything more than his head. He strained his ears to hear all the sounds; his eyes darted into every corner and shadow, as if expecting to find something, finding only darkness and stillness.

He had emerged from the water at the edge of what was left of an old dock. The street ahead and the buildings all around him were overgrown with greenery. Several buildings across the street from his position had been consumed by fire before he had arrived at Lima Charlie, possibly years before.

"The last recorded instance of humans inhabiting the city was in a quarantine zone two kilometers from your current location," Charlie advised through his audio piece. "The city was abandoned just over fifty years ago; the quarantine zone holding out for another ten years before it was recorded that all survivors left for the Citadel," Charlie finished.

"Fifty years," Christian said in hushed reverence. It was a sight to behold; the measure at which nature had moved to reclaim this once bustling city and a monument to man's nature to build and conquer. The City was in ruins. Christian was curious as to the marvels he would find, the relics of a civilization long past. Would the story be revealed, or would the past keep its secrets?

In no time, Christian began to see signs of conflict as he cautiously moved down from the remnants of a street. Craters from explosions and burn marks from a weapon's discharge were visible all around him. He examined them closely, eventually finding skeleton remains nearby. Human or Savage, he could not tell.

"Human?" Christian asked, pointing the camera from the portable interface at the remains. On the display, a sensor grid appeared and swept over the bones. A small spinning icon in the corner of the display took over after the grid retracted into it.

"So, it would seem," Charlie answered eventually. "Been there for decades," Charlie had finished speaking, as Christian resumed his search of the area.

The buildings in the area looked like they used to be family dwellings and a block of stores and light industrial buildings. Christian carried on in silence, sweeping his gaze with Charlie's sensors from left to right to inspect the buildings thoroughly. One of the building's front-facing walls had at one point been composed almost entirely of glass, the majority of which lay shattered on the ground, leaving the building open. Christian approached the building, turning on a light at the end of his weapon to help him see inside. He swept from left to right, top to bottom; seeing no threat, shrugged and stepped into the building.

"Curious," Charlie interrupted the silence. "There is a refrigeration unit in the back corner that appears to still have power. This part of the city seems to have been powered by a cold fusion reactor, similar to the one in the outpost," Charlie explained, having scanned the wiring and underground power lines and sub-systems.

"There may be items of use." Charlie's voice crackled and faded out of audible range. Christian backed up until Charlie's voice returned.

"There is some kind of interference, as well," Charlie cautioned. Christian hesitated for a moment before his curiosity got the best of him.

"Quick - wait!" Charlie started but was silenced by static. Christian moved towards the refrigerator and stopped, counting to three to help calm himself before opening the door.

A light inside the unit blinked to life, revealing a treasure trove before Christian's eyes. There were bottles labeled, *"Beer,"* he recognized them from his days at the Citadel. His father would enjoy this beverage on a Friday night. Christian had never been allowed to try it. It was the law that he had to be at least twenty years old before drinking it. Reportedly, this beverage would give anyone who drank it a warm, fuzzy feeling. He reached into the unit and removed two bottles, placing them in his backpack, securing them so as not to contact each other, hoping not to break them.

Next, he noticed four small bottles labeled "Penicillin".

"What is this?" Christian questioned, holding the bottle up to the camera, but when no response came, he remembered the interference.

"Right," Christian said with a shrug and put the bottles back. He found several freeze-dried bags of food labeled "Doritos," and he placed two of them in his pack, taking up almost all the remaining room.

Next, he grabbed a container labeled *"Coke 3000."* Christian examined the container and pulled a tab marked, *"Pull."* With a pop-fizz, the container opened, spilling some of the bubbly liquid onto the ground. He sniffed the container, the fluid smelled sweet. He rubbed a small amount between his finger and thumb, it seemed like dark water. He carefully licked a small amount of the liquid off his fingers, and a giant grin formed on his lips; he had never tasted the like.

Christian guzzled more than half the can and stood with his eyes closed, enjoying the moment. He giggled from the sensation of the bubbles, from the carbonation that burst on the surface of his tongue by the thousands. A few seconds later, his stomach rumbled, and Christian let out a tremendous belch, the sound echoing through the building. He laughed despite himself, turning back to the soda and drank the rest.

It took several seconds for Christian to hear the drops striking the broken glass on the ground outside; his elation quickly evaporated as a chill ran down his back. It had begun to rain. Christian dropped the can and readied his weapon. His nerves were ablaze with impulses as he scanned his immediate surroundings. Once it was clear, he moved to the front of the building, and as he did, he heard a crackle in his ear followed by Charlie's voice over his earpiece.

"Get out of there. Savages moving towards you from the southwest, dozens of them." Charlie was nearly frantic. Christian sighted them down the street through his scope; there they were, heading his way, too many to know if he could get them all, should he open fire.

Christian was back in the building, desperately searching for an idea or a hiding spot. A ladder in the back of the store leading through a hole in the roof caught his eye. He bounded through the shop, up the ladder, and up to the roof. He kept low and moved towards the edge of the building. He realized he had left the ladder standing to avoid making noise, but that meant leaving a means for the Savages to follow him.

Christian bolted from the edge, running and leaping to the next rooftop. He landed and crouched, removing the portable computer from his weapon and holding it up to use it to look over the side of the building, like a periscope.

The Savages were everywhere on the street below, sniffing the air and searching for him; at least that is what he figured.

Christian lay as still as possible while the rain poured on him. He was thankful for the protection of his glasses, allowing him to keep his eyes open. The heads-up display tagged each Savage in view and tracked them even when out of sight. Christian only had to point the hand-held unit at the group to receive the data.

He figured it was a little early to be optimistic, but it did seem as though they would pass by without noticing him. He felt himself relax slightly at the thought. A second later, there was another rumbling from his stomach - the Coke 3000.

Christian could not stifle the burp in time. Every target displayed in his glasses stopped and turned towards him in one fluid motion. Christian froze, his heart pounding in his chest, his blood turned cold. They had heard it, but would they realize he was on the roof?

As though to answer his unasked question, he noticed a group nearing the area of the shop where the ladder had been; the targets jostled around slightly in the display, and he could hear their grunting. Seconds later, one of the Savages appeared on the adjacent roof.

Christian forced himself to breathe deeply to calm himself. He sighted through his scope, aiming for the creature's chest, and fired, vaporizing the Savage in one shot, the plasma rifle being set to maximum power.

"Run!" Christian heard Charlie's voice yelling in his ear. He found his feet and fled across the rooftop away from whence he had come. The Savages were now in pursuit, and some clawing their way up the ladder, fighting more with each other to be the first to the roof than with anything else. Others still followed Christian's path from ground level. Christian leapt from one rooftop to the next.

"You will be out of rooftops in half a block," Charlie warned. "If you can make it to the ground without injury, you will still have four blocks to cover to get back to the water and the relative safety of the hover board.

"I need ideas, Charlie!" Christian yelled back.

"I'm working on it."

Christian jumped to the last rooftop. He ran along its edge and could see he had managed to stay a few hundred feet ahead of the horde.

"We can overload the rifle," Charlie finally spoke after what felt like an eternity, although it had only been a few seconds.

"Turn this knob all the way around to the right and pull this lever," Charlie raised his volume level. Christian had to look down at the rifle before the Augmented Reality overlay showed him how to carry out Charlie's instructions. Christian did as he was instructed, and the weapon began to vibrate. He had reached the edge of the roof and, without hesitating, jumped from the edge to the ground. He landed and tucked into a roll, springing back to his feet without missing a stride.

Christian yelled into his earpiece. "Now what?"

"Get rid of the rifle, throw it behind you right now!" Charlie barked.

Christian swung the sling over his head and whipped the rifle into the air, again without losing pace. No sooner had his rifle left his hand, he drew his pistol. He turned and fired quickly, dropping two of his pursuers before resuming his sprint towards the water.

The rifle landed amidst the gang that was less than twenty feet behind him. One or two of the Savages stopped to look, as the rest ran by. The air was split by a blast that rocked the ground; the shock wave knocked Christian over. He tumbled and rolled, getting his feet under him again, but his pace was stunted as the blast had popped both of his eardrums, changed his equilibrium was causing him to stagger. He stopped and turned again, only to see two targets remaining in his heads-up display. One of those targets soon fell and disappeared, succumbed to its wounds.

Christian struggled to hold his weapon up; he fired several shots before he dropped the last Savage where it stood. Without hesitation, Christian turned and continued running slower back to the water. Blood streamed down his cheeks, and his vision was blurry, to say the least. It was pure determination that kept his feet moving, one in front of the other. Had it not been for the threat behind him, he would have given in to his injuries.

"There are several heat signatures near the building you originally entered," Charlie reported. "They are heading this way, but are several hundred feet behind you. If you can keep going even at this slower pace, you should make it to safety without them catching up."

Christian nodded and swallowed the pain, forcing himself to carry on; he was injured. But knew he could make it another two or three blocks.

"I'll keep talking you through until you reach safety," Charlie explained, though Christian could barely hear Charlie's instructions over the ringing in his ears. "I've ordered the hoverboard to move towards you. It will be able to transport you faster than you can run, Quick. It should be in view now."

Christian was happy to see the hoverboard streaking towards him. As Christian came up to the board, he dropped onto it, not even trying to stand for the ride back to the outpost. The hoverboard spun round and headed back towards the water.

The hover board floated at top speed across the water, up the bank on the far side, and into the waiting open door of the outpost. Christian struggled to maintain consciousness until he saw the door of the outpost closing behind him.

***   ***   ***

Christian awoke several hours later, his head pounding and a throbbing pain in his left leg. He forced himself to sit up. Charlie lowered the room lights in response to Christian's squinting, before the young man had even said anything.

"You've sustained damage to your upper left leg. It would appear that a piece of shrapnel from the weapon explosion managed to miss every Savage and lodge itself in your leg."

"It would appear - damn - my head," Christian stammered, nearly yelling.

"You also have sustained damage to both eardrums. The damage will heal in time, and your hearing should recover almost completely," Charlie explained.

"Almost!" Christian spat and wiped the dried blood away from his ears, shaking his head.

"I guess I did ask for ideas," he continued, calming himself. It was most likely that the only reason he survived the day was due to Charlie's suggestion, if he had to suffer a few bumps and bruises. He thought, it could have been much worse.

Christian got to his feet; the weight transfer caused a shooting pain up his left leg. He nearly collapsed, but managed to steady himself. He limped to the mirror in the bathroom and found the hole in his pants about eight inches above his knee, thankfully, right in the meaty part of his muscular leg. He stumbled over to the nearby counter and reached for a pair of scissors and a first aid kit. He cut the side of his pants off, exposing his leg without having to pull the garment over the piece of shrapnel.

Once exposed, he hesitated and looked around, hoping to find something other than the obvious solution for pulling the debris from the wound.

"Do I just pull it out?" he asked Charlie, hoping the computer would give a different answer for him.

"Pull it out as straight as possible, then douse the area with the alcohol, then as quickly as you can, put the dressing over the opening and wrap it tightly," Charlie kept his voice clear and calm.

Christian looked around the room again and took several deep breaths, then ripped the shrapnel from the wound and poured the alcohol. The alcohol stung, well, burned a lot, and Christian could not stifle a grunt in response to the pain. He winced and tilted his head back, trying to keep the room from spinning. The hole in his leg was at least two inches in length; blood spewed from the opening and mixed with the alcohol, making a puddle on the floor.

Christian's stomach turned, and his vision grayed; he shook his head and slapped the dressing over the wound with his last bit of strength. He collapsed from the ordeal, but Charlie had placed the hoverboard next to him in preparation. Christian slumped onto the board, which slowly floated across the room and slid him onto his bed, where he lay unconscious for several hours. Charlie monitored the young man's vital signs closely and raised the temperature in the outpost to eighty degrees, keeping him comfortable.

Chapter XIV

Almost a year had passed. The winter had been long, with temperatures too cold to do anything much out of doors. Christian had recovered from his injuries and resumed his training with a renewed passion. His last experience in the city had not gone as well, and he vowed to return and explore more in the spring and summer.

He diligently planted his garden, tended the crops well enough, and waited for them to mature. The days had grown long and warm, it was early June. Christian had been on his own for over a year. He had a combination of circumstances, such as aging, proper nutrition, and ample exercise led him to put on nearly forty pounds over the past twelve months or so. Christians' physique was in top athletic form.

The morning workout consisted of swimming a lap around the island. He felt particularly safe in the water, knowing that Savages were afraid of it and were notoriously bad swimmers. The resistance of the water offered a full-body workout and kept him cool at the same time.

Christian rounded the bend from the southern tip of the island into the channel between the outpost and the city. He stopped suddenly and held his position, treading water with just the top half of his head protruding from the surface of the water. He spotted movement on the far bank that had caught his eye.

He remained there for ten minutes without seeing anything; perhaps he had been mistaken, figuring it was just a wild dog or another animal. He reluctantly resumed his swim, finally climbing up the bank where he had left his towel only an hour before. As he dried himself, he stared into the city, putting the Augmented Reality glasses to see if maybe Charlie's sensors could see something his unassisted eyes missed, and still nothing.

He turned to return to the outpost to come face to face with a figure holding a blade.

"Picking up a heat signature near you, use caution," Charlie's voice his earpiece.

"Yeah, thanks," Christian answered, putting out his arms, palms towards the person in front of him. It was a woman, looking to be roughly his age. She was crouched slightly, raising her weapon into a high guard position. She did not strike, but did appear to be ready for a fight.

Christian was only mildly concerned; he didn't like the fact that he was unarmed, but clearly, this was not a Savage. She was quite attractive. Her face and clothes were dirty, but looking past that, Christian saw a woman. She had short blonde hair, and faint freckles on her cheeks; her eyes were sharp and piercing, silver, like two small moons staring back at him.

"Easy, I.." Christian spoke, trying to calm her,

and she attacked as he did. Her movements were experienced but weak. She swept her blade in tight, directed arcs, which Christian avoided, thanks only to his training. He paused to think how this exchange would have gone a year ago.

The woman changed her attack to a thrusting motion, and Christian saw his opening. He was able to grab her wrist and hold it while stepping in close to grab her by the throat.

"There's no need to fight," Christian said, and was about to loosen his grip when he felt her body go limp. She collapsed, dropping her sword, and Christian moved swiftly to catch her from falling. He picked her up into his arms, leaving her weapon where it had fallen, and carried her into the outpost.

"Are you sure this is a good idea? She was just trying to kill you," Charlie cautioned, as Christian brought her through the main door.

"So has everyone I've ever known," Christian answered, under his breath. "But she wasn't trying to kill me; I think she was trying to scare me off. Check her vitals and scan for injuries." Christian ordered.

There was a brief silence as Christian carried her to one of the beds and lay her down. Charlie's voice came back after completing his task.

"No sign of injuries, but her pulse and respiration are weak. She appears to be."

"Starving," Christian finished the sentence before Charlie could.

"Indeed!" Charlie answered.

"She was trying to scare me away from the food," Christian explained. He walked towards the galley and busied himself with boiling water and some bones left over from a few pheasants he had recently hunted.

"Let me know if she wakes up. She'll be scared, and I don't want her to hurt herself." Christian said, then turned back towards the bed she had been placed in, only to find her standing behind him, armed again with a kitchen knife.

"She is awake," Charlie said plainly.

"You're not very good at this, I guess," Christian said sarcastically to Charlie, before looking the woman in the eye. The woman appeared confused by Charlie's voice. She was not quite sure who Christian was speaking to. Her eyes darted around the room looking for a third person, but quickly zoomed back in on Christian, the laser focus in her eyes.

"Hi! I think we got off on the wrong foot," he quickly explained, not hiding his nervousness, all while raising his arms in front of him again. The woman twitched nervously but did not attack. "I'm making some soup," Christian continued, trying to remain calm. He turned back towards the stove, thinking that the fact that he was willing to turn his back on her might make him seem less of a threat. "Figured it would be easier on your system since you haven't eaten in days? Weeks?" he asked softly, he cocked his head slightly, studying her face for the slightest reaction, but none came. She stood poised to strike, her face hard, as though chiseled from stone. After a few cautious moments, Christian finally saw the corners of her eyes and mouth soften slightly.

"Eight days," she finally answered, her voice weak and gruff.

"If you haven't figured it out yet, I'm not gonna hurt you," Christian said, and turned back towards her. He lowered his arms slowly while gesturing to a chair with his right hand.

"Why don't you sit down before you fall?" he asked, then reached his hand out, gesturing for her to give him the knife.

"I need to cut some potatoes." He pointed over his shoulder to the kitchen.

"Unless you don't like potatoes." He was trying to get a reaction from her, which didn't come.

"Quick," he said, pointing to himself. "My name is Quick," he said. he felt a twinge of guilt knowing he had given her a nickname instead of his real name. he was, after all, trying to gain her trust. He shrugged, more for himself, and thought, *What's in a name?*

The woman spun the knife around and handed it to Christian, handle first, and lowered herself into the chair.

"You give yourself that name?" she asked, trying to sound defensive.

"Yeah, I guess," Christian answered, preparing his soup.

"Yes, I like potatoes," she answered eventually, and quietly.

"That's a funny name, even worse than Quick," Christian quipped. He looked up to see her smile slightly, then force the smile away.

"Mary," she said after a moment. "My name is Mary."

Christian looked up and smiled. He put down the knife and wiped his hands. He walked towards her and offered to shake her hand. Mary looked at him for quite a moment; Christian wasn't sure if she was sizing him up or mustering the strength to lift her arm. She finally raised her arm and shook his hand.

"It really is nice to meet you," Christian said, and smiled as warmly as he could. Christian slid the potatoes from the cutting board into the broth, then selected some mushrooms he had found growing in the shaded corner of one of the buildings on the island. Charlie checked them out to make sure the mushrooms were safe to eat. Christian chopped the mushrooms, followed by some onions, dropping them all into the pot before putting the knife down on the counter. Wiping his hands again, walked to the refrigerator, took out a bottle of water, and walked back to the table, placing the water in front of Mary.

Mary eyed the bottle for a few seconds, then snatched it from the table. She opened it and drank heavily from the container.

"Easy," Christian cautioned.

Mary stopped with a gasp and put her hand on her chest. "Been a few days without water, too, I guess."

Mary nodded and pulled her feet up onto the chair, hugging her legs, sitting almost in the fetal position. She rocked slightly and put her chin on her knees while staring at Christian. The two sat in silence. Listening only to the pot boiling on the stove for several minutes. Soft instrumental music started to play, and Mary looked around for the source of the sound, while Christian rolled his eyes.

"Mary, say hello to the residential A.I.; his name is Charlie."

"I thought music might help make the situation less tense," Charlie explained, his voice coming over the built-in speakers in the ceiling. His voice surprised Mary: she snapped her head around, looking at the facility, before she remembered Christian had introduced him as A.I.

"Hello, Charlie," Mary said, sounding confused and relieved.

"Welcome to Lima Charlie Outpost," Charlie said proudly.

"Thank you," Mary said, smiling warmly for the first time.

"Quick, I believe the soup could use a splash of garlic, and it will be ready to serve. Mary looks hungry." Charlie did not want the silence to continue.

Christian got up and grabbed a clove of garlic from a rack near the stove. He skinned it and crushed the garlic, throwing it into the broth. He removed the bones, threw them in the recycler, and stirred the soup, wafting the smell towards his nose; he looked over at Mary and shrugged.

"Not bad," he said, with a self-assured grin, and pulled a ladle full of broth out and blew on it, then sipped from the spoon. After swallowing, he looked around as though waiting for something.

"Not bad at all," he finally said, then grabbed a bowl, served a healthy portion, and placed it in front of Mary.

"It's really hot, though." Christian cautioned, then watched in amazement as she picked up the bowl and drank down the soup.

"Don't wait for me, I'm fine," Christian said with a grin, as he reached for another bowl. He filled it and crossed back to the table only to find that Mary was close to finishing her portion. He slid the bowl in front of her and winked as she looked up at him.

"You need it more than I do," he said, smiling to reassure her that he meant it. Christian slowly dropped onto the chair across the table from Mary and stared as she ate. He studied her intently and noted even the slightest movement while she ate.

"What?" Mary slammed her bowl on the table and dropped her feet on the floor. She was irritated, apparently from the staring.

"It's a little creepy," she explained, and made an exaggerated staring gesture to emphasize her point.

"Sorry, I just_" Christian was at a loss for words. "I just don't - how are you here?" he asked finally. Mary shrugged but didn't answer; instead, she resumed eating, slowly.

"I've been out here for over a year and have not seen another living soul other than Savages or wild dogs - I mean - I almost feel like I'm hallucinating," Christian explained.

Mary slowly chewed a mouthful and swallowed. She now found herself staring at the man across from her.

"I get it," she explained, with her mouth still partially full. She swallowed and went on. "I've been out here for - well, I don't know how long."

"The current date according to the Julian calendar is June seventh, 2964," Charlie interjected.

"Almost two and a half years," Mary whispered in shock; her eyes welled slightly, but she held the tears back before continuing.

"I left the Citadel in the east with nine others and have watched them all die." Mary turned back to her bowl and spooned another scoop into her mouth as tears began to slowly slide down her cheeks. She tried to focus on the food in an attempt to distract herself from the memory, with no success.

Christian allowed her to finish. The pair sat in silence for a time, getting accustomed to the presence of another living person around them. After the meal, Christian saw that Mary was exhausted from her journey and directed her to a bed. She reluctantly lay down, then looked around nervously.

"You are safe here. Why not get some rest, and we can figure the rest out after." Christian tried to look as reassuring as he could.

"I'll be outside if you need anything; you can also ask for Charlie, he has audio sensors everywhere."

Mary smiled, and Christian couldn't tell if it was sarcasm or not. She fidgeted, and her mouth opened; a slight sound erupted from her throat. She attempted to resist, not feeling comfortable enough to sleep with a strange man watching over her. She turned her head to the side, but quickly submitted to her fatigue. Christian watched as she flopped onto her back. It may have been a rudimentary cot, but it was the most comfortable thing Mary had been on in quite some time. She closed her eyes, then opened them slightly to watch Christian march straight towards the door.

"Is everything okay, Christian?" Charlie inquired over the earpiece. "Your vitals are slightly askew."

Christian didn't answer at first; he waited until he was outside.

"Yeah, I think so, Charlie; it just feels really odd to have another person around after so long."

"Indeed," was all that Charlie responded.

Christian paced back and forth outside the door in the early afternoon sun. He closed his eyes to help calm himself and enjoyed the cool breeze coming off the water against his face and bare arms. After several moments, he felt less nervous, but could not get rid of his pent-up excitement or anxiety.

For lack of a better idea, Christian walked to his training dummy. At first, he leaned against it for support and hung his head low. Almost as if it were second nature, his hands began to move through the forms, striking and blocking the rungs protruding from the figure. His eyes still closed, he moved faster and faster until his movements were only a blur.

Christian lost all track of time as he pounded his emotions into his poor training dummy. Finally, his muscles burned, his hands ached, and his clothing was soaked with sweat. He collapsed to the ground and lay panting. Christian opened his eyes momentarily and realized that dusk was upon him. He had been at it for nearly four hours, without stopping.

He sat up, still breathing heavily, and turned his face into the breeze. The evaporation of the moisture on his face was accelerated by the wind and cooled him quickly, certainly a welcome feeling. He placed a hand on one of the practice arms and pulled himself to his feet.

"I wondered when you were going to stop," Mary's voice came from over his shoulder and startled him; he spun to face her.

"Sorry," he panted. "I didn't realize you were here; I mean. I'm not used to…"

"You do this often?" she asked, raising an eyebrow, not wanting to acknowledge his nervousness. She didn't want him to know she thought it was kind of cute.

"Every day," he replied.

"You train until you collapse?"

Christian was caught at a loss. "No, I." he stammered, but stopped as Mary smiled.

"I feel much better after some food and rest. I can't thank you enough," she smiled. Christian could feel his face getting warm again.

"The only thing missing would be clean clothes, and maybe a shower?" Mary pulled at her tattered clothing and waved a hand past her hair, allowing the wind from her hand to shake free some dust from the road to illustrate her predicament.

"Ah, yeah." Christian's eyes widened, and he remembered how much he enjoyed his first shower after being out in the world. He knew Mary would love it; he had a hard time containing his excitement. "We can help with that - totally. Charlie can fix you up with some clothes, and I can help you shower, I mean show you where the shower is." He blurted out, while scrunching his face up, embarrassed, not believing the slip of his tongue. Mary smiled quietly, not bringing unwanted attention to it, and walked slowly back into the outpost.

Charlie had already produced new garments for Mary, having heard the conversation from outside, had already done a complete scan of her earlier, and knew her sizes. Christian opened the door to the shower and got Mary a towel; then he pointed out the soap and liquid cleaners and stood there smiling awkwardly. After several moments, Mary smiled as well.

"You're not planning on standing there all night, I hope," she said with a grin, though she wasn't completely convinced that would be a problem.

"No!" Christian yelled, then turned sharply towards the door. "Sorry!" he waved behind him, not even wanting to turn to look at her again; if he had, he would have seen Mary's playful grin and hushed giggle as he walked out.

***   ***   ***

Christian waited nervously, sitting on the edge of his bed. After only ten minutes, but what felt to him like an eternity, the shower shut off. Christian jumped up and put a sweater over his head, realizing he was still shirtless since his impromptu workout, and figured it was a good idea to cover himself.

"Are you sure you're okay, Quick?" Charlie asked after several moments.

"Yeah, I'm good, I'm good," Christian answered anxiously.

"She is rather attractive," Charlie said, as if agreeing to a statement Christian hadn't made. "You have to remember I can monitor your vital signs and pheromone levels."

"Uh, really?" he replied, and jumped to his feet and paced the floor quickly.

"You disagree?" Charlie asked, then turned one of the wall monitors on, showing a live feed from the shower room, displaying Mary in all her naked splendor.

"Shut that off. What the hell, man? Christian barked, raised his hands to block his view, then lowered them again slowly and found himself staring at the image on the screen for longer than he figured he should have.

"Seriously! OFF!" he barked again.

"Sorry," Charlie said, and shut down the monitor. "I thought it would help you past this awkwardness."

The door to the shower room opened a second later, and Mary walked out holding her original clothing and donning the one-piece coveralls Charlie had produced for her. Her hair was still wet from the shower, but she was not concerned about it.

"That was heavenly," she said, and stretched.

"Yes, it was," Christian said, then realized what he had done. "I mean, I bet it was. My first shower when I got here was awesome; that's what I was thinking of - yeah."

"Okay," Mary answered, unaware of what had transpired while she was in the shower room.

"Perhaps a tour of the facility would be in order," Charlie offered, trying to help Christian out of a proverbial corner.

"Yeah," Christian's voice cracked nervously. He cleared his throat and continued. "A tour, great idea."

Christian spent the next few hours showing Mary everything about the outpost that he could think of for food storage, his garden, weapons, vehicles, all of it. Mary listened intently and asked questions when needed. They talked for hours, eventually returning to the sleeping quarters of the outpost. They lay down across from each other and continued to talk until Mary could not stay awake any longer. Christian stared at her, afraid to sleep for fear that when he awoke, she would be gone, like something from his imagination.

They were well suited for each other, similar in age.

They were the same in many ways, she had been able to use a weapon without turning into a Savage. Christian was happy she was there and hoped that she felt the same.

Chapter XV

The next day, Christian awoke and quietly exited the outpost to begin his workout routine, without waking Mary. He stretched and slowly started his jogging laps of the island. He enjoyed the stillness of the morning, only the noise of the gulls around the bay interrupting the soothing sound of the water lapping the shore. Christian had finished the northern leg and turned west, starting to pick up the pace a little.

"How many laps are we doing?" Mary's voice came out of nowhere, and Christian jumped, his heart pounding. He slid to a stop and braced himself for attack before realizing what had happened. Mary covered her mouth and giggled softly, pleased with herself for sneaking up on Christian.

"You! Uhm." Christian stammered and bent over to place his hands on his knees to brace himself and catch his breath.

"Yes, me," Mary answered coyly, knowing she had taken him by surprise. Christian looked up and smiled.

"Three! And the loser cooks breakfast," he said, and took off at a jog, though faster than before. Mary easily matched his pace and ran along with him, both of them in silence for several minutes before Christian's curiosity took over.

"Are there others out there?" Christian asked. Mary slowed as they neared the outpost, only one lap down. Mary slowed to a quick walk and put her hands on her hips. She paced, trying to catch her breath. Christian slowed to match her pace.

"Like us?" she panted, coming to a stop.
"Are you looking for a friend?" she asked sarcastically, but Christian scoffed and turned away from her slightly. He found himself caught in his memory, feeling the need to explain himself to Mary.

"I had friends once; a family even." He cleared his throat after his voice cracked. "Then one day they all turned on me and drove me from my home, forcing me into this world all alone, with no concern for my existence, a moment after that. Such fear and hatred in their eyes. I've had my share of friends."

Mary stood; mouth slightly agape; she truly hadn't expected that response. She had mourned every friend she had lost in her journey and felt horrible for Christian.

"I'm so sorry," her voice hushed. "I hope that doesn't include me?" she asked innocently.

Christian turned back to face her and forced a smile; he wanted it to look as genuine as he meant it to be, but wasn't quite successful. "I'm willing to make an exception in your case. Well, so far anyway." The mood had already turned.

Christian knew he had seen no sign of another human in his short travels north from the Citadel, but knew that didn't mean anything.

"Out there, you mean?" Mary questioned, turning the conversation back to where it had begun.

"Yeah, there has to be something, someone out there," he said desperately.

"Oh, there has to be?" she questioned, then turned back to Christian. "There is death and terror and ugliness, that is for sure, but others?" She shook her head slowly. "If there are, they are hidden," she said quietly.

"Come on," Christian said, putting his hand on her shoulder. Mary turned slowly to look him in the eyes, her eyes moist from tears she struggled to conceal.

"I'll cook breakfast," he said, and walked towards the outpost.

"If there are," Mary said again, then trailed off. She walked towards Christian's sparring dummy he had been using the day before. "I need you to train me so we can find them." She said and punched the figure.

Christian walked to her and again put his hand on her shoulder in an attempt to calm her.

"But first, breakfast; I never train on an empty stomach." Mary eventually turned from the dummy to face him and smiled.

"First we eat, then we train," she said, forcing a smile.

"Like a beast," Christian assured her. They walked quietly back towards the main building, each reflecting on their pain and curious about the other's story. Mary didn't like the dark undertones of the morning so far. She thought back to Christian's earlier comment.

"Are you admitting you lost the race?" She bumped her hip into his jokingly. They looked at each other; Christian chuckled slightly.

"I wouldn't go that far," he answered through his laughter.

***   ***   ***

Weeks turned to months as the pair lived and worked together. Christian shared the video and Augmented Reality videos to train Mary in the Martial Arts. Mary would share what she had learned from necessity from her travels. They would also spend hours training with the rifles and pistols, all the while getting to know each other, their fears, their hopes, their quirks; they shared everything. Whether it was due to a lack of choice or something far more meaningful, the two had become very close with each other.

By September, Christian was ready to venture out to the city again; he was confident that Mary was, too. She was certainly keen on the idea. They had finished harvesting much of the garden and prepared for the coming winter. The last day of the harvest was upon them, and they had gathered plenty of food.

Christian had prepared a meal while Mary finished preserving the red peppers, with Charlie's help, of course.

"So tomorrow, then." Mary pleaded as she

217

flopped into the dining hall chair, awaiting Christian to bring in the meal, plated.

"Yeah, I guess." Christian shrugged and raised an eyebrow. "Just gotta avoid the coke 3000," he said with a chuckle.

"What do you mean?" Mary asked.

"Long story," Christian said, waving his hand to gesture an end to the topic.

"Indeed," Charlie spoke up.

"Never mind," Christian said with his mouth full.

They ate quickly, as they usually did. Mary cleared the table, scraping the scraps into the recycler before washing the dishes. Christian walked up to help as she put the last dish in the drying rack. He toweled the dishes off quickly and hung the towel to dry. He turned and wrinkled his nose.

"Whew, I guess I need to shower," he said honestly, and peeled his shirt off over his head. When he looked up, he noticed Mary looking at him, not as she had any other time, though.

"Yeah, you do that," she said softly, then shook her head and added, "Stinky," to try to draw attention away from the way she was looking at him. He threw her an awkward grin and walked towards the shower.

"Should I lower the internal temperature, Mary? You seem to be very warm in the cheeks," Charlie said. Christian froze, recalling a similar conversation with Charlie not long after Mary arrived. He said nothing and hurried into the shower room.

"Make it nice and warm, Charlie," Christian said, shaking off the whole exchange while he stripped down to walk under the water stream. He left his head under the water for some time, enjoying the feeling, then rubbed his face and head to wash away some of the sweat of the day. Christian then turned in the shower to grab his shampoo, but instead he put his hand on Mary's wet skin. He opened his eyes, surprised by her presence, but not surprised at the same time. She stood before him naked, in all her glory. Far more beautiful than he could recall from the image Charlie had shown him months before.

Christian had taken notice of her beauty from day one, stealing a glance at her form when he could. She was a friend, a partner, and he had always feared taking the relationship beyond that, but had always wanted to try. He was not alone, apparently, in that desire.

Mary smiled nervously, then pushed Christian back slightly so she could enter the water stream. She put her head back to allow her hair to slick back as it got wet. Mary softly moaned, enjoying the water temperature, then leveled her gaze at Christian, whose eyes were big with surprise. Mary was happy to have caught him off guard, yet again, but he was not objecting, not even slightly. Mary leaned in close to him and reached up to put her arms around his shoulders, and pulled him in for a kiss.

"I..." Christian started, but soon his mouth was

occupied with activity other than talking.

They kissed deeply and warmly. To Christian, it felt familiar and welcome, but so exciting at the same time. They had formed a healthy friendship over the past few months, and this felt like the natural progression.

Mary felt completely swept up in the moment. She had often thought of intimacy with Christian, but never confident enough to try. The fact that he reciprocated felt so good to her.

The warmth of the water was nothing compared to the heat from their naked bodies. Their limbs and lips intertwined in a passionate frenzy. Their hands explored and touched each other as any lovers would, but with the wonder and excitement that came with this first experience.

Christian lifted her into his arms and lowered her onto his form; she wrapped her legs around his waist. The excitement weakened his knees slightly, and he found himself needing to lean her back against the wall for a moment. The heat from the water and their emotions soon found them both out of breath. Their skin was hot to the touch, it was almost more than they could bare.

Christian lifted Mary slightly, moved to cradle her in his arms, and walked out of the shower. He moved out into the main room and straight to his bed. He lay her down and quickly crawled over her, kissing every inch of her neck, ears, and lips as he entered her again.

The house lights dimmed silently, and one of the

walls' displays turned into a fireplace, which soon became the only light source in the room. Mary stopped from their activities, pausing at the setting, and smiled back into Christian's eyes.

"You program that?" she asked quietly.

"Huh, maybe, I don't know." Christian panted and resumed caressing her skin, moving his mouth slowly down her neck and across her breasts. She quietly moaned, which was enough to block the rest of the world from his senses; all he could see, smell, taste, and feel was Mary.

They continued for nearly an hour, Christian collapsing on the bed next to her after he had reached his climactic point. Mary rubbed his chest and turned on her side, and continued kissing him. Moments later, she crawled on top of him and the whole experience started all over again.

***   ***   ***

Hours later, they found themselves on blankets they had dropped on the floor in front of the makeshift fireplace, both panting for air. Each of them was completely caught up in the other. Neither could stop touching or kissing the other, though barely a word had been spoken since the shower. There was no need at the moment; they only needed to look into each other's eyes until neither could stay awake in the wee hours of the morning; the entire day had passed.

The next morning started the same way. They had both awakened at the same time, the same smile still on both their faces. The rest had led to renewed vigor in both of them, and the effort was rewarded with powerful climaxes.

They lay in each other's arms again, and Christian looked into her beautiful eyes, and he smiled as she did.

"Whatever should we do today?" he asked quietly.

"Well," she answered, running her hand softly over his manhood and smiling. Christian raised an eyebrow in surprise. "Oh yeah?" He answered. Genuinely surprised by his tone.

"Actually," she kissed him slowly before continuing. "As much as I would like to, I'm afraid of losing the ability to walk," she said playfully.

"Perhaps a rest would be in order, or a workout?" teasing. Mary looked around the room and the disarray they had caused the night before.

"Of course, but first we should clean up, I think."

They lingered in bed a bit longer before Mary got up. "I have to pee anyway," she said.

"Well, thank you for getting up first." Christian is never lacking in wit. He got up and dressed in a pair of shorts while she walked to the bathroom. He stared at her until she reached the doorway. Mary turned back, as if to make sure he was watching her.

"I'll be right back," she smiled, and closed the door behind her.

Christian had difficulty containing himself. He had never been in love, but he felt as though his heart would burst from his chest. He couldn't stop smiling. He put the blankets into the laundry equipment for cleaning, then walked to the fridge to grab a bottle of water. He guzzled half its content before Mary emerged from the bathroom. She had donned a sports bra and panties and walked to Christian, took the bottle from his hand, and finished the water.

"I had to pinch myself; I thought I had dreamt the whole night," she said, after swallowing the water.

"I know how you feel," Christian answered, and leaned in to kiss her again. She grabbed the back of his head, then pulled away after a couple of seconds.

"That's gonna put us right back where we came from, young man," she warned, stepping back from Christian. "And I believe we have a workout to finish first," she explained.

"Aaaaahhhh!" Christian whined and stomped his feet like a small child, pouting. "You're right," he said, and led her towards the door.

"Charlie – thanks for the mood lighting, but can you?" Before he could finish, the house lights returned to their normal settings.

"Thanks."

"Indeed," Charlie answered.

They paused to put their jumpsuits on for training, and Christian grabbed his pistol and nodded for Mary to do the same.

"We spar for thirty minutes, then it's target practice. Winner gets to be on top," he said playfully.

"You are so on," Mary replied, following Christian outside.

***   ***   ***

"I thought I was the only thing you stared at like that," Mary said sardonically. They had made it to the sparring area, and though she had only known him for a few months, had already noticed Christian tended to stare across the water into the city any time they had come out from the outpost.

"What do you see?" she asked, as he hadn't responded yet.

"A cute little red-head," Christian answered, just to be a smart ass. Mary slapped him on the butt in response.

"Sorry," Christian answered. "My curiosity gets the best of me." He spun to face her. "But you are the only girl I'll ever stare at again; I promise you that."

"Or I'll kick your ass," Mary answered and dropped into a crouched stance.

They sparred for over an hour; Mary would manage a victory, her style was rawer and more brutal, having been developed on the road, dealing with the Savages. Christian was talented and capable, but when fighting, even practicing, Mary had a survival instinct that would carry the day.

"Why don't we go and check it out?" Mary asked as she blocked a high kick from Christian. "It'll give us something to do."

"I can think of plenty of things to do," Christian

grunted, answering. He made a quick hop and struck again with a high roundhouse kick that Mary ducked. She leapt from the ground, sweeping his leg, and throwing him to the ground.

"Well, yes, but we need to do something other than that," she answered with a smile. "Besides, I can see how curious you are." Christian had no comeback; she was right.

"My last outing didn't go so well," Christian thought back to his burp heard around the world.

"Yeah, but now you'll have me to protect you," Mary said, punching him in the shoulder. She landed the punch as Christian was distracted by the thought of going to the city.

"Ow!" he said, rubbing the area she had punched. Indeed, he would have someone with him who had proven herself capable. They would watch out for each other.

"Okay, okay; you don't need to beat me to get your way," he pleaded, raising his hand in a motion for her to stop.

"Maybe I like it rough," she winked, then turned to walk away, knowing full well Christian would be focused on her round rear curves, and he was.

"We'll need to shower before we go, though," she said, then turned to confirm that he was staring. She lingered long enough for Christian to raise his gaze to her face. Mary raised her eyebrows several times, He knew full well what was meant by that, and seconds later, Christian broke into a sprint, chasing her back into the outpost.

Chapter XVI

After another rather pleasant shower, Christian and Mary busied themselves preparing for an outing into the city. They performed system checks on the Augmented Reality, the portable computer interface, and weapon systems. Each carried a rifle and sidearm. Having had time to familiarize herself with both weapons, Mary proved capable of using them over the past few months.

They climbed the ladder to the roof hatch and proceeded into the early afternoon light of a beautiful sunny summer day. Christian uncovered the scout vehicle, instructing Mary, who was eager to help. They both agreed that access to a quick escape vehicle was desirable for the outing.

"Is this thing fast?" Mary asked while helping secure the tarp cover into a storage bin. "I like fast, at least I think I do," she smiled. "I remember being in a transport drone as a kid. It was exciting."

"Yeah...it does okay, I guess," Christian answered, knowing very well he was understating the situation. Christian seated himself behind the controls after stowing his rifle in the weapons rack. Mary climbed on behind him and wrapped her arms around his waist.

"So – So-AAAAHHHHG!" she screamed, as Christian hammered the accelerator. The scout bike leaped from the roof and blasted across the island and out over the water.

"Holy Shit!" She yelled. Christian answered with a devilish laugh.

They slowed to a more manageable rate, closer to fifty miles per hour, as the scout ship turned back to the city, gaining altitude to clear the buildings, or what was left of them, close to the shore. They weren't looking for anything in particular, maybe supplies or curios, and dare they imagine, survivors. They cruised around the once-flourishing city in silence as they looked around.

They left the outskirts of town, heading towards an area cluttered with much taller buildings, some reaching several hundred feet into the air. They looked like bizarre hanging gardens, stretching into the sky. Wildlife, mostly birds, wildcats, and even reptiles, were visible on all the different levels of the skeletal remains of the buildings.

"How 'bout there?" Mary said, pointing to the rooftop of a building, a two-story flat top still void of vegetation somehow. The idea was that the structure would support their weight and the weight of the scout bike. It also had a fire escape ladder on the side of the building that appeared intact.

"Yeah," Christian answered, and lowered the craft slowly to come to rest in the middle of the roof. Both dismounted, each taking the time to examine the cloudless sky.

"Mic check Charlie. You got us?" Christian spoke into the comms, receiving a nod of confirmation from Mary.

"Check two," Mary spoke, receiving an affirmation from Christian in the form of a thumbs up.

"Both signals strong, loud, and clear," Charlie answered.

Christian pulled his rifle from the weapons rack, checked it one more time, slung it over his shoulder, and let it hang from the tactical sling while he powered his sidearm up and re-holstered it. He pulled out a very large and menacing-looking knife from a sheath built into his vest, ran his thumb across the blade to make sure it was razor sharp, then put the blade back and took up his rifle again. Mary left her rifle over her shoulder, preferring her pistol at the ready.

They made their way from the rooftop and to street level without incident.

"Mark the building, Charlie," Christian instructed, and the building took on a yellow glow through his heads-up display in the glasses. "Thanks. I would hate to lose the bike," he said, throwing Mary a grin.

At street level, it was silent. The calm summer breeze was barely enough to move the grass, which, for some reason, was not as long here as they had seen in other sections of the city. The composite road material was still visible in large sections in some places.

The buildings, with all things considered, that lined the street were in decent shape. Most of the windows remained intact. Doors still hung and, in many cases, closed. Signs from storefronts had faded or broken free from the buildings. They walked along in silent awe of where they were and what they were seeing.

They reached a roadway intersection; the building on the northwest corner was fronted all in glass. They approached to peek inside; they each had to wipe a section clean of years of dirt to get a look inside. They found multiple tables and chairs inside. Simultaneously, they looked at each other.

"A restaurant," Christian explained, seeing the confused look in Mary's eyes.

"I've been studying historical documents and news video clips that Charlie has on file. Been going over them as much as I can, as often as I can over the past year." Christian looked back through the glass, as did Mary. Charlie superimposed an image of what the restaurant would have looked like a hundred years ago, displaying people sitting at the tables, or wait-staff taking people's orders.

"They would come here and pay money to have the people who worked here cook them a meal," Christian continued. "They were either treating themselves or were otherwise too busy to cook for themselves. They would gather in groups to celebrate special events or take each other out as part of a courtship," he said, then motioned for Mary to follow him inside. The door to the building had fallen off.

"They didn't have to grow their food or hunt

it?" Mary asked, confused, compared to life within a Citadel. They had access to technology, yes, but there had been a sweeping movement to return to a simpler or meager existence. People would help in communal gardens or the raising and slaughter of livestock. Nothing was done to excess. Money no longer existed.

"Nor clean their dishes or even their clothes." Christian pulled out a seat for Mary at a table, and she sat down. Christian sat across from her, pretending they were on a date, caught up in the moment of the past.

"They had jobs or other means to make money, which could buy you anything, and for which people would kill. History records that greed for money was one of the driving forces that led to Mabus gaining power. People would lie, cheat, even kill for this,... money."

They sat for a moment in silence and looked around; the overlaid scene provided by Charlie faded away after a few moments. Mary was the first to get back to her feet; something had caught her eye behind the counter on the far side of the room.

Lights flickered dimly overhead as she approached the bar. The city's power grid was still active in places. Charlie had explained that the cold fusion reactors were still producing electricity, and areas where the cables and conduits had not rotted or been chewed through by rodents were still live.

Mary walked behind the bar and opened a small cupboard door that was a refrigerator unit. She smiled and reached in to grab two bottles of beer. She leaned the top of the bottle on the edge of the counter, allowing the bottle cap to catch on the countertop, then smacked the top of the bottle in a downward motion, prying the bottle cap from its seat with a pop. She then repeated the process for the second bottle; all the while, Christian watched in silent curiosity.

Mary crossed the room again and placed one of the open bottles on the table in front of Christian.

"If it's a date, let me buy you a drink," she said with a wink. "At least I believe that was the custom."

Christian sniffed the bottle and took a small sip. He felt the cold but bubbly liquid touch his tongue. The flavor was beyond anything he had ever experienced, but he paused and put the bottle down.

"Gotta be careful with this stuff; it'll mess with your stomach, and you'll make a noise. That'll bring the Savages down on us." He recalled the Coke 3000 incident as he squinted his eyes at the beer, as if giving it a warning look. Before his words had fallen silent, Mary lowered the bottle from her lips and let rip with a loud, low rumbling belch.

They both went silent and looked around, waiting for a response. After several seconds and nothing had come of it, they both giggled happily, and Christian guzzled back a healthy gulp or two from his bottle. Within a few seconds, he opened his mouth and released a loud burp.

They sat and drank for several minutes, and giggled at the noises they would make, almost forgetting where they were momentarily. They both finished their drinks, then sat and enjoyed the warm glow from the alcohol; not enough to be inebriated, but enough to take the edge off.

"People would kill so they didn't have to cook for themselves?" Mary said in disbelief and fidgeted in her seat. Christian shrugged and nodded a disapproving nod.

"How did the world get so broken?" she asked as she stood and walked towards the door, Christian following close behind. The moment they had allowed themselves had passed; Mary's question had brought them back to reality.

They walked to the edge of the building. Mary stopped, covered her mouth as she gasped in surprise, and closed her eyes, turning away from the alley behind the restaurant.

Christian could see the bones; human bones piled in a heap. They had been there long enough to be all but cleaned of their flesh; there had been no one to carry the bodies away, or to bury them. Had they died in the struggles that had beset this town, rendering it nearly void of human life? Had survivors been trying to make it to Lima Charlie Outpost or the Citadel? They would never know.

"Broken indeed." Christian led her away from the alley, further down the street. They wandered into a building, a residence at one point, and looked around.

"Cursed Mabus," Mary spat, still trying to get the image of the dead bodies from her mind. Christian put down an object he had been studying, not knowing what it was. He had left his rifle to hang from the sling at his chest. Both of them were more comfortable being away from the outpost, now. "Constantine is as much to blame," he said plainly, looking at her across the room. Mary cocked her head to the side and turned to face Christian.

"How do you figure that?" she demanded.

"Think about it." Christian shrugged. "If the Savages are the way, they are because of their 'faith...' he said, making air quotation marks as he said "Faith."

"Then it stands to reason that people are the way they are because of their faith."

"And how are they?" Mary asked.

"Helpless," he answered, shaking his rifle for effect. "Think about it. If any of them were to take up arms, they would have been stricken with incapacitation. They cannot even defend themselves from those who would hunt them down. Making us something, something else." He let those words fall silent before carrying on.

It had occurred to him that Mary had never actually answered his question. How was she able to fight? Was she like him? Or was she something else?

"The Citadel," he said, pointing in the direction he thought it was. "The Citadel is as much a prison for those who live there as it is a deterrent for those who seek to end them."

Mary had to think about that, her emotions flaring as she did.

"It may be fancy, and very big, but it is a prison

nonetheless," he said.

Christian then spotted something on the counter on the other side of the room. He crossed the floor and picked it up. He knew what it was. He flipped the lid open, hearing a satisfying "Clink" as he did, and turned the wheel quickly with his thumb. Sparks flew from the wheel, and flame slowly grew from the nozzle underneath the wheel.

"Cool lighter," he said, then closed it and put it in his pocket, taking any opportunity given to him to change the subject. Without another word, they turned towards the door and walked back to the street. The fact that the sky was now starting to cloud over was not wasted on either of them.

Christian looked down the street, noting the highlighted building Charlie had marked, indicating where the scout ship was.

"Maybe we should head back," Mary suggested. Before Christian could answer, Charlie's voice rang over the comms.

"Danger close," Charlie cautioned, but not before Christian was sent tumbling to the ground, struck from behind, the Savage having jumped from the building above them. He could see Mary turn to face her attacker before it had struck. She pulled her rifle off her shoulder, striking her Savage with the butt of the rifle just before having it knocked from her hands.

Christian made it to his feet on time to block a feral strike from his attacker. "Thanks for the heads up!" he yelled at Charlie while countering two more wild attacks from his enemy. From the corner of his eye, he watched Mary draw her sidearm and finish the other Savage definitively. She then turned towards Christian. The remaining Savage paused, unsure which target to address first now that he was alone. Mary aimed but was stopped by Christian.

"Wait!" Christian shouted. "Let's finish this," he yelled at the Savage, beckoning it.. Christian realized that all his training had paid off; the Savages may be strong and vicious, but they lacked training.

The creature lunged toward him, and Christian countered, redirecting the Savage past him, striking the creature in the neck with his other hand in a clothesline-like move, sending the creature to the ground. Mary still had her weapon trained on the Savage.

"Keep an eye out, in case there are others," Christian said as he unclipped his rifle from the sling and dropped it lightly to the ground, his voice calm given the circumstance. He was learning, using this as a training exercise. He figured that, should he fall into trouble, Mary would come to his aid.

He allowed the Savage to get up; the creature was furious, now. It charged at Christian, attempting several desperate haymakers as it did. Christian blocked each attack and countered, landing several skilled blows to the Savage's chest. The creature was so enraged that it barely reacted to Christian's attacks. It set upon Christian, thrashing and biting to thwart the young man. Christian was unaffected, deciding that this training session had gone on long enough. He got inside the Savage's reach, driving a stunning blow to the creature's jaw. Christian then used the time he gained from stunning his opponent to circle behind the Savage. Wrapping his arms around the creature's head, he twisted it violently, snapping the Savage's neck, killing it instantly as it dropped to the ground in a heap.

"And we won't be burying this thing, either," he said, panting slightly. He was satisfied with his performance and looked to Mary to ensure she was still okay. She smiled nervously; her confidence had grown from the exchange as well. They each stood motionless and silent, allowing their breathing and nerves to calm to normal levels. The summer breeze lapped at their skin, cooling them. The vegetation on the sides of the buildings swayed gently in the breeze as it carried the pollen and dust through the air.

Birds circled lazily overhead, possibly scavengers, landed on the rooftops around them, staring down at the two fresh kills lying on the street.

"Are you both okay? What the hell happened?" Charlie's voice interrupted the moment, causing them both to jump slightly. They each looked at each other and grinned.

"Yes, we are both fine, Charlie; thanks for asking," Mary answered eventually, moving to pick up her rifle and sling it over her shoulder again.

"The world may be broken," Christian said, retrieving his rifle and clipping it back to the sling. "But maybe that's why we're here," raising an eyebrow toward Mary.

"Let's not get ahead of ourselves, shall we?"

she said, rolling her eyes slightly. She walked over to take Christian's hand. "That was pretty hot, though," she smiled warmly at him. "But maybe we should get going?" she asked.

Christian looked around and at the sky. The clouds had begun to separate. He smiled, then smiled at Mary.

"Perhaps we should," he agreed. They started back toward the building marked on their glasses.

"I just mean, maybe, if Constantine won't defend the people, maybe we can," Christian continued his earlier thought.

"Let's just focus on keeping us alive, defending us... for now," Mary countered, then smiled before she winked at Christian. "Maybe we can save the world tomorrow."

Christian nodded, appreciating her humor, then leaned over to kiss her.

A wisp of movement caught their eyes at the same time, and both spun in unison, drawing their weapons, and finding a small girl standing frozen in the street near the door to the restaurant. She was trembling and pointing at the two of them. The girl didn't look more than twelve, maybe fourteen years old.

Mary dropped her weapon and fell to her knees, attempting to disarm the frightened child. "It's okay," She spoke softly. Mary motioned for Christian to lower his gun, keeping it in his hand.

"How?" The girl's voice trembled. "How did

you do that?" She managed to string a sentence together over her nerves and pointing at the dead Savages lying in the street. It was obvious to the couple that the young girl had watched the entire fight.

"We stopped the monsters; it's okay," Mary said again, beckoning the girl to come to her with her hands. After several seconds, the young girl walked towards them.

"I know, I saw," the girl said as she walked. "I want to know how?"

Mary looked up at Christian; he had little help for an answer. He raised his eyebrows and shrugged to show his state of mind.

"It's a long story. Where did you come from?" Mary tried to change the subject.

"We had to leave a Canadian settlement," she answered.

"Had to?" Christian asked. "Did they chase you out for being different?"

The girl stopped just short of where Mary was kneeling. "No." She wiped her nose with her tattered sleeve and sniffed. "There was a sickness that was killing everyone," she answered with a shrug.

"Charlie. Scan her vitals; is she sick?" Christian asked, not even trying to hide his question.

"No sign of pathogens or infection," Charlie answered, almost instantly.

"I'd like to get out of here," Christian warned, starting to feel exposed. Mary turned and looked up at him again, giving him an angry look before addressing the young girl again.

"My name is Mary," she said with a warm smile. "What's yours?" she asked. The girl stood quietly for a moment, then looked up at Christian.

"You're gonna protect us?" she asked, obviously having overheard their earlier conversation. Christian looked down at her for the first time since they first saw her. He tilted his head, surprised by what she had said.

"What's your name?" Mary tried again.

"What do you mean, US?" Christian asked, not giving the girl time to answer. The girl wasn't fazed, but instead wiped her nose again with her sleeve and looked up at Christian.

"My name's Kelly," she said plainly. "My family and friends are trying to make it to a place called Lisa Charlie." She mispronounced the name, but they both understood and looked at each other.

"I've been broadcasting a signal to advise people to come to the outpost," Charlie explained.

"Thanks for that," Christian answered, his voice not hiding the fact that he wasn't happy about the signal, turned back to Kelly.

"You better take us to them, Kelly; it's gonna be dark soon, and I don't wanna be out here in the dark if I don't have to," Christian explained and reached out towards Kelly. The young girl took his hand and led them towards another alley. Toward where she had come from.

***   ***   ***

"How is it that you can defy me?" Constantine's voice boomed through the church. Rafeo paused only for a moment; he wanted to put the would-be god on notice.

"Because the authority that binds me is more powerful than you," Rafeo warned. He resumed his march towards Christian. He held his walking stick out in front of him like a shield. Constantine grew concerned as he wanted to finish his task uninterrupted.

"I meant what I said, I mean them no harm, nor you, but I will stop you if I need to," Constantine warned, causing Rafeo to stop again and look up. He offered only a smug grin in response.

Constantine shook his head, his eyes growing large, showing his disappointment and frustration.

"Remember your place, mortal," Constantine warned, then raised one of his hands. Rafeo's grin quickly melted away as if he knew what would follow.

An energy bolt burst from Constantine's hand, catching Rafeo in the chest and launching him through the air, back through the doors of the church.

Not a soul, not even Constantine, noticed Christian's eyes move, following Rafeo as he flew through the air. The memories that he was reliving paused and scattered throughout his mind. While in the moment, Christian was confused as to why Constantine would be so interested in returning his lost memories, but figured there must be something trapped in his mind that Constantine wanted.

Christian wasn't sure if he was in any danger, but as he wanted his memories back, allowing Constantine to continue, and hoped that Rafeo would be ok and wouldn't interrupt.

Rafeo landed with a thud and slid to a stop against a tree in the front yard of the church, his body crumpled and broken. Rafeo was not convinced one way or the other of Constantine's intentions. Rafeo didn't know if Constantine knew who the boy truly was; he didn't care either. Rafeo's only concern was the mission; he couldn't risk losing Christian again.

Satisfied, Constantine refocused his energy back upon Christian and Mary, not noticing Rafeo slowly start to move. His injuries healed almost instantly. In just a few minutes, Rafeo was back on his feet. Beginning his trek back towards the church and his friend.

Chapter XVII

Christian saw his memories flash from summer, where he had been interrupted by whatever was going on between Rafeo and Constantine, to the next winter. The settlement they had built around Lima Charlie Outpost had grown. 11 other survivors with Kelly were found that summer and were offered food and shelter. Two of the members of their party were like Mary and Christian; Magi is what Christian figured.

He remembered a ship appearing in the harbor later that spring, and their colony grew again by another eight. They grew and tended crops. One of the new arrivals was a doctor and a Magi, along with the two other Magi.

Christian would help train those who could fight. He watched as his memories unfolded in his mind's eye. They grew together, all of them in friendship with Christian and the Magi going on more and more scavenging missions, searching for survivors and hunting Savages. The more Savages they killed, the more that would come. Christian often preferred to use swords that he had found when engaging the enemy over firearms, and leaving the rifles for the others.

Mary and Christian had to sneak away to a small building on the island if they wanted alone time, which they did regularly. The days blurred together, from hunting, to chores, to the hours and hours of love making. He watched his memories like a movie kept in the archives of Charlie's memory banks, but this movie was about him.

The flashback slowed as Constantine had vanquished Rafeo. at least for the time being. Christian allowed his current reality to slip away and lost himself in his past. It was November, and the start of a very cold winter. Their food stores were full and seemed sufficient to see everyone through the winter. It was becoming cramped in the outpost, as most days, no one chose to venture out of doors and into the cold.

Christian and Mary followed their routine, running a few morning laps and more often than not sneaking into their love shack for some additional physical activities. That morning, they finished up and got ready to leave for the outpost. Christian noticed a fox standing in the middle of the Channel to the east of the island. The water had nearly frozen between the island and the mainland, which meant the Savages would soon be able to reach their Island.

"Well, that's a problem," Christian said, staring out the window at the fox.

"I don't think the fox is gonna hurt anyone," Mary answered, as she nuzzled next to Christian and rubbed her hand across his chest. He turned, looked down at her, and gave her a twisted grin.

"Not what I meant," he said with a wry tone.

The fox scampered across the rest of the ice and up the bank on the far side. Christian and Mary followed the red-haired canine with their eyes until it darted behind a building and out of sight. Their gaze continued to the horizon, and some very black clouds to the east.

"Shit," Mary said, now understanding Christian's concern for the ice. They both threw their clothes on and bounded out the door back towards the outpost.

"Did you see that cute little fox?" It was Kelly's voice on the comms. Christian looked up to see her atop the outpost with Jack, one of the other Magi, who was taking a turn in the lookout. Charlie's sensors could warn them of approaching problems, it gave people structure to have tasks and duties, and they would each take shifts in the lookout.

Christian completely ignored the girl and spoke to Charlie instead. "How thick is that ice, Charlie?" Christian barked.

There was a brief silence before Charlie answered. "At the thinnest point near the middle of the Channel, it is still several inches thick. The ice could support the weight of multiple creatures should they wish to cross, even hundreds." Charlie again grew silent. "I'm also picking up hundreds of Savages to the east, heading this way."

Christian and Mary had made it back to the outpost. They rushed into the building through the main door.

"That was quicker than usual. Everything

okay?" Linda, one of the women who had been on the boat, said. She had figured out, right away, what Christian and Mary were up to after their morning run. She usually had a comment for them when they got back, which would lead to a whimsical conversation about carnal knowledge and innuendo, but today Christian ignored her and ran straight to his gear.

"Charlie – what kind of explosives do I have access to?" Christian demanded. Many others now perked up and started paying attention to what was going on. They all gathered around the table that Christian was using to lay out his equipment.

"I have an idea, but you're not gonna like it." Christian winked at Mary while he loaded a rifle and handed it off to Jack, who had come in from his perch on the roof.

"I need everyone out on the Ark." Christian didn't give time for Mary to comment. The Ark was the ship on which the second group of refugees had arrived. It had been moored at the edge of an old dock that was still intact, on the north end of the island. The main harbor had been kept clear of ice from the current that flowed through.

The ship had a functional nuclear power plant, but it had been underutilized as the crew had never had a destination.

"You should be able to make the open water."

"Why? We like it here, I thought you said we could stay." A voice from the back of the small crowd brought everything to a halt. Christian looked up from the weapon he was fiddling with and took a deep breath.

"This place is about to be overrun," he said plainly. "Unless my plan works," he added, letting out his breath.

"Magi – take every weapon you can carry and get everyone safely on board," Christian ordered.

"It'll take twenty minutes to fire the drive unit up." This is from Gabriel, the doctor who had come in with the ship.

"Then let's not waste time talking to me," Christian grunted, brushing past the man and making for a weapons locker on the other side of the room. He paused and turned back to the others who stood dumbfounded around the table.

"Move, now!" Christian yelled. The group dispersed and grabbed their personal belongings, then rushed towards the Ark, led by the other Magi.

"Let me help!" Mary pleaded amongst the fray. Christian paused and kissed her.

"No," he smiled, as warmly as he could. "I need to know you are safe. And..." He raised his hand over Mary's mouth as she formed an objection. "...and you can cover me from the deck, I hope."

He kissed her again, patted her on the bum as he ran back to collect several plasma rifles and power packs, and stuffed them into a satchel he had slung over his shoulder.

"I love you," Mary shouted from across the room. She snatched up a rifle and headed for the door.

"I love you, too," Christian answered. He continued through the door, out of the outpost, and the others followed right behind him. Christian watched as the group ran as fast as they could down the island and to the Ark. Gabriel had run out ahead, and he could already see that lights were coming on around the bridge as the doctor worked at getting the ship powered up.

Christian ran out onto the ice, tossing items from his satchel as he moved towards the far shore. He crossed to the other side and sprinted up the bank, then launched himself up the fire escape of an old building, darted across the roof, and leapt to the next building. Christian quickly scaled the side and came up onto the third-story roof. Making it to the east edge of the rooftop, he looked out across the city as the storm raged overhead.

The lightning strikes were the only source of light as the clouds darkened the sky. When the lightning would flash, the streets to the east seemed to move on their own. The Savages were closing in, shoulder to shoulder, as they advanced towards his position.

Another bolt of lightning lit up the sky, and the figure of a man who appeared to be floating forty feet in the air along with it. Christian was unable to stop a shiver from running down his back. He had faced the enemy many times before, one on one and in groups, but this was a little different, and he could only assume the flying figure was none other than Mabus himself.

If there was a power for good, and many knew Constantine to be that. Mabus was the polar opposite.

Constantine revealed himself to the world a year after Mabus had. He offered humans hope and guidance, but in so doing, humans had evolved to become so pious that they lost the ability to defend themselves.

Christian reached into his pack and grabbed the last power cell. With a running start, he threw it hundreds of yards to land amidst the advancing Savages. He then cranked his rifle's power output to max and fired on the power cell. The resulting explosion was powerful enough to collapse a nearby building, which added to the carnage. The kill count was over one hundred, and Christian held his breath as he watched the Savages try in vain to avoid ending up under the falling building.

The street below fell silent for a moment as the dust settled. Christian was quite pleased with the results from his initial volley; knocking the building over wasn't in his original plan, but he was proud of it nonetheless. The silence, however, was short-lived. Christian saw the Savages climbing over the rubble, as though it were little more than a bump in the road.

Christian barely leapt out of the way as a lightning strike flashed from Mabus toward him. He had almost sensed the attack a moment before it came. He had seconds to make it to the edge of the building and jump back to the neighbouring structure before it collapsed. He landed, rolled, and got right back to his feet. It was definitely time to fall back. was that if he could not stop the Savages, he would at least lead them away from the Ark. He uncovered the speeder bike as a last resort; he wasn't ready to give up the new home he had built.

Christian jumped from the roof he was on, dropping to the ground. The Savages were now on the run; Christian could hear the noise from the creatures behind him. He reached the opening near the top of the bank, leading down to the frozen channel. Several plasma bolts whistled past him, catching several Savages, closer than Mary liked. She and the other Magi were now firing steadily, building the gap between Christian and the mob behind him. Had he been able to see behind him, the image would have been bleak: a single man running from a horde of hundreds.

He slid down the bank and found his feet again on the ice. The snow on top of the ice offered some traction, enabling him to make good time as he ran out on the ice. He could now hear maniacal laughing like thunder behind him. He dared not stop to look, but knew it was the laugh of Mabus; truly, he believed he was to be victorious this night.

Christian pumped his legs like never before, as a constant spray of rifle fire poured from the deck of the Ark. He was glad to see the ship had cleared its moorings and was safely out in the open water of the bay.

Now halfway across the channel heading back towards the island, he could hear the ice echo the thunderous noise of the many feet from the Savages on his heels. He noticed one of the power cells lying on the ice; he could only hope that Charlie's calculations were correct.

"Do it now!" Christian yelled into his mic.

"You're still on the ice," Charlie warned. "I fear you may not be clear of the blast."

"Just fucking do it," Christian yelled. "I can swim – they can't, remember?"

"But the temperature of the water."

"Charlie!" Christian demanded.

There was a high-pitched tone that Christian heard for about three seconds, then the surface of the ice erupted in fire as eight plasma rifle power cells overloaded all at once. The slippery snow and ice prevented any of the Savages from changing their direction of travel in time. Those who weren't on the ice at the time of the blast slid down the bank and into the chaos in the channel.

The ice surface fractured from the blast, and now, under strain from the weight of hundreds of bodies, it began to heave and shift. As the one end of the ice sheet sank under the weight of the Savages, the other end slowly rose into the air. Christian could see the edge of the ice and could only pray he would make it before sliding backwards into the fury of bodies now slipping below the water's surface.

Mary and Kelly watched from their separate positions on the ship's deck as Christian struggled against the gravity of his situation. In desperation, they both closed their eyes.

"You can make it!" Kelly said aloud while

forming fists with her hands. She knew she believed, as Mary did, that Christian would make the jump to safety.

Mary, in turn, did not take her eyes from the scene; she drew a deep breath and let it out slowly, while whispering, "Go... go... go... I believe in you; you will make it."

Two more massive strides. Christian suddenly felt a strength he had never known, and leapt from the ice. His momentum was just enough for him to reach the edge of the island and solid ground. He slid to a stop, having landed on his back, and turned to watch his plan come to fruition. The channel swallowed hundreds of creatures and gave not a single one back.

Christian lay on his back where he had landed; he pulled his pistol from the holster and looked to Mabus now. The hooded figure let out a howl. He seemed weakened by the event. He appeared to lose the ability to defy gravity as the loss of his forces seemed to force him to the ground; he also seemed smaller in size and stature. There was a definite, indefinable connection between Mabus' power and the lives of his followers.

The rifle fire from the Ark turned to rain down on Mabus. The strain seemed more than he could handle, and the dark figure vanished from sight. As he did, the storm dissipated before Christian's eyes. They had done it; somehow, they had stood against a god and carried the day.

"I can't believe that worked," Christian sighed. He was happy to be alive, still lying on his back, panting from exertion.

"What?" Mary screamed over the comms.

"Oh, I mean, I knew that was gonna work," Christian corrected himself, and grimaced slightly, forgetting she could hear him. Christian didn't want her to know that his whole plan had been based on a hunch. "But all things equal, I think I'd rather sleep on the Ark tonight," he said, as he got to his feet.

"Uh-huh," Mary replied. He could tell she was upset with the risk he had taken.

"Christian. It's Gabriel. Come and see me when you have a minute; there's something I'd like to show you."

"Sure thing, doc." Christian welcomed the change of subject from Mary's anger. He hopped into a small launch at a pier, having made it to the North end of the island, and set out for the Ark. Everyone, as it seemed, liked his idea of staying on the ship for the night.

Christian rowed his way out to the Ark, lashed his small boat to the base of the ladder, then climbed aboard. He was met by Mary, waiting right at the top, her arms crossed and wearing a scowl. The look on her face was hard to read; Christian could tell she was happy and relieved, but also unhappy at the risk he had taken. She grabbed him by the cheeks and held his face to hers.

"Don't you ever dare be that reckless again," she growled, her expression quickly turned to a smile, and she kissed him deeply.

"I'll try," Christian answered, through their kiss. They both stopped and looked up as Gabriel ran onto the deck.

"Yeah, doc, coming." Christian kissed Mary again and put his arm around her; they both walked towards Gabriel. He motioned for them to follow him, and he bounded back into the room from whence he had come. The room looked like a lab of sorts, with various workstations set up and a myriad of equipment spread throughout the room.

"Have you ever wondered why it rains whenever they are around?" Gabriel asked, barely hiding his giddiness. Christian and Mary looked at each other with a puzzled look.

"Well, no, actually," Christian spoke with a shrug. "But now that you mentioned it, I can't stop wondering." He and Mary nodded together and walked a little closer to Gabriel.

"I've never had to, nor had the opportunity to safely collect samples until this evening. That's the closest I've ever been to a Savage, ever. I've never been so terrified." He trailed off and was caught up in the memory. His eyes began to dart around the room nervously.

"But, it's safe now," Christian spoke slowly, attempting to bring Gabriel back to the topic. "And you were able to find?" Christian wanted to know what was going on.

"Ah. Yes," Gabriel said, shaking off the memory. Charlie was able to confirm my suspicions within a few seconds." Gabriel paused and picked up a mason jar full of a clear liquid.

"Looks like water, doesn't it?" he asked. Mary and Christian nodded in agreement.

"That's cause it is, basically," Gabriel's answer annoyed the other two, and they didn't try to hide their expressions. "With one major difference. This water contains a highly addictive and frankly dangerous hallucinogen." Gabriel explained. The other two let the information sink in and processed it.

"So, the Savages are?"

"Drugged," Mary answered Christian's unfinished question. Again, the room fell silent.

"Slaves, in fact," Gabriel spoke, after what felt like an awkward moment.

"But what about us? We've been in the rain several times – it hasn't affected us. Right?" Christian looked at his hands for lack of a better idea.

"No, you're right," Gabriel continued, "I had tested the rainwater with my blood samples. I have them here; anyone who is Magi seems to have a natural immunity to the drug?" He pointed at Christian, his clothes still wet, then he looked at Mary. "You and the others who were on the deck of the ship don't seem to be affected. Not to mention your abilities to use weapons."

"Holy shit!" Mary whispered in disbelief.

"And swear," Gabriel continued with a raised eyebrow, "As Magi, we are different from humans, I believe on a genetic level, though I lack the equipment to prove that here."

"So, the mystical Magi are people who have developed an immunity to a drug." Christian spat the words, as though he didn't like the taste of them in his mouth.

"And Mabus, for all his parlor tricks, is little more than a drug dealer," he scoffed at the idea.

The room fell silent for a while. Christian finally nodded, looked up at Gabriel, and thanked him. Without another word, Christian walked back onto the deck and stood looking at the moon rising into the cold winter's night sky. He could feel the anger grow within him. All this time, he had lived with killing the Savages as he believed them to be little more than animals, unholy beasts. But now there's a possibility they are victims in all of this, as well. He placed his hands on his hips and arched his back to stare into the night sky.

A moment later, Mary ran out of the room after Christian. She found him on deck, staring into the sky. She slowly approached him, wrapped her arms around his waist, and pulled him in. She could feel his tension.

"What have I done?" he asked, with a tear slowly sliding down his cheek. "Am I a monster?"

Mary smiled, her eyes welling with tears, as well. "Only a good man would question what he has been forced to do. Regardless of the circumstances of how they got to be the way they are, there isn't one of those Savages that you have killed that would not have taken your life in an instant," she reassured her lover.

"And if any of the others had been on deck tonight, we would have had to kill them, too." Christian was so upset that he hadn't noticed Kelly; she was standing on the stairs, five feet away.

"But you didn't," Kelly said, in her matter-of-fact way.

Christian and Mary both looked up to see her and tried to smile. Without another word, Kelly walked to them and gave a three-way hug.

"But it's cold out here," Kelly said after several moments had passed. "Do you suppose we can go inside and warm up?"

Chapter XVIII

The next morning, Christian lay in bed, or was he in a church with Mary and Constantine? Was it a dream, or a memory? Was it real? Seeing Mary's face before him, staring at her as if it were the first time he had seen her. Taking in her beauty, memorizing every minute detail of her face, down to the last freckle. He felt happy in this moment, wanting desperately to kiss her, holding her for all eternity.

He reached out for her, but as he did, Mary drew away; the distance opened between them. Christian was now running, trying to catch up with Mary. Her face had turned from smiling and playing to a look of sheer terror. Mary's screams faded as her face disappeared, engulfed by darkness from all around her.

Christian bolted straight out of bed, jolted awake by a haunting dream. Finding solace in the fact that Mary was lying next to him. Kelly had fallen asleep with them as well. Both women stirred slightly from the commotion he had caused, but failed to wake from their sleep. Relieved to still be alone as the others slept, giving him time to process what he had just seen in his dream.

Crossed the room, found his sweater, and put

it on in the dim morning light coming through the windows. He stared out through the porthole and watched the winter sunrise. He did not want to go out in the cold anytime soon and was happy to feel the boat move in the current of the bay. The movement assured him that they were still in open water, and therefore fairly safe, at least for the moment.

But what was the next move? Their activities caught the attention of Mabus. Regardless of how Christian felt about him, he was very dangerous. He did not want to stay if it meant being responsible for twenty other people, most of whom could not lift a finger to help defend themselves. But he could not return to the Citadel, he could not give up his freedom.

Mary awoke to find Kelly still snoring and Christian staring at her from across the room, smiling. She got out of bed, wrapped a robe around her, and motioned for Christian to follow her quietly, not to wake Kelly.

They went down the hall to the next room and went in quietly. The room was empty. Mary grabbed Christian and ripped his sweater off while dropping her robe. They kissed like two people possessed; hands rubbing and touching each other's forms as if they were touching for the first time. Mary pulled him onto the bed and on top of him; Her desire and intentions were clear. For the moment, Christian forgot that he wanted to talk to her about leaving, or anything else for that matter; surely it could wait.

"Sorry, I couldn't help myself. I know you wanted to talk, but I figured," Mary quietly whispered, still out of breath from the preceding. She paused playfully, knowing full well that the apology was not necessary. The love-making had perhaps been brief but had certainly satisfied both. Mary lay down and cuddled up close to Christian, rubbing his chest gently.

"It's okay – believe me, feel free, anytime. Feel encouraged." Christian said in jest, eliciting giggles and a playful slap from Mary. "But you're right. We should talk." Christian cleared his throat before proceeding. His face turned from elation to something far darker in a second. "Last night was a game changer," he said, then flipped the covers to expose Mary's naked backside. He grabbed it and giggled. "But I'm having a hard time concentrating."

Mary flipped the covers back over herself and kissed Christian on the cheek. "Game changer," she repeated, trying to get Christian back on track.

"I've only heard stories about Mabus; it's quite another thing to see him in person," Christian began. He exhaled, trying to gather his thoughts. "He lost last night, and I imagine Mabus won't take long planning his revenge. He'll bring more foot soldiers next time." Christian fidgeted slightly as he imagined the scene in his head. "He can drown hundreds of thousands of Savages in the waters around the island, then the rest can walk across the corpses to the outpost." They didn't know how many Savages there were, but stories from their childhoods would have them believe that their numbers were in the tens of millions.

"We could take the Ark south and get them to

the Citadel," Mary offered. Christian thought about it and nodded; he had considered the same idea.

"But I can't go back there," he exclaimed. Mary didn't say anything for a moment; she had enjoyed the life they had made on their little island. The outpost had become home to her and Christian. Compared to the regimented life within a Citadel, she felt truly free, and it was exciting, with a little element of danger; at least that's how it started. Now the risk was too high.

"So, what of us?" Mary asked; she didn't want to join the ranks in the Citadel either.

They stayed quiet for several moments, both fidgeting slightly, uncomfortable with the obvious thought that they didn't want to speak aloud.

"If we stay here, he'll have us," Christian answered, finally saying out loud what they were both thinking. Christian slowly ran his hand along her naked back, sending a shiver running through Mary. She looked up at him and smiled, but the smile faded quickly.

"We should tell the others and then prepare for the journey." She was concerned but tried hard to put on a brave face and smiled again. "Besides, we can't just lie around naked all day," she said playfully and got up to get dressed.

"Those were the good old days," Christian said sarcastically.

"What were?" Mary paused and turned to look at Christian.

He eyed her carefully; she was still mostly naked, having only managed to put her pants on before pausing. He drank in her beauty like manna from heaven.

"When we could lie around naked all day." The sincerity in his face was unmistakable. Mary tried again to smile. They had many fond memories of the outpost. Mary was not eager to leave either, but understood the need to.

***   ***   ***

Mary and Christian joined the rest of the others in the galley once they had dressed. The conversations in the room fell silent as they walked in. Christian tried to make a point to try and smile at each face that greeted him, and was relieved to receive a smile back.

For a moment before entering the room, Christian feared he would find the same looks of hatred he had seen the day he was cast out from the Citadel. relieved to be wrong was evident with each smile and nod he received from the people awaiting him in the galley.

"Good morning," Christian said quietly to the crowd around him, as he poured a coffee and sipped from his mug. All at once, the crowd began to speak. Some questioned what was going to happen; some asked if Mabus would be back; still, some questioned if they were leaving the island. But over it all, Christian could hear Gabriel.

"How did you make that jump to shore?"

Christian turned and stared at Gabriel. He had

262

felt the same at the time of leaping from the ice the night before, but dismissed it. He had assumed that his perception of the distance he had jumped had been skewed by adrenaline or his eyes playing tricks on him.

"What?" Christian questioned, causing everyone to repeat themselves. He held his hand up to gesture for them all to be quiet, while keeping eye contact with Gabriel.

"No, no, sorry," Christian said, shaking his head. "Gabriel – what was that?"

The room fell silent, and everyone turned to look at Gabriel. He swallowed and looked around at everyone in the room. He wasn't one to enjoy being centered out, but his curiosity overpowered any feelings of shyness.

"It had to have been over thirty feet if it was an inch, from the top of that ice shard to the shore," He said nervously, licking his dry lips as he looked around the room again, before his eyes came to rest on Christian.

"I thought I had imagined that," Christian said quietly, shaking his head.

"It was very far," Kelly confirmed. The room fell silent. Christian looked around at the faces again, fearing a change in their hearts, friendship for fear, but it didn't come. He looked at Kelly before he spoke again.

"Just luck, I guess," he said with a shrug.

"We have to leave this place," Mary said to

break the awkward silence, and to direct the conversation back to a matter at hand. The group anticipated the news, no one appeared to be surprised.

"We'll have to collect what supplies we can," she continued. "We'll head out of the bay here and make for the Citadel." As she spoke, a map appeared on the wall display behind her. Charlie had already linked with the ship's systems and plotted a course south, down the coast, highlighting the route on the map.

"If the seas cooperate, the trip should take less than two days," Charlie explained, his voice playing on the ship's speakers. Until that point, Christian hadn't thought about Charlie. He would be alone again.

"We will take the speeder but leave the hoverboard. We will leave some rations and weapons for anyone else who might make it here."

Christian nodded. "Charlie," Christian called out and paused, though logically he knew the emotional attachment was ill-founded, but like it or not, he actually felt a friendship between himself and the A.I.

"I will simply go dormant again, no need to worry about that."

Christian wished he could take Charlie with him; he had been the only other voice around for over a year before Mary came to the outpost.

"Sorry, Charlie," Christian said quietly.

"Appreciated but not necessary, Quick; I am, after all, only a computer simulation," Charlie said.

"Not to me," Christian answered.

"Many hands make light work," Mary instructed and clapped her hands as a way to try and break up the meeting and get everyone moving to the task at hand.

Gabriel turned on his heel and headed for the bridge of the ship. He took to the controls and sank into the seat behind the helm. He maneuvered the ship with great skill along the dock and slipped it into a berth. Others on deck tossed mooring lines to shore, then jumped to the dock and tied off the ship. They lowered a plank into position to act as a gangway.

"We want to be out of here in two hours." Mary stood at the edge of the plank, stopping the group from disembarking. "We need food and weapons. You two!" She pointed to the other Magi. "You come with me for weapons detail. The rest of you gather whatever food and other supplies you can," she said, and turned to Christian.

"I'll get the scout," he said, then bounded down the plank to shore and jogged towards the outpost.

***   ***   ***

Christian lingered in the outpost. He had parked the scout on the deck of the ark and had gone back in to make one last check for things he may want to bring from the outpost. Mary joined him and wrapped her arms around him from behind.

"We've got everything on board. We can leave any time," she told him, as they swayed back and forth slightly.

"Please take one of the mobile devices and the glasses." Charlie startled them both as he activated a large wall display, bringing up a map of the West Coast. "That way, I can still help." Charlie highlighted a route south again. "I'm transferring the coordinates to the bridge of the Ark. You should make for Eureka," he explained, highlighting a dot on the map. Then head inland to the southwest entrance of the Citadel, this will take you past the sight of at least two other Lima Charlie Outposts." The locations popped up on the map near the towns of Willow Creek and Weaverville.

"They will provide you shelter and possible re-supply points, as I have not received notifications that those sites have been compromised."

Christian slipped a mobile display into his cargo pockets and looked up at the display in front of him. He was choked up slightly as he spoke. "Thanks, Charlie, for everything."

"Do not despair, Quick. I will transfer my AI to the other locations. Between that and the mobile device, I'll still be able to offer whatever assistance I can." Charlie's A.I. sounding almost emotional.

"Sure thing, Charlie," Christian said.

"Come on," Mary prompted him towards the door, but Christian hesitated; he looked almost angry.

"What is it?" Mary asked, wanting to be direct.

"I feel like we are running away," Christian said quietly, but there was anger in his tone.

"If we just had more time, more people – we could raise a small army and go run that son of a bitch down." Christian pointed towards the city as though Mabus was still there.

Mary suddenly realized that he meant what he had said the day they met Kelly, that Christian wanted to fight back to protect the people that Constantine had forsaken.

"Well, there aren't enough people, and there isn't enough time," she sighed, sharing his frustration, but resigned to the reality of the situation.

Christian turned to look at her and nodded, then grimaced. He put his arm around Mary and led her towards the door.

"Lock it up behind us," Christian ordered, trying to shake off his feelings as they watched the light go out behind them.

They passed through the door one last time. The door slid shut and locked. They jogged out towards the ark without looking back.

***   ***   ***

The ship lumbered into motion, pulling away from the dock. Christian and Mary stood on the deck to watch and say a final farewell to their island. They headed north past the city, towards the channel that led to the Pacific Ocean. All were relieved to be sailing under clear skies. It was cold, but still, the warmth of the sun was noticeable.

Mary turned to leave the deck, though Christian lingered slightly. He waited until the island was completely out of sight before returning to the galley. He had never been on a boat before; the sensation was different. The ship was large enough, two hundred and sixty feet in length, with sleeping quarters for thirty or more passengers. It handled the slightly rough waters with little noticeable swaying, a fact which Christian was thankful for, although noticeable to him.

The ship ran itself once the course was accepted by the navigational computer. Gabriel spent most of his time on the bridge monitoring systems, just to be safe. They sailed roughly twenty miles from shore, hoping for less turbulent waters, but kept the shore in sight; something else Christian was thankful for.

Christian found himself on the bridge, though he didn't really have a clue how to control the ship or operate any of the equipment; he felt better on the bridge than sitting in the galley or in his room.

They moved along at twenty-five knots. With each passing hour, the air seemed to get warmer and warmer as they made their way south. Gabriel and Christian sat quietly on the bridge, occasionally making small talk, getting to know each other better.

Late in the afternoon, Gabriel jumped from his seat as though having remembered something. Christian tensed up, surprised by his sudden movement. Not sure if it meant trouble, not until Gabriel put his hands up to reassure him.

"Sorry! Everything's okay. I just wanna grab something." Gabriel slipped out of the room. After several minutes, he returned, carrying a bundled towel or blanket under one arm.

"When I first came across the Ark, here, it must have been over ten years ago, now," Gabriel explained. "I've lived on board all this time. I'd make landfall occasionally when I needed to collect supplies or seeds for the gardens." He pointed to the deck where Christian could see two large empty planting boxes.

"Can't live on fish alone," Christian nodded, acknowledging Gabriel.

"Anyway, one day I met an older man, a traveler. He said he had been out in the world alone for some time. He asked if he could join me on the ark for a while, and I agreed. He helped with growing and gathering food. He was a great fisherman. He said he needed a rest from the world – and who wouldn't?" Gabriel said, his eyes getting larger as he nodded.

"After about a year, though, he tells me he has to leave, cause he's looking for someone. So, he left, and I've never seen him since, but I found these in his room and thought you would like them."

Gabriel unrolled the material, revealing two swords. Christian raised his eyebrows, obviously intrigued by the weapons.

"Katanas," he said, having recognized their design. He picked one up and removed the blade from its sheath. The blade caught the sun through the windows, splashing the surrounding area with light that looked like it emanated from the blade itself. The blade was engraved with intricate and detailed scrollwork, perhaps a foreign language, and some pictograms. Christian stared, studying the blade for a long time, then put it on the table next to the scabbard, and took up the other blade and studied it.

"The old man had shown me these once before; he told me they were nearly two thousand years old. He used one to cut through a two-foot-thick concrete block without even scratching the metal of the blade."

Christian looked up from the blade in astonishment. "Say that again!"

"Two-foot concrete block," Gabriel gestured a slicing blow. "Like it was nothing."

They both stood in silence for a while, admiring the weapons like they were a form of ancient art or a mystery to be solved.

"I just figured if anyone could use them, it would be you," Gabriel said quietly, then sat back down in the captain's chair.

Christian placed the swords back in their coverings and noted that the scabbards were connected to a belt harness. He picked up the whole thing, attempting to mount it around his waist, but it felt awkward. A thought occurred to him, and he released the buckle and moved the blades to rest across his back, the handles protruding above his right shoulder. He secured the belt diagonally across his chest and around his midsection. The weapons looked as though they belonged to his body, like another appendage he had been missing.

"Definitely you," Gabriel said quietly, admiring Christian's new look.

"Thank you," Christian said with a slight bow, wanting to express his true appreciation for an amazing gift.

"Well – thanks for saving my ass. How many times, I've lost count." Gabriel gave Christian a wry smile.

Christian left the bridge and walked out into the early evening air on the open flybridge. The temperature had risen to a pleasant level. He took a deep breath and held it in, closing his eyes and enjoying his surroundings. The warm ocean breeze met his skin gently as the Ark plodded along its course. After letting out his breath slowly, he opened his eyes and reached up for the swords, pulling both from the scabbards, then slowly lowering his arms to his sides. Gabriel sat forward in his seat so he could see Christian completely.

Christian began slowly moving through forms and stances with the swords, getting faster and faster in his movements until the blades were no longer visible, only as a blur of movement. He battled an invisible enemy across the deck of the ship. It was a sight to be seen and did not go unnoticed by the others on the ship. Most of them had gathered in the wardroom on the main level so they could see Christian through the large windows. A hush fell over the group, as each of them became mesmerized by the display of Christian's sword mastery.

As abruptly as he had started, Christian ended in a killing stroke, holding his final pose for some time. In his mind, he had just ended his final enemy, perhaps Mabus. He envisioned the dark, hooded figure at the end of his blades, his body limp and lifeless, falling to the ground.

Christian finally sheathed both the blades, not bothering to wipe away the sweat pooling on his brow. He stood, staring past the imagined scene, onto the serenity of the setting sun reflecting from the calm ocean surface. He consciously tried to regain control of his breathing. After several moments, he turned back toward the superstructure, only then realizing that he had attracted a crowd. Without a word, he walked to the nearest hatch and made his way to his cabin.

Chapter XIX

It was late morning when they felt the ship change its heading east, towards shore, and the entire crew gathered on the main deck. They had arrived, coming into port at a town once known as Eureka. They slowed as they passed the breakwater and moved into the channel that led to the dock.

It was apparent that Eureka had experienced a higher level of unrest in the times leading up to its abandonment. Like many other cities, its inhabitants would have left in favor of the Citadel. The remains of many ships, partially sunken in the harbor, were easily visible; many appeared to be military. Bodies of people that had fallen in the struggle and had not been washed away by weather or the sea lay where they fell; their remains added an eerie feel. No one spoke as the ship neared its birth. The images around them were one thing, but the wall of the citadel, though partially obscured by early morning fog, loomed in the distance. The sheer mass and scope of the structure were enough to give even those who had seen it before pause to absorb the scale.

Mary nodded to Christian and moved to the scout ship. They had previously discussed that she would scout ahead and report back if there was trouble; Christian would stay with the group for obvious reasons. Christian slipped his augmented reality glasses on and had to admit he welcomed hearing Charlie's voice, even if it was only through the mobile unit. He watched as Mary took off and flew over the hill and the town.

"I see a big mess, must have been a battle at one point, but not seeing any movement down here," Mary reported.

"Ya, this was a perimeter town. It and several others were garrisoned to help protect the building of the citadel, at least until the walls were finished. The fighting was always the heaviest in these areas." Christian explained, showing how much of the history he had retained from Charlie's historic files.

"I'll circle back around, but you're safe to get off the ark and make your way inland once you dock," she finished as Christian watched her maneuver in the distance.

"Thanks, babe," he said into the comms, then turned to the group. "We're clear," he assured the others, and lowered the board to the dock, allowing them to walk off the ship. Christian made eye contact with Gabriel.

"I'm sure she'll be safe here now." He forced a smile, noticing Gabriel seemed hesitant to leave. "Who knows, maybe we'll come back someday, and go for a fishing trip." Christian placed his right hand on Gabriel's left shoulder in an attempt to cheer him up.

Gabriel smiled. "I'd really like that."

Christian nodded, and they made their way to

the dock. The group headed east, guided by Mary and Charlie, towards Willow Creek and the first of two Lima Charlie Outposts. They would cover half the distance to Willow Creek the first day, having to make camp for the night, and were happy to find an old transport truck they could use for shelter, posting a rotating guard on the roof of the trailer for the night.

The next day, the group was visibly relieved to find the outpost not only intact but still stocked with food, power, and hot water for showers. The third night was spent in a train car. The group's spirits remained high as they traveled, some emboldened enough by their escorts to sing as they walked on. The mood didn't last as the sky on the fourth day became cloudy.

"Good news. You're only about two miles from the outpost at Weaverville," Mary reported, causing Christian to smile. The smile didn't last, though.

"Bad news is there's a hunting party of about twenty-five of our friends headed in with this rain." Mary continued. "If you don't pick up the pace, they might catch up to us."

"How's the outpost?" Christian asked.

"We should be good to go," Mary answered.

"'K, folks, I don't want to worry you, but we need to do some jogging," Christian instructed. He was pleasantly surprised that not one of the others panicked; they just started running.

"Should I engage and slow them down?" Mary asked.

"Negative. I'd rather sneak past them than attract attention to us. We might handle them, but we still have to be here for two days until we reach the Citadel. The next group will be bigger." Christian answered as he ran.

"Good point," Mary agreed. "I'll land on the roof of the outpost and warm up the place."

***   ***   ***

"This is gonna be close," Mary's voice came over the comms twenty minutes later. "It just started to rain here," She explained.

"Yeah, I know. We're a block away to the south of the outpost." Christian answered and waved. She looked to her right from her perch atop the outpost and saw Christian's wave.

"Thank god," she whispered to herself, but Christian still heard it. "Door's open, let's go." Mary barked.

"Coming, dear," Christian answered and broke cover, running straight up the street to a building across from the outpost to cover the others as they ran diagonally across the street towards their destination, around the barricades, and into the front door. Christian reached his position, gun drawn and ready. He checked around the corner and down the street as the rain fell heavily. He turned back to watch Kelly, the last of the group to reach the barricades.

A Savage jumped from the rooftop across the street, landing right next to Kelly and scooped her up, throwing the girl over its shoulder. Neither Christian nor Mary could shoot without risking hitting Kelly.

The Savage stood its ground as if daring them to shoot.

Mary scampered down the ladder as Christian stepped away from the building he was up against, and slowly walked towards the Savage.

"Take the shot if you got it," Christian barked, as he squinted against the rain to keep his eyes focused sharply on the Savage, who just stood there holding the girl. He noticed the rest of the hunting party file in behind this one.

"Yes! Please take the shot, and I'll feed her to the others."

Mary and Christian were frozen in place; the fact that the Savage spoke shook them to their core. The creatures outnumbered them, but Christian and Mary always kept the advantage because the Savages were simple, unable to speak or use weapons. They were just mindless, ferocious creatures. But this one had spoken.

"I didn't think they could do that," Christian said sarcastically, moving closer to Mary; she didn't answer, not appreciating his cavalier attitude. Christian holstered his gun, figuring he wouldn't use it, anyway. He watched as the Savage slowly pulled out a long and jagged-looking sword.

"So, what shall we call you? Chatty Kathy, perhaps?" Christian needed a moment to process what was going on and to give time for the others to get into position. He figured getting him to talk might buy them the time they needed.

The other's form was large; he stood three to

four inches taller than Christian, heavier by at least forty pounds. His left arm appeared shriveled, disfigured. Over his black shirt, across his chest, there was a field dressing over a wound. The bandages were dark with blood, and the wrappings were dirty. His left eye had a scar running over and through it, seeming to render the eye useless.

"I am Balthazar!" the other said, raising his sword to a mid-guard position and staring down the blade into Christian's eyes.

Balthazar launched Kelly into the air and the awaiting arms of the other Savages and rushed with tremendous speed towards Christian and Mary. He leapt into the air and slammed a devastating overhead blow, driving his blade right to the ground, just missing Christian and Mary as they dove to avoid the attack.

Christian drew his swords and rushed to battle, attracting the enemy's attention. Mary had a chance to evade and regather herself. She focused on Kelly and freed her. Mary was surprised to see the other Savages not joining the fight; instead, they stood as though guarding their comrade and quarry.

Christian's attacks were so fast they were impossible to see with the naked eye, but his adversary blocked with even greater speed. The Savages did not notice the remaining Magi sneak from the outpost and move to a flanking position on a rooftop to the group's left. Mary had seen them, thankfully, and wanted to be ready when they were in position.

Christian's attacks became even faster as he

became angered by the fact that his opponent was defending himself. The Savage also carried a grin on his face as though it were a game to him, which angered Christian further. Their swords' clattering filled the night air and echoed through every raindrop.

Mary opened fire seconds before the others did. They killed the Savage, holding Kelly and a number of the creatures closest to her. Kelly dropped to the ground but sprang to her feet, dashing towards Mary, running past her straight to the outpost, and was blinded by a flash. Her body was thrown to the ground by the concussive force of an explosion that ripped through her allies on the rooftop. Christian's quarry was not only able to defend against his attacks but had lobbed a grenade right into the faces of the other Magi.

The blast caused Christian to stumble, and Balthazar was able to grab him by the scruff of his neck and throw him across the street and through a window that was still intact. Christian landed in a heap on the floor in the building. Seconds after landing, he heard a series of metallic clattering, and watched another grenade land on the floor next to him. He leaped behind an old stove, narrowly escaping the blast.

Another grenade followed; Christian sprinted to the other side of the building and jumped through the window, seconds before the explosion.

He landed hard on the ground. This time, he knew he would not be getting right back up again. Debris from the blast landed on top of him, covering him almost completely. Christian could still see Balthazar through all the debris and a hole blown through the building. He watched as, amidst the confusion, the lead Savage scooped Mary up over his shoulder, and he and what remained of the enemy turned and ran into the night, leaving Christian for dead.

***   ***   ***

Constantine ceased his hold on time, releasing Mary and Christian from his power. The congregation around them had noticed a little flash of light. The people barely reacted, not noticing the slowing of time nor the return to its usual passage. Rafeo burst through the doors of the church, causing nearly everyone to jump, and many gasped in surprise. As the bewildered congregation looked around, they became aware of Constantine's presence, dropping to their knees and bowing their heads.

Christian had been overwhelmed by the process. He had dropped to one knee from the strain, but slowly struggled to his feet.

"I remember," he whispered as he looked around him. In what appeared to be only a second, Constantine had allowed him to relive several lost years of his life, regaining his lost memories. He saw Rafeo charging towards him, but Christian held his hand to reassure his friend.

"I remember!" he yelled, failing to contain his excitement. His voice thundered through the church. Rafeo stopped next to him and put a hand on Christian's shoulder.

"Christian," Mary sobbed quietly, unable to keep her emotions in check. She had gone through the same memories as Christian had. She knew that he remembered her now; she knew she had him back.

Rafeo noted Christian's name. Rafeo had always known the young man by his assumed name, Quick, but he had to admit that Christian seemed to suit him better.

Christian turned to Mary. He stared into her eyes. "Mary," he whispered as a tear rolled down his cheek. He was seeing her again as though it were the first time.

"I thought I lost you." He grabbed her face in his hands, which were noticeably trembling.

"But how – how did you get away? Balthazar took you; I saw it – I remember."

"Balthazar? What?" Rafeo's inquiry went unacknowledged.

Mary smiled and pulled Christian closer. She kissed him deeply. "It's a long story, but she didn't finish her thought, as she noticed Christian's gaze move past her to the young girl behind her.

"The best part was the cool light," Charlette said, staring off into space.

"Charlette!" Christian said with hushed awe. He now realized she was his daughter, his and Mary's.

"She's my - our" Christian trailed off as Mary nodded, confirming what he already knew in his heart.

"Be at peace, my people." The words came from Constantine. Everyone turned to look at the figure at the head of the church; everyone except the family and the old man standing in the aisle.

Constantine appeared drained from the experience, though he held up his right hand and gestured, as if bestowing his blessing on the assembled crowd. Again, everyone, except Christian, Mary, and Rafeo, bowed. The three left standing watched as Constantine disappeared before their eyes.

Mary picked up Charlette and brushed her hair out of her face with her hand. "Are you okay, baby?" she asked, then kissed her on the forehead.

"No. The best part was when he disappeared," Charlette corrected herself, not answering her mother's question.

"All of that to give you your memory back?" Rafeo was puzzled. He had convinced himself that Constantine had an ulterior motive behind what had happened, but for the moment, anyway, it appeared as though he had been mistaken.

They stood and looked amongst themselves. The crowd around them dispersed without affecting Christian and the others. They stood, steadfast in the aisle, looking at each other as though the explanation they sought would appear on their faces. Despite getting his memory back, Christian had many other questions, as did they all.

"Are you alright?" Rafeo asked; they were now all but alone in the church. Christian looked around.

He smiled at Charlette and Mary, though even to him, the smile felt forced.

"I need time," Christian explained, then motioned for them to move towards the exit. They walked in silence, still processing the day's events. They made it outside; Christian took in the walls of the Citadel and how peaceful the surroundings were. A light breeze brushed through the crops in the nearby fields; the sound of it conjured more memories from his childhood.

"Let's go." Mary paused as she looked up at Christian while she leaned on his arm that she had been holding. "Home," she finished, with a look in her eyes that Christian did not recognize. He nodded and gestured for her to lead the way.

"Are we going home, Mommy?" Charlette's voice was a welcome interruption.

"That's right," Mary said.

"Good – I'm super tired," Charlette answered, as if having already forgotten everything that had happened.

Christian paused and turned back to his old friend. "There is more I will tell you, but I need," he hesitated, thinking of what to say next.

"Time," Rafeo finished Christian's thought with an old self-assured grin and a nod.

Chapter XX

Leaving the church, the entire group was under a shroud of silence. Rafeo stayed quiet to fulfill Christian's request; he did not want to pressure his friend. They made their way down the street on foot, led by Charlette, the only one who spoke. She did enough for everyone, barely letting a minute go by without saying something.

Christian focused on the young girl while he tried to get over his surprise and awe at the fact that he was a father. She was wondrous in her curiosity, and even more amazing, she spoke her mind. There was no questioning what she was thinking because she would tell you, whether you wanted to hear it or not.

She had her mother's looks, but Christian was beginning to see himself in the girl. It was a welcome surprise, but a surprise nonetheless, and he would need time to come to terms with everything. After all, he had awakened this morning not knowing who he was and would go to bed that night with his identity and memories intact, a woman he loved, and a daughter he wanted desperately to get to know.

It wasn't until Charlette stopped in front of a house at the front door that Mary realized they were home.

"Mom, you have to open the door, cause I can't open it. Maybe Dad can open the door. Is he feeling better, now, Mom?" Charlette rambled on.

Christian had heard her call him Dad, and his heart melted.

"Yeah, I'm feeling better now," Christian said. He tried awkwardly to rub Charlette's hair as a sign of affection but didn't quite pull it off. He felt bad for failing, but was happy he had tried.

Mary came out of her daze and realized she had to use her thumbprint to open the door. Afterward, she looked back at everyone and noticed Rafeo, looking out of place.

"I know this was a hell of a weird night, but Master Rafeo, please stay with us," Mary said softly.

"Mommy swore," Charlette said, before anyone could respond.

"I don't wish to impose," Rafeo answered, though focused solely on Charlette, and smiled warmly.

"No! Please." Christian started, then paused and looked back at Mary. "I guess it isn't really my place to invite people to stay," he stammered, but Mary smiled warmly.

"I hope it will be, soon enough; I hope you will see this as your home too," she answered.

Christian nodded awkwardly; he wasn't sure if the Citadel would ever be home to him, though this house, and more so the people who lived there, it was very tempting.

"Bath time." Charlette bellowed, as though wanting to break the silence, and ran into the house. Mary took Christian by the hand and followed.

Rafeo took a deep breath and entered the house. He still had his mission to keep in mind. To restore the true Guardian, to deliver the Book of Power, and complete the mission he accepted over twenty-five hundred years earlier, the mission that kept him alive for such an unnatural length of time, his only release would be by the will of the Guardian.

He set his staff down near the door, leaning it against the wall and hanging his cloak upon it. While doing so, his thoughts replayed the events of the evening.

"Christian," he said aloud to himself. The boy's name conjured his memories of his life long ago, of an old friend long gone. He wandered into the living room from the doorway, still deep in thought, to find Christian sitting alone on the couch with his head in his hands. Christian slowly looked up to see his old friend and smiled.

"There is so much I need to tell you; I just don't know where to start," Christian said slowly, then lowered his head into his hands again. Rafeo gradually crossed the floor and sat next to him.

"When you are ready." He tried to sound reassuring and placed his hand on Christian's shoulder.

"But can I suggest that you have already missed so much; your daughter is getting ready for bed, and you might want to help with that." He suggested with a warm smile.

Christian stood up quickly. "Yeah, yeah!" he stammered, unsure what that meant. "I, we'll be right back," he answered, and slowly walked down the hall towards Mary, who stood in the doorway to the bathroom, illuminated dimly in the dark hallway by light coming from the room from which he could hear Charlette splashing in the tub and talking.

"The best part is the bubbles," she said, as Christian entered the doorway, slipping his arm around Mary and watching Charlette blow bubbles from her bath into the air. He could not stop the tears streaming down his face. Mary could sense his emotions brimming and squeezed him a little tighter to reassure him.

***   ***   ***

"Do you remember the night we found that bubbly wine?"

"Oh shit. You were so funny," Mary spoke up and laughed for the first time in hours; perhaps it was the fatigue from the late hour, the events of the day, or both. They had been sitting in the living room, talking about their experiences at Lima Charlie for hours; a glow from the approaching sun was visible in the sky.

"I've never seen the like; I couldn't shut up, but you, you couldn't keep your clothes on." Mary had tried to wave Christian off, being embarrassed by talking about their sexual activity in front of Rafeo. He was more like a father to Christian, though, so he was fine with it.

"I think we both passed out in the middle of a go," Christian continued. They all laughed and slumped back in their seats a little.

Christian bolted up for a third time after a noise from Charlotte's room was heard. Again, Mary had to insist that he not go in to check on her, as it would reinforce a bad habit. He agreed begrudgingly and sat back down.

"So, what for you now?" Rafeo asked, honestly curious. He knew of Christian's skills and knew that he would need his help if Mabus were to be dealt with.

Christian tensed up again and sat forward; Mary did as well.

"Not saying you need to make that decision right now," Rafeo said defensively. "All work and no play," he finished with a shrug.

"I need some more time to figure this all out, but I hope you'll stay on with us in the meantime; you know, to help me," Christian remarked.

"Of course," Rafeo answered with his disarming smile.

"One thing I had thought of; those outposts," Christian said tentatively. Rafeo was excited that Christian was still thinking in terms of the mission and Mabus.

"All those supplies and weapons; we could collect them and distribute them among the other Magi." The idea was sound, but it felt like an attempt for Christian to let Rafeo down easy; either way, he had to admit it was a good idea. They knew of three outposts, and surely there were more.

"Perhaps in a day or two; maybe." Christian stopped and looked at Mary. He smiled as she squeezed his arm. "Maybe we could make a supply run and rendezvous with the Magi. Once we get to an outpost, we can search Charlie's database for the location of others. Then we can go, or the Magi can go, and check them out, or I can help, or whatever." Christian was unsure of either decision.

Rafeo told Christian when they met the Magi. If they could form a fighting unit, they could face Mabus head-on. The weapons from the outposts would go a long way to helping them win.

Rafeo told Christian over the years that Mabus and Constantine gathered their strength from the power of prayer and faith channeled to them from their followers. It was like food, or more accurately, a power source. If they could kill enough of the Savages, it might weaken Mabus to the point that Constantine might be emboldened to make a move. Getting the two deities to fight was the best hope for mankind. Maybe then the world could be fixed.

"Perhaps resting will help clear everyone's head," Rafeo offered. They all exchanged glances, and each had to admit that fatigue had taken them. Without a word, they each stood.

"I think sleep would be a great idea." Mary's voice was scratchy from the late hour. "Rafeo, let me show you to a guest room." She led the old man down the hall, leaving Christian alone in the living room. Mary's house was a far cry from the simple farmhouse he had come from or the cold but secure surroundings of the outpost. He could barely remember being in a real home.

The silence swirled around him, different from the security of the outpost. He had always been slightly on edge, weary of an attack that never really came. The farmhouse was the same; he knew at any minute the rains could come.

Here in the Citadel now, he felt a sense of security, despite the attack the night before. The automated defense system would have eventually taken care of the Savage threat, even if he had not gotten involved. The feeling was foreign to him, and if he was honest, not something he could see himself getting used to. He felt conflicted and could remember so vividly vowing to never return to the city after being rejected, even by his family. But he had a family of his own. His daughter did not deserve to grow up in the wilds of the world outside these walls.

Mary walked into the kitchen and stood behind Christian. They both stood silently before Mary turned gently to Christian to face her. "So, all that time we were together at the outpost, you never told me your real name?"

Christian turned back and leaned over the sink, both hands on the counter. "When I was cast out, I believed there was something wrong with me. I hated myself for a while. When I got to the outpost, I took on a nickname, but it was more than that. It was an escape from myself. I didn't want you to see the monster." He fell silent, and Mary could feel the pain in his voice.

"Hey," Mary whispered from behind, as she slowly ran her hands across his midsection and up onto his chest. "I think we should go to bed." There was no judgment, no disappointment. She had heard his answer and understood completely.

Christian turned and smiled, realizing it had been over five years since they had shared a bed. Becoming instantly excited and nervous, all at the same time, he followed Mary slowly up a spiral staircase that led to a loft, where their bed awaited. They stripped down and slipped into each other's arms. Sleep found them shortly thereafter, as it had in the days past, safe in the knowledge that they were together again. All other thoughts faded from Christian's mind, and he surrendered to slumber.

Christian slept, somewhat restlessly. His mind raced, leaping from dream to dream. He processed information and allowed his self-consciousness to wander as it needed. The images slipped back in his mind to where Constantine had stopped his vision quest earlier that evening. He saw Balthazar, then Mary, being carried off. As with all dreams, the story was not congruent, but fragmented, and even within his subconscious, he strained to connect the pieces. The next moment, he saw a dam and a city, though the *City* wasn't the right word for it. He yearned to see it again, and the image morphed again; he could see the dam and millions of Savages gathered at its base.

It had to mean something; his subconscious mind was processing information and assimilating it for his conscious mind. Again, he saw the dam, then he saw himself as though he were a spectator in his own story. He was covered in mud and leaves and other debris, camouflaged. Christian snuck into the dam, into the city. Next, the images flashed to row upon row of Savages, ranks of an army. Their faces were those of vile, wretched creatures; then, before his mind's eye, they changed, becoming more human.

Mabus appeared before him, his eyes flaring red. Christian wanted to wake up as his subconscious pulled away from the cloaked figure. As he did, he could see the dam again, spreading out behind his enemy. The dam was the location of Mabus's seat of power; the memory revealing his location. That must have been what Constantine had wanted him to see.

He felt his eyes slowly opening to acknowledge the daylight. His mind was anything but rested, but a little clearer from having processed some information from his memories. He felt a slight unease creep into his conscious mind and turned his head.

"You snore really loud," Charlette giggled, standing right next to the bed watching Christian sleep, her face inches from his own.

"Fuck!" Christian yelled, having been taken completely by surprise. He sat straight up and pushed back away from her until his eyes could focus, until he realized who was at his bedside.

"Fuck!" Charlette said loudly, imitating Christian, but with hardly any facial expressions.

"No, Sweetie." Christian tried to take it back.

"Fuck!" Charlette said again.

"That's not a good word to say," Christian was nearly panicking.

"You have big muscles," Charlette replied and abruptly turned on her heel and headed down the stairs. "The best part was when he said fuck," Charlette said, as she disappeared down the stairs. Christian slumped in defeat.

He felt Mary stir next to him, thinking that he had been at least lucky enough not to have her hear the last exchange. He put on a happy face and rolled over to look her in the eye.

"Good mornin', baby," he said softly, kissing her forehead and brushing her hair out of her eyes.

"Are you done teaching our daughter how to swear like an old sailor." The obscurity of the reference was lost on Christian. He cringed and moved out of the way as Mary sat up. She hopped out of bed and pulled her clothes on.

"That was funny, by the way," she reassured him. "Come on; we need to get breakfast on. I think all the loud swearing woke Raf up, too," she said with a chuckle, and disappeared down the stairs. Christian sighed and reached for his shirt and shorts. In a few seconds, he was downstairs.

"Who was swearing so loudly?" Rafeo bellowed from down the hall, knowingly reinforcing Christian's guilty feelings.

"Daddy," Charlette answered before Christian could form a rebuttal.

"Guess he'll have to make up for it by cleaning

up the breakfast dishes," Rafeo said quietly, wearing a Cheshire cat grin. He walked by and sat on the couch next to Charlette, daring Christian to say something, though he knew he wouldn't, not in front of the little girl.

"Don't push it, old man," he answered playfully, then rushed into the kitchen to help Mary with breakfast and coffee.

Chapter XXI

Christian stood in the kitchen in front of the sink, still wearing his apron from cooking pancakes earlier. The mound of dishes on the counter next to him, yet to be cleaned, seemed like such a daunting task. He found himself staring out the window. The house, as it happens, was across from the farming district, and the kitchen window looked out over a field of cornstalks, and leaves were moving gently in the late summer breeze.

He was still struggling to make sense of everything that had unfolded around him in the past twenty-four hours. "The dam," he whispered out loud, as he crushed the glass that he had been holding in his hand. Christian looked around, confused in the moment as to where he was. It took a few moments before he looked down at his hands. A shard from the broken glass had sliced the end of his finger. He now stood, entranced by the spectacle, as he watched his blood mix with the water in the sink, not knowing how to stop it.

"You're gonna wash the colour off the plates." Mary's voice from behind him seemed to bring him back to the moment, slightly; then he looked around nervously, as she ran her hand slowly up his back. "You've been washing the same glass for twenty minutes," she continued, then stopped short as she saw the blood in the water.

"What is that?" Mary asked, her expression changed from playful to concerned, as she remembered what had transpired for Christian recently. She felt for him, knowing he had lost his memory; he had lost time with her and his daughter that he would never get back. He had, from what she had heard from Christian and Rafeo, spent the last several years living a harsh life out in the wilds, fighting the Savages as though on a crusade.

She had missed him, but he had truly missed out. Mary had to admit that, if it hadn't been for her daughter, she would have wanted to be with him out there, despite the danger and the sacrifice, to have lived and fought the good fight.

Christian forced a smile, more for Mary's benefit. The smile was fleeting, and within a few seconds, Christian's gaze turned back to the window.

Mary quickly reached for a first aid kit and wrapped the wound on his finger with a sterile wrap. Christian barely noticed, but there was no sense in him bleeding all over the kitchen.

"Perhaps some training would help." Mary and Christian turned quickly, not having noticed Rafeo's entrance to the room.

"If not for the activity, perhaps I can knock his head back into adjustment with my staff." Rafeo sounded gruff, but he was truly concerned for the young man.

"Perhaps," Christian muttered, his mind still

clearly somewhere else.

"Why don't you two go? I'll finish up here," Mary said. Now it was her turn to force a smile, though she was more successful than Christian had been. She squeezed Christian's finger, finishing up with the bandage, perhaps the slight pinch of pain brought Christian back to the moment. He bent down and kissed Mary softly.

"Okay, then," he said, and peeled off his apron and handed it to Mary. He jogged past the old man, through the living room, and up the stairs to the loft. In a few seconds, he slid back down the railing, like a controlled fall, dressed and carrying his swords slung over his shoulder. He stopped short once in the living room again and gestured with his hand for Rafeo to wait for a moment. Christian then bent down and kissed Charlette on the head. She barely looked up from her digital tablet, then yelled. "Have fun, Dad," she said, indicating that she had overheard the discussion in the kitchen.

"I'll try," Christian answered. Once opening the door, not hiding his confusion, he continued outside, and Rafeo fell into step behind him. They walked back towards the medical tower and entered a building a block away, the same building where the store was. Once through the hallway, they came to an inner courtyard that was empty and nearly half a kilometer square; large enough for a sparring session, and private enough that they might not attract unwanted attention.

Christian began to stretch, preparing for the challenge ahead. Rafeo stood across from him and took his robe off. Rather than prepare, he leaned on his staff; Christian hated it when he did this.

Rafeo was a master at combat, having had several millennia to hone his skills, but Christian figured that the least he could do was pretend that he needed to stretch. It was one of the ways Rafeo got into the young man's head. Today, however, Christian did not say anything about it.

They turned to face each other, and Christian assumed the high guard, poised with both hands tightly gripping the hilt of his sword. Rafeo, as usual, held his sword with one hand in a very lazy rendition of a low guard. Another tactic by the old man, knowing his lazy approach to combat, enraged Christian even more.

Rafeo gave a lazy nod, indicating he was ready. Christian, though silent, offered a very sarcastic look to the old man, letting him know his attempt to upset him had worked, at least a little. Christian lunged forward, slicing the air with his blade. Rafeo blocked and evaded the attack effortlessly. Christian stopped and spun around to face the old man again.

"So, out with it," Rafeo ordered as he blocked another savage attack from Christian.

"Constantine gave me back my memory," Christian barked, as he swung furiously several times at Rafeo, and each time, his attacks were blocked.

"You had mentioned that," Rafeo answered. "You said your real name was Christian – I knew a man named Christian, nearly a millennium ago," Rafeo said with a smile. Christian stopped short; a memory flashed through his mind. A memory of him being shot, but he did not recognise himself in the memory. The confusion took him out of the moment, and Rafeo capitalized on the weakness; he went on the attack. He cleared Christian's blade and landed an elbow in the young man's chest, knocking him back with a grunt.

"Keep your guard up," Rafeo said as he circled Christian, who raised his weapon and circled. He told the young man, always keep his mind in the fight, but right now, he wanted Christian to work through his memories.

"He also gave me other memories that are not mine. At least, I don't think they are mine. They are from another life," Christian started. He swung his sword in a figure eight. "I can see them, smell them, and taste these images as though they were yesterday, but it was a different time, a different world, many times over." Christian crossed swords with Rafeo and used his slightly larger form to push the old man back, a way of showing some dominance and his frustration.

"The one that I see the most, the world, is like it was, open, free. No walled cities. Cars and people everywhere. We are in a market, and people start to shoot at us.

"We?" Rafeo asked, letting his guard down and stumbling backwards, in the wake of another attack from Christian.

"Yes, we. You, me, Mary, and others who feel so familiar, but I can't place their names."

Rafeo stopped completely and lowered his weapon. "A market, you say." He looked away in thought, turning his back on Christian. "And you say Mary was there." He blocked an attack without even seeing it. Rafeo then turned to look for Christian's continued attack, but nothing came.

They both stood and stared at each other, unaware that a crowd of spectators had gathered around the courtyard and on the roofs of the surrounding buildings.

"What else did he show you?" Rafeo demanded and swung his weapon, catching Christian slightly off guard.

"Everything from the moment I had been cast out of the Citadel to falling from the dam and losing my memory," Christian explained with a grunt, as he drove Rafeo back again with a flurry of blade strokes.

"The dam?" Rafeo questioned as he halted the attack; they stood once again, swords crossed.

"After they took Mary, I tracked them back to where the Savages live." Both men lowered their swords; the conversation suddenly became more important than the training.

"I had only one thought: I wanted revenge." Christian was nearly ashamed of what he had just said. "For all I knew, they had killed Mary, and I would be the reckoning they so deserved," he finished, still breathing heavily from the sparring. "I found them, millions of them, in squalor. They were massed around the spillway of a massive dam. I could smell the stench from the water over a kilometer away."

Christian walked towards a bench where he had put a bottle of water, drank from the container, then placed it back on the bench. He slowly walked back towards Rafeo; his head hung low. As he approached, he looked up; there was a darkness in his eyes, the likes of which Rafeo had never seen. He wanted Christian to finish his story and said nothing of it.

"I made my way into the dam structure; I guess they could produce electricity there, and the Savages held several human slaves inside to operate the equipment." Christian's eyes grew distant as he went back through his memory. "I planted several explosives I had brought left over from the outpost. I wanted to blow up the dam and wash them clean from the face of the earth."

Both men withdrew slightly at the sound of Christian's voice faded from the air around them. Christian was conflicted, his eyes welling up, though he would not allow for a single tear.

"What stopped you?" Rafeo was notably non-judgmental in his response, which surprised Christian a little.

"The Savages." He struggled to find the words. "Those creatures that I had met in battle so many times, the ones that had been relentless in their quest to end my life and Mary's, and anyone else I had known. They were... calm." He turned and paced away from Rafeo. "They even looked like men and women, not monsters. There were children there as well," he explained.

Rafeo had never bothered to seek out the

Savage camp. He never required knowing where Mabus was. He had the Book of Power; he searched for the Guardian. Christian words were difficult to hear. Christian had not come to the worst realization yet; Rafeo feared he may have to tell the young man what was to come.

"Most of them didn't even have homes or shacks. They stood in their place, as if waiting for something; their next order to attack." Christian sheathed his sword, slinging it over his shoulder, before looking up at Rafeo again; the anger and darkness had left his eyes. "I watched them for hours, and couldn't bring myself to do it. So, I left, or at least I tried to." He kicked at a pebble on the ground. "I guess a sentry noticed me, and then I was running for my life. They stopped chasing me after I fell down the cliff on the far side of the dam. That's when you found me," he said with a smile.

"Indeed," Rafeo confirmed. "I damned near killed you too, mistaking you for one of them." Rafeo laughed.

"Not exactly how I remembered it. We fought, but you didn't almost kill me, old man," Christian answered in jest, a desperate attempt to change the mood.

"We shall see!" Rafeo yelled and leapt into the air, his sword poised and aimed right at Christian. The young man drew both swords, crossing them to catch Rafeo's blade between them with a renewed burst of energy. Christian attacked; his swords moved like a blur, both finding their targets each time; Rafeo had to use every ounce of his mastery and strength to block the attacks. The thought of a counterattack was not possible under the assault he faced.

Sparks flew from the blades as they clashed and dragged across one another. The crowd had gathered and was on their feet, and moved closer to see the display they had never seen before.

"If you had blown the dam, you would have crippled Mabus, you know," Rafeo yelled over the fray.

The words enraged Christian again, and his attack became feral and more powerful.

"I didn't know that then," Christian yelled, as though the words would defend him. Christian was overcome with emotion. "Don't you think that decision is ripping me apart right now? Yes, it would have ended this, but at what cost?" Christian screamed; his eyes flared. Rafeo could see the internal conflict within the young man. He also felt the attacks he faced getting stronger, as Christian's rage built to a crescendo. Christian lashed out, spinning and thrusting his swords. The one sword connected with Rafeo's, knocking it out of the old man's hand, and the second blade sliced through his throat. There was a spray of blood, and Rafeo dropped to the ground. The shriek from the crowd was the first time Christian had noticed that other people were there.

The young man dropped his swords and fell to his knees next to Rafeo's body. He felt like a monster, having believed that blowing the dam would have been the right thing to do.

As he knelt and tried to regather his composure, Christian watched a pool of blood grow under Rafeo., Christian began to hear people's voices around him for the first few moments. They were hushed in horror, having just witnessed what could only be described as a murder.

Christian stood and turned to face the others; he put his hands up defensively. "It's okay." He tried to calm the hysterical crowd. Seeing that it wasn't working, he walked over to Rafeo as two robotic security droids rushed in behind him.

"You must surrender to us." Christian heard the mechanical voices but couldn't mistake the sound of weapons being loaded behind him.

Christian looked back down at Rafeo, noticing the pool of blood shrinking beneath his fallen friend. Christian's head cleared from the thoughts of Mabus and focused on the new problem he faced. The security droids were known not to be trifled with.

"Get up, you big baby," Christian said quietly through pursed lips. His comment was intended only for Rafeo, lying at his feet. Christian planted the biggest, albeit completely fake, smile on his lips as he raised his arms and turned slowly to face the droids.

"He's fine!" Christian smiled, hiding his emotion as though his would somehow sway the robots from arresting him.

"You will surrender to us," the droid said again.

"That won't be necessary, will it?" Rafeo grunted as he got to his feet, all evidence of an injury gone from sight. "I'm fine. We are sparring, training," he explained. Christian had never been happier to hear the old man's voice.

Several seconds later, without so much as another word, the droids lowered their weapons, turned, and left in the direction they came.

"I was thinking about letting you spend the night in a cell, but you'd probably only seduce your jailer, again," Rafeo joked as he put his hand on Christian's shoulder.

They both burst out laughing, then made their way to the bench and sat down. The laughter only lasted a few seconds, and the courtyard was left in silence again. Christian drank from his water bottle. They were both thinking the same thing: what if Christian had blown the dam?

"Constantine and Mabus did not come by their power knowingly.' Rafeo broke the silence after a few minutes had passed. "They were fighting when the power, a beam of energy, meant for the Guardian hit them instead."

Christian sat up and turned to look at Rafeo, with a puzzled look on his face.

"I should know; I was there," he snickered. "Almost twenty-five hundred years ago. The sight of my true and utter failure that has cursed me to walk the earth until I fix it."

"I think that's why your memories are a little scrambled. Constantine tried to restore your memory, but as he doesn't know the power he wields, I think he gave you memories from all of your past lives," Rafeo finished, and stayed quiet, allowing Christian to think about that.

Christian thought back to the image of his face in the historical records he had seen back in the outpost. Was that a coincidence? It could not have been. If that had been him, if he had lived that life a thousand years ago, could he have lived other lifetimes?

They gathered their things and prepared to return home. Christian slung his swords over his shoulder and waited for Rafeo to put his robe back on and take up his staff. Christian looked around the courtyard and was happy to see that the majority of the assembled crowd had left. His eyes scanned around the rooftops, then back to the doorway they had entered.

He noticed a man walking towards them from the doorway; this triggered another flashback in his mind. He saw himself in the market again, amidst a gun battle. One of the people with him was the man who now walked towards him. Christian winced as the flashback took him over, but straightened up as it subsided, just as the man-made eye contact with Christian and waved.

"I would know those swords anywhere," he bellowed, then reached out his hand to embrace Christian.

"Son of a bitch. I never thought I'd see you again," Christian yelled and hugged his friend. They released their embrace.

"Gabriel" Rafeo nodded, then turned to make

sure he hadn't forgotten anything.

"You'll have to forgive me, Gabe. The other night, at the church must have seemed pretty strange. I've been having memory issues." Christian explained.

"You must come with us. Mary will be so happy to see you," Christian suggested.

"I'd love to join you; we have much to discuss," Gabriel answered, and the three of them walked from the courtyard.

Chapter XXII

They walked down the quiet streets of the Citadel, back towards Mary's house. It was difficult for Christian to see it as his home just yet.

"Did you know we were here, or is this a chance meeting?" Christian asked to break the silence and to distract himself from everything else. Gabriel chuckled and shook his head.

"Yeah. You guys were sparring in my back courtyard; I live right there. I just looked out the window, and there you were. What are the odds?" he chuckled again.

"Really?" Christian stopped walking and looked at Gabriel, trying to imagine the odds of happening upon Gabriel in a city of over fifty million people.

Gabriel let him dangle for a moment before his laughter overcame him. "No, of course not. The media was all over the attack the other night. I saw you on the stream; Rafeo too. I knew I had to find you."

"Oh, yeah, that makes more sense," Christian said and shook his head. He giggled slightly, feeling quite gullible at the moment. They continued walking, and within a few minutes, they arrived back at the house. Mary met them on the front step, "I guess we are feeding the neighborhood," She teased.

"After all the excitement the other night, a rumor that Constantine had made an appearance, I figured I'd better come check on you all." Gabriel hugged Mary after joining her on the front stoop.

"And Kelly? She's okay?" Mary's voice faded.

"Yes, she is fine. Everyone from the outpost made it here and is safe, thanks to you both," Gabriel explained, more for Christian's benefit than anything else.

"Oh, do come in," Mary insisted, after looking around. They could talk more in the comfort and privacy of the house. They filed in and sat on the couch.

"Well, thanks to Master Rafeo." Gabriel continued. "After that last battle when Mary was taken, we all stayed in the bunker, terrified. We had just watched you die..." he pointed to Christian, "...along with the other Magi, or so we thought." Gabriel cleared his throat and continued, "We saw those creatures carry you off," he said, looking back at Mary. "None of us knew what to do." The room fell silent for a moment before Gabriel continued.

"The next morning, Master Rafeo met us at the door. He promised to get us here. We did a quick but cautious search for survivors, but only found Tyriell alive."

"Tyriell" Christian said his name with a hushed and shocked tone. That night the explosion had been so violent; they were amazed anyone had survived.

"Master Rafeo escorted us here, then left us at the gate to go after you. But that was a few years ago. Never thought I would see you again, Quick." Gabriel finished his story and sat back a little. He looked the couple up and down, as though looking at a miracle.

"Oh, it's Christian, that's my real name, but either will do." Christian's face wrinkled slightly, betraying the tinge of guilt he had for lying about his name to everyone.

They all exchanged a smile. This had brought back some painful memories, but they were also elated and relieved to learn that Christian was getting his memories back.

"I woke up in a pile of rubble with a head injury I probably should have dealt with, but instead took off in search of Mary. I tracked the savages that had carried her off. Found myself at their main camp." Christian struggled; he was still putting everything together. He fidgeted in his seat but continued.

"I found no trace of Mary, managed to fall, and hit my head, completely losing my memory. When I woke up, I was on a farm with Raf. Couldn't remember my real name – a real mess." Christian had a hard time keeping eye contact with anyone.

"That is why I seemed like I didn't recognize anyone at the church the other night, I guess, cause I didn't." Christian cleared his throat and looked up at the others. "Which raises a question – what the hell were you all doing outside the walls?"

"We had gathered all the Magi we could find and were planning,.." Gabriel started but was cut off as Charlette bounded into the room and jumped into Christian's lap. Mary nodded her head as if in answer to the question Gabriel hadn't asked.

"Wait, he knew? You knew she was pregnant?" Christian turned from Mary to Gabriel. The other man bowed his head, feeling guilty that he had never told Christian, but then neither had Mary.

"I was the closest thing to a doctor in the whole group. She wanted to make sure the baby was okay, and she was," Gabriel explained, then smiled at Charlette.

"What's your name?" Charlette demanded, as she stared back at Gabriel.

"My name is Gabriel," he answered, smiling a little more.

"Mom, I'm hungry." Charlette changed the subject as though she didn't want the answer to her Question. Gabriel smiled even more at her innocence. Mary paused, smiling as well. There had been much good news this day.

"Yes, dear, supper time," Mary sighed. "Gabriel, you will stay?" Mary hadn't left any room for him to disagree. Gabriel smiled and nodded.

***   ***   ***

Dinner had been wonderful. It had been one of the small but notable pleasantries since coming to the Citadel, food was readily available. The steak was fresh and grilled perfectly, falling off the rib bone, salad, cheeses, fresh fruit, and best of all, wine.

They had all finished eating and sat quietly,

sipping their wine. Shortly after she had finished, Charlette got up from the table, announcing she was going to play. Christian gave her head a rub as she walked by. He looked around his table and felt how he did as a child, before being cast out, in a normal family. The thought unsettled him greatly, as he fidgeted in his seat. Christian suddenly felt a need to do something. He was just about to bound from his seat when Gabriel, noticing Christian's strife, blurted out: "I know why it rains when the Savages attack." He had wanted to wait for Charlette to leave the room.

Christian froze and stared at Gabriel, who seemed to be comfortable here. Gabriel was a father, a husband, a regular man, but he was anything but a regular man. Christian had left much unfinished, and the last thing he wanted to do was give up his life at the Citadel. But at the same time, he knew he had to do something about Mabus. This was the route of his internal struggle since he had gotten his memories back. He knew what he wanted. He knew what he had to do, but didn't know how to choose.

"You had said something about the water samples," Christian straining to remember the conversation he had previously with Gabriel.

"The rainwater contains a powerful hallucinogenic neurotoxin that is incredibly addictive. The neurotoxin is absorbed through the skin, or any mucus membrane, and it turns those susceptible to it into those Savage creatures we have come to fear." Gabriel stated.

The room fell silent. Each of the others needed

time to process the information, particularly Rafeo. It explained so much. Mabus needed the energy from his followers to add to his power, and he had taken steps to ensure he would have as many followers as possible. It had been thought that it was purely a question of faith.

Rafeo stood and walked slowly from the table as he processed the information. All these years, he had blamed humanity for allowing this to happen.

"And the people in the Citadels, they're immune?" Christian spoke in a hushed, though enraged tone. Rafeo turned back to the table to hear the answer to the same question he had formed in his mind.

"The only people who are immune are the Magi," Gabriel answered. "My preliminary data shows that less than one one-hundredth of one percent of the population is immune. And only less than fifty percent of those are even aware that they are immune. They would have been cast out of the Citadels, or, if they were born within the ranks of the Savages, they may have escaped or been killed by their parents."

Christian's memory flashed, being thrown from the city gates. Christian stood and leaned on the back of his chair. He gripped the spires at the back of the chair so tightly in anger that everyone could hear the material stressing under the pressure of his hands.

"And the rest of the people in the Citadels?" Christian growled, aware that Gabriel had side-stepped the question earlier. Christian had been looking at the floor, and looked up to make eye contact with Gabriel.

"Daddy, I want a glass of water," Charlette spoke up from her bedroom, as if on cue. Christian looked at Mary, his anger draining almost instantly. Silently, he walked into the kitchen. He filled a glass with water and took it to his daughter. The thoughts of facing Mabus left his heart completely as he gave the girl the glass. She had no understanding of the conversation going on in the dining room, nor did she need to. His place was to be her father, protecting and raising her, like any normal father.

Charlette finished her drink and gave the glass back to her dad, and she hugged him. His eyes welled with tears.

"Come on, young miss; you should brush your teeth and get ready for bed." He led her to the bathroom. Charlette closed the door, wanting her privacy, and Christian returned to the dining room.

"There is something in the food and water here, and it blocks out the neurotoxin in the rain." Christian heard Rafeo say as he re-joined the conversation. The old Magi must have pieced it together.

"Correct," Gabriel answered, trying to smile. Before Christian could continue the conversation, the door to the bathroom opened.

"Dad, come tuck me in," Charlette ordered as she walked across the hall. Christian turned and walked back into her room, the conflict within him diminishing.

"You all settled in, Miss?" he asked, walking into her room. Charlette wiggled her way a little deeper into her blankets and smiled.

"Yup, all ready," she answered. Christian leaned down and kissed her on the forehead.

"Are you gonna fight the monsters again?" The question was innocent, but it struck him completely off guard. He thought about it for a moment before he answered.

"Not if I don't have to, and they better hope I don't have to," he said, playfully made a fist, and smiled at Charlette.

"The best part was when Constantine fixed us, the light was cool," she blurted out. Christian cocked his head.

"Okay, good night, Daddy," she said and turned on her side. Christian slowly backed out of the room, turning the main light off at the doorway, leaving her night light on. He slowly walked back to the dining room; he would speak to Charlette in the morning about the incident at the church. He looked at Gabriel, smiled, and walked back into the dining room.

"But?" Christian said as a hint for Gabriel to continue their conversation from earlier. Gabriel knew he wasn't going to let him off that easily; he couldn't stifle the sigh. "But, there is also a highly addictive mind-altering substance in the food and water here in the Citadel, and I assume in the others as well," Gabriel finished. The room fell silent. Christian lowered his head as though in defeat, then looked up and nodded as though hearing it spoken out loud made it better.

"Is there anything we can do with this info, or are we just talkin' here?" Christian asked after a moment to recompose himself.

"Well, actually, I've been working with one other scientist. We believe we have developed an antidote that will nullify the neurotoxin and that we can use rockets to seed the clouds. The re-agent would mix with the rain and leave the Savages self-aware and quite confused."

"Would also leave Mabus weakened tremendously," Rafeo added. He was excited by the prospect. Mary had moved from her seat and stood next to Christian, cuddling into him.

"A good defensive strategy, if they were ever to attack the city eon-mass." As Christian spoke, Rafeo realized Christian was out of the fight. Rafeo couldn't blame his young friend. Rafeo knew he couldn't ask the young man to return to the impossible mission, fighting a god. Despite his suspicions, Rafeo was already trying to justify losing Christian's help. "And in that moment, Mabus could be weakened, and maybe even eliminated." Rafeo didn't register what Christian had said. His mind was occupied.

"Neurotoxin – huh; makes sense, I guess. Can you blame them?" Rafeo asked.

"Damn right I can," Christian spat back. "Both of them, actually; it would have been noble for Constantine to put an inhibitor in the Citadel water, but as soon as he developed his neurotoxin, he became as guilty as Mabus."

"They are trying to hold onto a power that isn't theirs, they want to survive, just the same as any other man."

"Any other man?" he had said. Christian had known Rafeo long enough to know there was more he had to say, but he was having a hard time getting it out.

As if on cue, Charlette's voice came from the bedroom. "Daddy, there's a monster in my room." She didn't sound distressed, but Christian looked at Mary, returning to the role of a father in his mind. He smiled at her. "She asked for you," Mary said with a grin.

Christian shrugged, then turned and walked down the hall. he had not bothered with his weapons as he had in the past at the first mention of trouble.

"I'm sure there is no monster in here, young Miss," he said as he opened the door to her room. He was taken aback slightly at how Charlette was sitting very still on the edge of her bed, her window open behind her, the curtain billowing slightly in the evening breeze. The hair on the back of Christian's neck stood on end slightly, just before he heard the voice from behind him.

"Oh, but there is." The voice lingered in the air like tar on a hot roof. Christian spun round, reaching for his sword that wasn't there.

"Balthazar," he whispered. They stared each other down for a moment before his enemy burst from the corner where he stood in the shadows. Christian met his attacker, grabbing his arms, when another Savage he had not seen clobbered him over the head, knocking him unconscious.

The others heard the commotion and rushed down the hall to the bedroom, finding only Christian, sprawled out on the floor, and an otherwise empty room.

***   ***   ***

Christian awoke sometime later, his head pounding, his mind racing. In a way, he felt relief, as this certainly provided some clarity to his path.

"Balthazar," he said, as he became fully awake. Rafeo was distressed over the mention of that name. He reached between Christian and Mary and pulled Christian out of bed.

"Are you certain of that name?" His eyes were ablaze in a way Christian had not seen.

"Yes – how could I forget?" Christian answered and watched as Rafeo withdrew slightly.

"You said he was disfigured, his left arm shriveled?"

"Yeah – and an open wound across his chest was still seeping. Who is he, Raf?"

Rafeo turned to look out the window as if lost in his thoughts. "He was one of three who started on a mission nearly twenty-five hundred years ago. But he was killed, I swear, or else I would have looked for him – I would have saved him."

"Raf? Who the hell is he?" Christian demanded.

"He is a Magi – like me. Rafeo, Quintus and Balthazar. We three were the heralds of the Book of Power would restore the Guardian."

Christian had heard this before, but figured it was just a bedtime story. It had only really gained credibility in the last few days. He had seen Rafeo sustain several mortal wounds and recover as though they were nothing. He had Constantine magically return his memories. Maybe this wasn't a "bedtime story" after all. Maybe, all that had happened had been for a reason.

"Gabriel: you need to get those rocket delivery systems ready," Rafeo was barking orders like a man on a mission. "Mary, rally the other Magi to meet us at the Lima Charlie outpost."

Christian had to admit he was a bit surprised by the last statement, more so by the fact that Mary was not caught off guard.

"And you." he looked into Christian's eyes. "You, come with me."

***   ***   ***

Rafeo led Christian through the streets, back to what remained of their wagon in a garage. He had been met by a man at the door to the shelter. They exchanged no words, just a nod before Rafeo entered and removed a locked strong box from the foot well of the wagon. They entered a small cellar door and down a ladder. The room opened up slightly, and Christian could see another door at the far end of the room, which he believed to be their destination.

Once they were through the door, they were

met by a series of seven passages in front of them. Rafeo did not hesitate, heading straight towards the passage, third from the right. It led them down several stairs, several hundred feet down. The air grew cold and damp as they descended.

Finally, the narrow stairwell opened into a large, cavernous room like an underground rail system center.

They continued across the large open area and through another door on the far side.

"Is this from the world before?" Christian asked as he looked around the area.

"Yes, a subway station. I think this may be how Balthazar was able to get into the Citadel, but this was built over something much older," Rafeo explained, but did not go into detail.

"So, we are going after them?" Christian asked excitedly.

"Not directly."

"But they have my daughter," Christian yelled, his voice filling the large area they were in, but was silenced by Rafeo stopping and spinning in place to stare him down.

"But first, I need to give you the power you need to get her back; I need to complete my mission that I started two thousand four hundred and eighty-nine years ago." He spun and carried on through the door. More stairs headed down. They passed through history, through the corridors that followed; the deeper they went, the older the buildings were.

Christian was fascinated with the history had he not been singularly focused. The next opening was slightly smaller and looked much older. The designs were carved into the stone. It was unlike anything Christian had ever seen before.

The large hall was circular, rising in the center to what looked like a type of altar. There was an area all around it, which may have accommodated a congregation at one point. A series of large stone pillars formed a circular pattern matching the curvature of the walls. The pillars were ornately decorated with various carvings. The shape formed almost a large "T," the pillars widening at the top to a large head on the far side of the room, carved from rock that formed the outer walls.

Rafeo paused, placing his hand on a box. He opened the container and removed a very ancient-looking, large leather-bound book from it. He held the book in his left hand and placed his right hand, palm down, on the leather cover of the book. Rafeo lowered his head for a moment, and Christian could see his lips move briefly.

Christian reached into the box and pulled out a smaller leather-bound book, which he recognised as Rafeo's old journal. He had read it cover to cover several times, mostly when Rafeo was asleep or away from the house. He had read about different people Rafeo had believed to be the Guardian throughout the centuries. Some he had been wrong about, others he had lost before knowing for certain.

Christian had read and felt the torment dripping from the pages. He had seen the wisdom and experience gained by a man who was nearly twenty-five hundred years old. After a moment, he looked up at Rafeo. When the old man moved his right hand from the book, multiple torches were situated around the room, ignited, and illuminated.

Rafeo led them directly onto the altar, where he stopped and turned to Christian. "I told you earlier that I knew a man named Christian once before."

Christian nodded.

"He had a friend named Gabriel, and a woman that he loved; her name was Mary." As Rafeo spoke, Christian felt the hair on the back of his neck rise.

"Together, nearly nine hundred years ago, we fought to stop Mabus from destroying peace talks in the Middle East. We struggled to usher in a period of peace for mankind, and in doing so, I came to learn that Christian was, in fact, the Guardian, the one I had been searching for. Two and a half millennia have passed since I failed him, and in doing so, sentenced the Guardian to live in human form until I could find him and restore him to his power."

Rafeo paused and looked into Christian's eyes. There was a look of love, like a father and son, but also honor between true brothers. Christian arms were covered in goose bumps, and he was short of breath in anticipation.

"And tonight, after so, so many years, I will finally complete my mission," Rafeo explained and handed Christian the book. Rafeo then stepped back two paces and bowed, keeping his head down.

"Come on, Raf." Christian objected. "I'm not

some '*Chosen One,*' that's gonna save the world, I just want to save my daughter." Rafeo looked back up and smiled before he answered. "Saving your daughter." He paused and looked the young man in the eye. "Indeed," he winked and bowed again.

"Come on – you think I'm this guy? This Guardian?" Christian shook the journal to emphasize his point. Rafeo silently nodded, knowing this, on top of everything else to come to light in recent days, would be hard for this young man to come to terms with.

"How many times have we had this conversation, Raf?"

"Never," Rafeo answered quietly.

"Okay – not you and I, but you and the other Christians!" Christian left no room for semantics.

"Four, maybe five times," Rafeo quickly spoke.

"Four or five times." Christian scoffed, kicked the dirt, and turned his back on Rafeo. After only a few seconds, Rafeo could see Christian's shoulders lower and some of the frustration leave his form. The young man turned back around and looked at his old friend.

Christian looked slowly around the chamber, as though there would be something etched into the wall that would help him. He stood silently contemplating everything he had experienced in his time. "So we have done this before?" His back was to Rafeo, and the echo made his soft voice difficult to hear, but it did not take the fear out of the words.

"Yes, that is true." Rafeo's voice was meant to

soothe, but neither could imagine anything that would help in this moment.

"What do you think will make this time any different?" Christian turned to face his old friend so he could see the strain in his face as he tried to come up with something. It took a moment before Rafeo's expression turned to a slight smile. "'Cause I know nothing on this planet will stop you from getting Charlette back."

The words sent a chill down Christian's back. Rafeo could watch as the resolve filtered through Christian's blood, and the young man's face became like stone with determination. He turned and moved back towards the center of the room.

"I imagine it's probably been harder on you than it has been on me." Christian smiled and returned to where he had been directed by Rafeo. The old man nodded, trying not to get caught up in memories.

"Let's uh, let's do whatever it is you are gonna do." The calm expectance was undeniable in Christian's tone. He looked cautiously at the book, then back at Rafeo. The room fell silent. Christian felt a veil fall over him, though something separated him from reality. Through it all, he heard a faint whisper that he dismissed at first as an echo of his imagination. The whisper repeated, becoming more obvious and more insistent. The voice beckoned him to open the book. Christian hesitated, looked at Rafeo, then focused on the book in his hands, and slowly opened the cover.

The first page was covered in writing of a language he had never seen before, but he studied it carefully. As he stared at the page, the ink began to rise off the page as though it was still fresh, still liquid, and it began to move, alive, forming English words right before his eyes. The pages glowed, and the words then began to leave the pages. The letters flowed through the light as leaves floating on a stream. The liquid letters danced across his skin, forming words that were absorbed into Christian's flesh. He was bathed in the light, and Rafeo watched as every page emptied itself onto and into Christian.

Christian began to lift from the ground, the light becoming more intense, then suddenly going dark, dropping him back to the ground. He stood motionless for a moment, then began to look around as though confused. He leafed through the book, noticing the blank pages, but feeling the same.

"Um," he said slowly. The old man looked at Christian; his confusion matched by the younger man.

"Did it work?" Christian asked while scanning his arms and lifting his shirt to see if any words remained on his skin.

"I do not know for certain, we've never done this part before," Rafeo sighed.

"How can you be sure?" Christian continued to look himself over.

"If it had, I assumed I would be gone; no human body was meant to last twenty-five hundred years, and if it had worked, you wouldn't need to ask," Rafeo explained with a grimace.

"I fear that the book was just a catalyst, an absorption of knowledge that prepares you for the power of the Guardian, but others have said power."

"We will have to go get it back," Christian finished his sentence.

Without another word, Christian led Rafeo back out of the complex towards the surface, the same way they had come in.

Chapter XXIII

"Are we gonna walk to the outpost?" Christian asked as they emerged from the underground passageway. Rafeo placed the strong box back into the wagon before he stopped to answer Christian's question.

"No. I have a surprise for you regarding that," he said as he rummaged through a few boxes in the back of the wagon. A moment later, he emerged holding a rather impressive-looking weapon. It was the same weapon he had used a few days back, firing on Mabus from the security tower. He walked around the front of the cart and handed the weapon to Christian.

"No, that's not the surprise," Rafeo said sarcastically. He then turned on his heel and led Christian out of the garage.

Once outside, Christian came face to face with two waiting recon rigs. These vehicles were flying motorcycles, similar to the one he had found at Lima Charlie Outpost. He grinned when he saw them.

"Oh, thank God!" Christian released his breath. He hadn't realized he was holding and looked at Rafeo. "I didn't want to walk to Seattle again."

"Come on," the old man shouted. "We're

behind schedule."

Christian hesitated; he looked at the vehicle, ran his hands over the controls, but did not move from where he stood.

"Is there a problem?" Rafeo asked.

"How do I do it?" Christian asked hesitantly. "You saw it, the book thing, it didn't work." Christian hammered his fist down on the side of the vehicle next to him, then turned slowly to look Rafeo in the eye.

"How am I supposed to save the world?" he whispered, feeling defeated before they started.

Rafeo stood tall and looked his friend in the eye.

"You don't have to save the world; you need not even try," Rafeo spoke quietly. "All you need to do is save your daughter." As usual, Rafeo's wisdom was all that Christian needed. "All that other stuff – the Guardian – who or whatever else you are, forget about it all for now. All of that can wait."

"Thank you, my friend," Christian stared into Rafeo's eyes.

"Come, lad. Your daughter is waiting," Rafeo answered, then swung his leg over his ride.

Christian straddled the bike and fired it up. Rafeo took the lead, vectoring almost straight up in the air until high above the top of the Citadel walls, then cracked the throttle to full. Christian did the same, and both vehicles blurred out of sight. The craft, capable of accelerating so quickly that it felt like the wind and G-force would pull the drivers out of their seats, but both men held on. They hunched down behind the controls in an attempt to stay out of the wind. They stayed at an altitude of less than one hundred feet, traveling over three hundred kilometers per hour.

"We should be there in just over three hours," Rafeo said over the coms in their helmets.

"Not bad." Christian loved speed. The fact that he was able to escape and enjoy the moment was a good sign to Rafeo. Christian pulled up next to Rafeo with a grin.

"It took me just over three weeks the first time to get a handle on this machine," Christian finished in jest.

***   ***   ***

They arrived at the outpost just as the sun was coming up. Christian did a circle around the island to check the area over to familiarize himself with what had been home for so long. He then floated onto land next to Rafeo, just to the side of the main building. He got off the bike and pulled out the weapon Rafeo had given him.

"So, how does this work?" Christian asked.

"There's a lot of really boring science stuff behind it, so it's easier to just show you." Rafeo directed Christian to walk over next to him.

"I want you to think that you want to blow up that building over there," Rafeo told Christian, pointing to a building on the other side of the island.

Christian looked at the building and shrugged.

"Okay - And then what?" he asked.

"Pull the trigger," Rafeo said smugly.

Christian pulled the trigger, and a barrage of swirling cluster rockets burst from the weapon, shot across the island, and destroyed the building. Christian looked at Rafeo with a surprised but impressed nod.

"Now use fire to burn these weeds down," Rafeo indicated an old garden patch that had been overgrown with weeds. Again, Christian pointed the weapon and pulled the trigger; a stream of flame erupted from the barrel of the weapon, burning the weeds.

"Very nice, yeah; blowing stuff up is always better than boring science stuff," Christian said with a grin. Before anyone could speak further, their attention was drawn to the south, and the sound of an approaching vehicle, possibly several. Christian stepped away from the outpost to get a better view. Three older but military-grade transport ships came into view. Rafeo walked up next to Christian seconds later and looked south as well.

"Ah, looks like Mary had some luck," Rafeo said as if he knew exactly what was going on. The three ships came in and circled the outpost, landing to the north of the building. The ships were quite large once they were up close; each running over thirty meters in length. Once on the ground, a hatch on the side of each opened, and people began to emerge from the ships. Mary came out from the one in the middle. She ran over to Christian and kissed him.

"You seem different," she said after being released from his embrace. "You okay?" she asked.

"What do you mean? Yeah, I'm fine," he said with a smile. Not realizing the experience with the Book of Power may have changed him physically.

"I don't know, taller or bigger somehow; it's weird," she went on, but then stopped and turned to the crowd that had amassed behind them from out of the ships.

There had to be over one hundred people in each ship; all dressed similarly to the group they had met in the old church that night after leaving the farm. They all had on the best body armor and tactical gear they collected and saved from the ruins of the world before. Though somewhat rag-tag in appearance, the resolve in their eyes as they assembled, waiting for direction.

"The Magi?" Christian asked Rafeo, who was reviewing the troops assembled.

"Indeed, they are," he answered quietly. "And they will want to hear from you."

Christian turned and jogged towards the front door of the outpost. In a scene familiar to him, the building seemed to come to life; lights turned on, and a scanner grid ran over his body. Seconds after the main door opened, Christian disappeared inside.

"Christian?" Charlie's familiar voice came over the speakers inside, as all the lights came on.

"Yeah, Charlie, I'm back," Christian said with a

grin, as he ran towards the roof hatch ladder and bounded up and onto the roof. He walked out towards the edge, where he could see the entire group assembled on the ground.

"Charlie, can you amplify my voice? And project a map of the spillway for the hydroelectric dam to the northeast of us, here?" Christian asked as he placed his arms behind his back and looked at the group on the ground.

"I ah," Christian began, adjusting to hearing his voice over the speakers that Charlie had set up. Everyone on the ground tilted their gaze upwards and solely focused on him.

"I would like to thank you all for coming. I'll get straight to the point." Christian shifted to the left and pointed at the map Charlie had projected.

"Mabus has taken my child, and I'm going to get her back. To that end, I will be making a frontal assault on a Savage stronghold, as shown on this map." As he spoke, another older military ship could be heard on approach, and Christian watched as Gabriel piloted his smaller vessel to land next to the small fleet now assembled at the dock.

"We have the plan to release a chemical agent into the rain that will counteract the neurotoxin that makes the Savages – Savages." Christian indicated Gabriel's ship, equipped with what looked like a crop duster rig under it.

"The creatures we all know as Savages; each of us has probably encountered at least one of them." Christian watched the crowd for the vast majority to nod in agreement. "They are not Savages by choice. The rain generated by Mabus contains a chemical that fuels their rage and addicts them to their cause, effectively making them slaves. The result? Their rage in turn fuels Mabus," he hesitated, giving time for the others to assimilate the information.

"We are going to free the Savages, which we hope should leave the combatants that we encounter greatly diminished, and their leadership weakened. I will then go alone to rescue my daughter." He could hear murmuring ripple through the crowd.

"I would never be careless with your lives. All I ask, that you take up positions at the top of the spillway banks to cover my approach and escape." He indicated several points on the map where the Magi would have the high ground and be able to fire toward the enemy forces in the trench below.

"As you know, the Savages do not use ranged weapons, or any technology, so a small number of riflemen should be able to level the odds, even against their vastly superior numbers." Charlie provided a cheap animation to go along with Christian's plan on the fly.

"If they press your position, do not stay on the ground. These ships will provide a firing position that the enemy cannot get to." As he spoke, the hair on the back of Mary's neck stood on end. She could feel the energy of the people assembled, their courage seemed to build more and more as Christian spoke.

Christian could feel it as well. His spirit was inspired, his strength seemed to bubble within him, and his confidence was bolstered in a way he had never felt before. He had never seen himself as a leader.

"I will approach on foot, attempting to get as deep into the enemy camp, undetected. Once inside their borders, you will be providing a distraction and cover fire that should enable me to accomplish my mission: to save my daughter."

As if unable to control themselves, the crowd let out a roar of cheer. They were excited to take the fight to the Savages.

"Stay at a safe distance and choose your targets carefully. Just don't shoot me or my daughter, and we will be fine." Christian finished and raised his arm into the air, which brought another cheer from the crowd. He turned to go back down the ladder, then paused; he decided to jump down from the roof. He landed, feeling a renewed strength in his legs.

Gabriel had made his way through the crowd, and Christian walked towards his friend.

"I hope after all that, you have your reagent ready to deploy?" Christian said with a smirk.

Gabriel nodded and smiled. "You bet," he said and stepped to the side. A young woman was behind him; Christian took a second but recognized her almost instantly.

"Kelly?" He was taken aback by how much she had matured.

"It's me," she said quietly and hugged him. "You gonna kill Mabus?"

Christian noticed that many around them had turned to hear his response to this question. Christian looked at Rafeo, and the old man nodded.

"Kill the bad guy, save the world? I'm just one man. I don't even know if he can be killed," Christian answered, loud enough to address the crowd. "I'm just going in there to get my daughter. Saving the world may have to wait. Or maybe." his voice fell silent, as he thought for a moment, bowed his head as the words came to him, looked up and smiled at those gathered around him.

"Maybe that's how we win; that's how we save the world by looking out for that one person who needs us, by choosing for ourselves to do the right thing, only because it is the right thing to do. We lead by example and fight the good fight, not for fame or recognition, but to inspire one another. When we stick together and choose to care for one another, how can evil stand a chance?"

A hush fell over the crowd. Kelly stepped forward and hugged Christian, then turned and left with Gabriel to prepare for their flight. Christian caught a glance from Rafeo amongst all the faces gathered around him and could feel the warmth of his smile from across the tarmac. Slowly, but purposefully, the Magi returned to their ships for a final equipment check.

Walking back to the outpost, Christian put on the familiar augmented reality goggles. He grabbed the portable computer interface and placed it in a pocket on his vest. He secured his swords over his left shoulder and slung the hand cannon that Rafeo had given him into a large hip holster on his right leg.

"You know we could just blow the dam and be done with it," Rafeo said as he walked into the facility and grabbed one of the rifles left in the shelter.

"I'm not going to murder millions. They are slaves, and I will set them free," Christian objected. He had considered it, but for the same reason he couldn't bring himself to blow up the dam all those years ago, even for revenge, it would prevent him from doing it now, even to save his daughter.

"This plan will work, you'll see," Christian gave Rafeo a reassuring slap on the shoulder as he walked past him, back to the door. Rafeo stumbled backwards from the blow. Christian stopped short and looked with concern at his friend.

"You okay, there, old man?" Christian asked, keeping his concern in check.

"Yeah, I just feel ..." Rafeo trailed off. "Maybe I'm coming down with something. I'll be fine," he insisted.

Once back outside, Christian saw the others had loaded the speeders into Mary's transport. She had received confirmation from the other ships' commanders that they were ready to depart. Christian and Rafeo jogged up the ramp and into the ship, and the ramp closed behind them. Instantly, the ship began to lumber slowly into the air.

The fleet made its way to the first checkpoint five kilometers from the river valley. At this point, Gabriel broke off, gaining altitude, getting ready to seed the rain clouds over the Stronghold. The other vessels would drop Christian off and wait for him to cover the rest of the distance on foot.

Christian kissed Mary deeply. "Don't worry, this is gonna work," he told her to reassure her, having felt her tremble as they kissed.

"I know, just be careful," she warned. Christian smiled and nodded at Rafeo, then bounded down the ramp and sprinted away from the ships.

The sky darkened quickly, and Christian was running in the rain.

"You are feeling okay, babe?" he soon heard over his headset.

"Yeah, I feel great! Why do you ask?" Christian said as he jumped from the ground to the roof of a house. He chose to take the high ground as he passed through the remnants of a city just south of the dam site. He stopped and thought about that for a moment before carrying on.

"Cause our equipment shows you traveling at a speed of forty kilometers per hour, and did you just jump over four meters vertically?" Mary's voice was concerned.

"I think so," Christian answered with a shrug. "I feel great, though."

"I bet," Mary said quietly to Rafeo, who was also watching the monitor with awe. Perhaps the encounter with the Book hadn't been a complete waste.

Christian had covered the five kilometers in under ten minutes. He was barely breathing hard as he stopped on the edge of the river valley to look around. The floor of the valley seemed to move from the number of Savages that were huddled on both sides of the river. There weren't many structures in the area, and the Savages concentrated closer to the dam. The larger buildings were closest to the dam, and he figured that's where Charlette would be.

Christian continued across the top of the valley at an incredible pace. He drew his one sword and used it on several occasions to deal with sentry units he came across. The Savages barely had time to see his approach or react.

Christian keyed his coms. "I'm in position; gonna need that distraction now. Gabriel, what's your timeline?"

"About ten minutes out," Gabriel answered, just before Mary replied. "We're on our way."

"Ten minutes should do it," Christian acknowledged to his friend. He then waited, and within two minutes he could hear the rumble of the ship's engines. The Valley seemed to come to life, with Savages rustling and getting stirred up to meet whatever was coming towards them.

In the disorder caused by the approaching ships, Christian launched himself down the hill towards the building where he expected to find his daughter and his enemy. He had grabbed a scrap of sheet metal and used it as a surfboard to slide his way down the hill; it was more like a slightly controlled freefall. At the bottom, his momentum carried him at great speed toward the building; any noise he made was masked by the approaching ships.

Nearer the building now, he leaped over five meters to the first level roof and sprinted across its surface until he was at the center structure, which rose like the center of a stronghold or keep. He pulled out his hand cannon, took aim at the roof, and pulled the trigger; this time it fired a rope and grappling hook, just as he had desired. The hook lodged itself on the roof, and he felt his weight transfer from his legs to his arm as the weapon winched him upwards towards the roof. At the top, he landed and sprinted to the other side. From there, he could drop down to the balcony below, which he assumed Mabus would use as a reviewing stand to survey his minions.

Christian dropped to the balcony and kicked the door open. He cautiously walked into the room that was shrouded in darkness. He squinted, hoping his eyes would adjust more quickly to the low light as he slowly walked in. The A.R. glasses engaged a form of night vision, illuminating the surroundings for him. He was amazed at how much the distraction being made by the others was working, as he had met with little resistance.

"Daddy?" Christian heard Charlette's voice before he saw her, but within a second or two, his eyes had finally adjusted to the point where he could identify her, sitting in a cage at the foot of an ornate thrown. The chair was decorated with bones and skulls of humans. Christian then saw the eyes, glowing in the dark, the cloaked and hooded figure was almost one with the darkness, made of energy. So dark in fact that the light-intensifying effect of the glasses was useless to penetrate the shroud around the figure.

"Mabus," Christian whispered and cautiously drew his hand cannon. He walked slowly to the center of the chamber.

"I'm guessing since my daughter is still alive, that you want to talk," Christian said, and as he spoke, he could feel the tingle in his hand, indicating his weapon was receiving input and readying an appropriate ordinance.

"Yes," Mabus's voice boomed throughout the room. "You have been a particular pain in my ass," he spoke, as he slowly stood from the chair. He didn't seem to stand as much as float, but where his feet contacted the floor, there was a visible discharge of energy, like electricity passing from Mabus to the ground.

"So, I thought I would offer you one last chance to join me. This offer will not last long. I will need an answer now." He floated over to the right side of the room. Along the wall, he had several other beings, people, strung up. He reached the first body and held out his hand; a red glow could be seen flowing from the body to Mabus's hand.

Christian took the opportunity to fire a small, silent volley at the cage that held his daughter. The round hit its target undetected, and thousands of tiny robots, nanites, spread out from the point of impact and began dissolving the cage. Charlette had let out a slight gasp, but Christian held up a finger, gesturing for her to keep quiet. Christian kept his eyes focused on Mabus, searching for a reaction, but all the while he moved slowly closer to Charlette's location.

"You and your daughter will live like royalty,

of course," Mabus finished, before turning back to face Christian.

Christian slowly lowered his weapon and slid it into its holster. He continued his slow approach towards the cage, using the guise of considering Mabus' offer to stall and get closer to Charlette.

Chapter XXIV

Rafeo had positioned himself on top of the ship, lying on the top of the craft so he could add his rifle to the ship's weapons as they fired on the Savages below. Several others had joined him, turning the ship into a floating barrage.

He had watched Christian specifically and provided cover on his approach to the main building, while the others had randomly fired on any target of opportunity. Rafeo watched as Christian moved at inhuman speed to his objective, then dropped down nearly thirty feet from the roof to the balcony, seemingly uninjured, and walked into the darkness within.

Rafeo now looked to fire on any troops that would rush into the building to stop Christian from escaping. Much to his surprise, there did not seem to be many of the Savages heading to the aid of their master. Perhaps another drawback of reducing his followers to mindless Savages. They weren't smart enough to come to Mabus' aid, or he didn't feel as though he needed them.

Rafeo scanned the chaos, then felt his strength wane and his stomach turn as he zeroed in on one face in the crowd. It was someone he had not seen in a very long time.

"Balthazar," he said in a whispered tone, shocked.

Rafeo got to his feet, struggling against the movement of the ship, and made his way to the roof hatch. He clambered down the ladder and into the cargo area. Rafeo keyed the coms port on the wall, hailing the bridge.

"Mary, I need you to open the main hatch; I need to take one of the speeders," he said in as even a tone as he could. Mary was sitting in the co-pilot's seat, trying to operate weapons systems and targeting scanners. She went numb for a second.

"Is he okay?" she asked, swallowing her fear.

"Yes," Rafeo answered, as straight as he could. "I just have something I have to do."

Mary didn't like that he would not be covering Christian anymore. Assuming that it must be pretty damn important, so she pushed her doubt aside and keyed the main hatch to open.

"Godspeed," she said. The sentiment was not wasted on Rafeo. He chose not to answer, though he wanted to reassure Mary. He did not have the words; his mind was elsewhere.

"Godspeed, indeed," Rafeo repeated to himself, leaping onto the speeder. He blasted out of the cargo hold and raced towards Balthazar.

***　　　　***　　　　***

"I do not like to wait," Mabus's voice boomed again, as he turned to face Christian, his eyes glowing even brighter. "What say you, boy?"

Christian took another moment to think.

"Well, I," Christian started casually, as if to throw Mabus off, then in a blink, he raised his weapon and fired several volleys, striking Mabus with each round. The weapon had produced multiple metal rods that impaled their target, effectively anchoring Mabus to the wall behind him. The rods then proceeded to emit an electrical discharge to the area of contact between Mabus and the wall, resulting in a tremendous light show. Christian watched for a moment and secretly hoped the process was painful at least, but recognized this would not hold him for long.

Christian scooped up Charlette with one arm and sprinted back towards the balcony. A horde of Savages burst through a large door to the right of the thrown, having been held off by Mabus until the moment of Christian's attack.

Christian made it to the door of the balcony and fired once more from his weapon. This time it produced an explosive round. He holstered the weapon and leapt from the balcony just as the explosive blast ripped through the throne room, collapsing the roof of the building.

The blast was epic; large enough to vaporize the pursuing Savages, and then bring down the entire building. The resulting blast wave propelled Christian away from the area, deeper into the sprawling spillway settlement.

He was able to make a controlled landing,

surprising even himself. He swung Charlette around to his back.

"Wrap your legs around me and hold on tight to my vest," he yelled, indicating the webbing straps he was wearing over his jumpsuit.

"The best part was the explosion," she answered. Not worried at all about their current circumstance.

"Yeah, that was pretty cool." Christian took a moment to answer before he drew his weapon and sprinted away. He intended to try to make it to the waterway, figuring at least that the Savages wouldn't pursue them into the water. Now, only a labyrinth of shanty shacks and thousands of Savages stood in their way.

***   ***   ***

Rafeo landed in the middle of a courtyard just behind the main building, stepping away from the vehicle.

"Balthazar!" he yelled, attracting the attention of hundreds of Savages, along with his old comrade. The Savages moved in on him, then stopped as Balthazar bellowed.

"Wait!"

They all stood for several seconds, motionless. Rafeo was trying to believe his eyes; the Savages were longing to rip him apart. Finally, Balthazar raised his right arm and pointed to the building behind him.

"To the master," he ordered, and as a horde, the Savages rushed from the courtyard to the main building, leaving the two Magi alone.

"I thought you were dead," Rafeo whispered. The two walked towards each other slowly.

"I wish I was," Balthazar answered quietly. "For almost two hundred years I lay at the bottom of that chasm, bleeding to death but unable to die, starving to death but cursed with immortality," he spat. Rafeo's face drooped as he began to understand the suffering Balthazar must have endured.

"I could not call out, not that anyone was anywhere near that deserted spit of land. I lacked the strength to climb out, though I did try. My first fifty attempts were in a desperate need to help you; I feared you were in danger, brother."

"Indeed, I had my hands full. I did not know that he had forged a weapon from the nails that had held Christ to the cross. The Guardian should have destroyed them or reclaimed those artefacts after he regained his powers from that event." Rafeo was defensive. "I figured your wounds were mortal, and I had to go."

"After the book!?" Balthazar cut him off, finishing his sentence. He drew silent again, rubbing the wound that was still present across his chest from that day nearly twenty-five hundred years ago.

"But that is not the worst of it," Balthazar went on. "Eventually, Quintus came back for me. He must have known I was alive." Balthazar moved a few paces closer to Rafeo and stopped. Rafeo could see him tremble with rage.

"He and Mabus tortured me for another

hundred years, until I gave in." Both men had tears in their eyes now.

"I am so sorry, brother. If I had known," Rafeo's voice trembled.

"The hour is far too late for sorrow, brother." Balthazar's voice was cold and harsh as he drew his sword and dragged the tip in a half circle across the cobblestone; the sparks were visible despite the rain.

"I don't wish to fight you," Rafeo said, putting his hands up.

"Good, then you can die," Balthazar grunted, then lunged through the air, driving his sword from overhead to cleave Rafeo in two.

Rafeo managed to step forward and catch his opponent's wrist. "Please, we need not do this." He bade Balthazar to stop, but to no avail.

Balthazar managed to raise his shriveled left arm and slap Rafeo in the face, which was enough to break his grip, more by surprise than anything else. Balthazar managed to slice Rafeo on the left upper arm as he fell away. Rafeo landed and somersaulted backward to gain his footing again. He looked down at the wound on his arm, expecting it to heal as wounds like this always did, but this time, nothing happened.

"So, you have a weapon touched by the blood of the mortal Guardian," Rafeo figured, as the wound failed to heal.

"In fact, no," Balthazar answered, holding up his bandaged right hand. "I injured myself earlier today, and it did not heal." Balthazar picked up his weapon once more and watched Rafeo draw his sword.

"It looks like, for whatever reason, this is to be a final fight... for one of us," Balthazar laughed.

***   ***   ***

Christian managed to make it halfway to the river. He came to a halt as he entered an open area in the shanty town. Charlie's voice came over the coms as his heads-up display indicated he was about to be surrounded.

"Mary will try to cut a path to the northwest to get you to the river, but you are about to be swarmed," Charlie warned. Christian told Charlette to hop off his back and take shelter in one of the nearby shacks.

"When it's clear, we'll have to get out of here fast, but stay hidden until I call for you," Christian instructed her, as she ran across the open ground and hid in one of the unassuming shanties. She made sure she found a small opening, so she could watch the action.

Within seconds of Charlette reaching cover, the Savages poured in from every direction, like a flood. Christian heard the explosive rounds from Mary's ship landing to the northwest; he put them to his back, knowing he was covered at least from that direction.

He opened fire with his weapon from his right hand while using his blade in his left hand to deal with any enemy who got too close. I Savages fell by the hundreds, and for a moment, even Christian believed he could do it, that they would not escape this nightmare. The bodies piled up several feet high as the oncoming Savages would crawl over their fallen, desperate to reach their prey. Even explosive ordinance could not keep them all away.

Within thirty seconds, they were too close to use the cannon, and Christian dropped it back into the holster, in favour of two swords. There were too many of them, and the Savages were soon upon him. Christian disappeared under the waves of enemies.

Mary watched as Christian disappeared; she tried to see his life signs on the monitors, but there was no data. After several seconds, the torrent of Savages subsided, and they retreated from the area, revealing Christian's broken, lifeless body lying face down in the rain.

Mary's hands went limp, her eyes welled with tears that streamed uncontrollably down her cheeks. She felt a glimmer of hope as the scanners picked up human life signs from the area. Charlette was still alive, at least for the moment.

"There is no way this is over, Christian." She lowered her head and began to shiver. After several seconds, she looked up quickly. "CHRISTIAN! You have to save our daughter," Mary cried.

***   ***   ***

Charlette's view was obstructed by the multitudinous creatures swarming the area. After several seconds, she noticed the commotion outside the shack had slowed, and the Savages were retreating. Charlette's next view was that of her Father, lying face down in the rain; the water all around him growing more and more red.

Charlette was frightened and crying, unable to take her eyes off her father's body.

"No," was all she could whisper, repeatedly. Each time, the word took on a different meaning to her. "No" in disbelief and shock soon turned to a "No" of defiance. In her mind, in her heart, her father couldn't die.

***   ***   ***

Rafeo and Balthazar crossed swords again, each man's fatigue beginning to show. Their struggle had lasted much longer than either man could believe. They were at the point of leaning on each other just to stand, the strain and fatigue caused by their fight were almost more than they could bare.

Both men were unaccustomed to feeling weakness. They stood, heaving chests, trying to breathe deeply, their lungs and muscles begging for oxygen. Rafeo felt Balthazar's strength waver slightly. Was the fatigue taking its toll, or was there more to it?

Rafeo saw his opponent's expression soften, though slightly, it was noticeable. Rafeo had a moment of retrospect, recalling his old friend to be reasonable, even in unreasonable situations. Balthazar had always been a gentle spirit, peaceful. Rafeo allowed himself to hope that maybe, if this was to be their end, perhaps Balthazar wanted to meet it with a clear conscience.

The sudden absence of sound from the distant battle caught both of their attention. The sound from the guns had stopped. The ships were no longer firing, nor were the Magi on board.

"Oh. Perhaps the fool has finally fallen," Balthazar's voice dripped with contempt.

Rafeo used his other arm to punch Balthazar in the face, knocking him backwards while laughing hysterically, as though the pain from the blow was enjoyable. Rafeo took the reprieve to look around, and indeed, the weapons on all the ships had gone silent.

Before either man could say another word, both were brought to their knees by pain or sickness; uncertain of the cause, though it was clear, something was not right.

***   ***   ***

"No!" Charlette said again, this time much louder. Without thinking, she rose from her position and walked to the opening of the shack. She was still concealed by the shadows, but her voice had caught the attention of some of the Savages nearby.

"No!" she said again. This time her tear-filled eyes fixed on her father's left hand; it just moved.

***   ***   ***

"No!" Mary had repeated herself several times. She got up from her position, peeled off her headset, letting it drop to the floor, and wandered into the cargo hold. Many of the other Magi joined her in the hold, each had the same dishevelled look on their faces. Mary opened the cargo bay door again as the ship floated closer to where Christian lay dead.

"No!" Their voices were in unison, similar to a chorus. Each repeated their chant, voicing their belief in the man they had all come to know through story, reputation, or by meeting him. Whatever they knew of Christian, they believed that he would rise; they believed he could save his daughter; they believed in him.

As they stood in the opening of the hold, Mary saw a faint yellow glow from where Christian had fallen. It began as faint as a firefly, barely noticeable, but with each passing second, the glow was getting brighter.

Christian's body began to rise off the ground slowly, and the yellow glow around him began to intensify. The Savages that were withdrawing from the area stopped, and stared at what was unfolding before them.

Words began to form on Christian's skin as his body rose higher and higher in the air. He opened his eyes as more words scrolled across his face, moving into his eyes. The glowing light that encapsulated his body was undeniable now; it was difficult to look directly at him as the light coming from Christian could rival the sun.

The Savages in the area began to bark and howl, whether from fear or defiance; they were in a frenzied state.

Charlette had walked out into the open, though not a single creature moved against her. She stood only a few feet from where Christian had fallen, looking up at her father and smiling.

Christian looked at her and winked, pulled his swords, formed a cross with the blades in front of him, and slowly lowered himself back to the ground. He stood and took a deep breath as the Savages cried out in unison, howling in shock and disbelief. The enemy gathered and slowly began to advance on his position again.

"You are all really fucked now!" Charlette yelled at the top of her lungs to the approaching Savages, her face beaming, grinning ear to ear. This brought a wave of silence; the creatures were caught off guard by the girl's defiance.

"Charlette! Christian bellowed.

He stopped the Savages in their place, causing his daughter to jump slightly.

"Language," Christian said with a slight grin, then pointed for her to get back into the shack. She ran as fast as she could back to her hiding spot, giggling slightly.

Christian stood motionless, beckoning them to attack, daring them to try. There was a moment of hesitation.

The creatures had a hard time understanding what they had just witnessed. Soon their programming took over as the Savage's began to advance, again.

Christian waited until he could smell their sour breath, then released the glowing energy that had built up around him, knocking the creatures back in every direction like a tidal wave. Their lifeless bodies fell into messy, bloody piles. Without hesitation, Christian ran to the shack and dropped to one knee. "Come on, kiddo," he said, and Charlette ran back to him and hopped up on his back.

"The best part was when you weren't dead," she said and hugged him from behind.

"Thanks, little lady, I like that part, too," Christian answered, then resumed his sprint towards the river.

***   ***   ***

Mary felt her strength return. She turned to the others, smiling uncontrollably. She was met by looks ranging from surprise to elation.

"Did you know he could do that?" one of the Magi asked her.

"No, but I believed he could," Mary answered and smiled warmly.

"We still have a mission to complete," she said loudly. She headed back to the cockpit and could hear excited cheering behind her from the others.

Mary jumped back into her seat and put her headset back on. She brought the targeting scanners online, again, and watched Christian on the display, moving even faster than before towards the river.

There was a crackle over her headset, then a voice came through.

"What the hell was that bright light?" It was Gabriel. Mary had begun to fear that he would not make it here on time.

"Gabriel, thank the maker. Where have you been? You're a little late to the party," Mary exclaimed.

"Yeah. I had something chasing me, shooting lightning at me, and thought he had me, too, until he just disappeared a few minutes ago," Gabriel explained.

Chapter XXV

"Sorry, I'm late," Gabriel yelled over the noise in his headset.

"We can still make this work," Mary explained. "We've hit a snag, but Christian got past it. I bet he could use it for the Savages to stop chasing him right about now."

"I'm starting my run from the north," Gabriel explained, then his mic went silent. Mary turned to her right to try and see Gabriel, but he was deep into the cloud cover.

"Wait," she said, as a thought occurred to her. "Did you say the lightning guy just disappeared?"

"Yeah, 'bout two minutes ago, now. That's why I'm late; I was trying to lose, whatever that was. Why?"

"Then that must mean," she said slowly, and turned back to the fray in the valley below.

***   ***   ***

Christian had reached the river. He kicked a small board free from the roof of a nearby shanty and dropped it right next to the bank.

"What's that for?" Charlette asked as she

climbed off Christian's back.

"That is going to be a raft; we are gonna float down the river. Time to get the hell outta here," he smiled, then placed the board into the water, and held it still for Charlette.

"Come on, hop on." No sooner had her feet landed on the board than Christian had lost his grip; the board and Charlette were carried away by the current. Christian had been knocked clear by a huge bolt of lightning beside him.

"Daddy!" Charlette screamed, falling flat on the board while being carried away by the current.

"It's okay, baby; I'm right behind you." Christian had gotten back on his feet, running back to the water's edge to try and help Charlette, then turned and watched Mabus walk from the epicentre of the electrical blast.

"Oh, I'm afraid it is anything but okay!" Mabus yelled the last word for dramatic effect.

"Christian, Gabriel is about to start his run, but watch out, I think Mabus is coming for ..." Mary's voice was overrun by static on the coms.

"Yeah, I see that!" Christian tried wiggling his earpiece, knowing it wouldn't help restore the channel. "Can you get to Charlette?" he asked, but Mary wasn't going to get the message since he heard nothing but static in his ear. At least Charlette was safe on the water.

"Hey, glow stick, you made it." Christian tried to show he wasn't afraid of Mabus. "I thought I had you back there, but you are a slippery little bastard, aren't you?" As he spoke, he could hear Savages approaching his position. He considered jumping into the river and escaping, but running wasn't on his mind. After what had happened earlier, he felt as though he should stay, though he had a good chance at winning. He could hear the report from Gabriel's ship as it flew overhead; he looked skyward, hoping to see his friend, but could only see bursts of light from the charges. The rockets, if noticed, might easily be mistaken for more lightning. Christian grinned and turned back to Mabus.

"My followers will tear you limb from limb," Mabus grunted.

Christian looked around at the Savages; he noticed many of them began to twitch, then convulse, some even falling to the ground.

"Yeah. They tried that earlier, but I'm like a bad penny, I guess," Christian said smugly. He was emboldened by what was going on around him.

"What have you done?" Mabus dropped from his stance, floating just above the ground; his whole body looked like it was shaking, and weak.

Christian turned to the crowd around them, completely turning his back on Mabus.

"You are all free now; the rain is washing the poison from your veins and your minds. You are free to choose for yourselves," Christian's voice thundered through the valley. He could see most people around him straighten up, their eyes cleared, and their breathing slowed.

"Gabriel! It worked; it worked!" Christian hollered into the coms.

"Don't sound so surprised," Gabriel answered. "Oh! By the way, I picked up Charlette; she is a great little co-pilot."

Christian didn't have time to enjoy the thought of Charlette testing Gabriel on every control in the cockpit, and then choosing her favorite one. Instead, from behind him, he heard a devilish laugh. It started quietly and grew louder, and more horrible sounding, like thunder, the sound which would make you crawl under your bed as a child.

"Well played," Mabus chuckled, as he rose to his feet, then resumed floating just above the ground. "But I think you are about to learn a hard lesson about the true nature of man," he laughed again.

Christian turned to face the crowd surrounding him. He could see that in some cases, a few were running up the sides of the valley, trying to escape this place, but nearly the entire lot remained ready to do their dark masters' bidding.

"Now, stop me if you've heard it." It was Mabus' turn to be coy. "But my followers *will* tear you limb from... limb."

Christian could feel time slow all around him. r.

"Constantine," he said aloud.

***   ***   ***

Rafeo and Balthazar were in trouble. Rafeo fared slightly better than Balthazar in light of the ancient wound the man still endured. They were both succumbing to mortality. "Leave me, I don't deserve your help." Balthazar tried to throw Rafeo back, but the old man held fast. They were trying to crawl up the side of the valley. Rafeo knew that the dam might burst, and he wanted to try to get out of there. He hoped he could see Christian one last time.

"I left you once, my brother. I will not do it again," Rafeo said with a smile. "If we are to die, then we will die together."

The two held each other's gaze for some time. At that moment, Balthazar was overcome with all that he had done. Madness or not, torture or not, he should never have given in, he should never have lost his hope.

"I am sorry, my friend," he said gravely, choking back tears.

"As am I, old friend," Rafeo smiled. "Now, put some effort into it, you old fool; I don't want to die here, today," Rafeo barked, spurring them both on.

***   ***   ***

Everyone that Christian could see was again frozen in place and time.

"He is too strong for either of us, I'm afraid." A portal opened from thin air, and after a moment, everyone watched from their statuesque poses as Constantine stepped through. He walked through the portal and joined the conversation as though he had been there the entire time. "If he destroys me, he could take my power and add it to his own. He would destroy the Citadels with a thought," Constantine explained to Christian.

"It's about time, nice of you to drop by," Christian said, with some contempt. He quickly understood what was going on. He could see the horde starting their rush towards him, but they all appeared frozen in time.

"But together." Christian was cut off.

"I'm sorry, but it is up to you. It is taking all my power to do what I have done." Constantine smiled, but it did not last. "You had the opportunity once before but chose not to do it; you took pity on them. But I believe they have proven unworthy of that kind of love."

Christian looked past Mabus. He was also frozen in time, to the dam in the distance. In his mind's eye, he suddenly saw five distinct areas of the dam. Critical areas where he had placed explosive charges all that time ago.

"Those charges," Christian whispered to himself. Even when freed from the addiction, thanks to Gabriel's science, these people were still choosing to serve Mabus. Christian knew what he had to do, not out of malice or spite, but out of necessity. He nodded to Constantine.

Constantine released time, but before he disappeared, he used what power he had to drive the Savages back and away from Christian. In the confusion, Christian drew his cannon; again, he felt the tinge in his hand. He watched as Constantine vanished back through his portal; his energy was nearly completely spent. Christian took a deep breath and spun towards Mabus. As he did, the cannon unleashed a volley of rockets that spread quickly, completely going around Mabus.

"Young fool." Mabus laughed again. "You had your shot! One opportunity, and you completely missed me."

Christian let out the breath he was holding and holstered his weapon.

"You know, for a guy who claims to be omnipotent, you sure have a problem seeing the big picture," Christian answered as flippantly as possible. Before Mabus could even turn around. The dam in the distance erupted into flames and hellfire. The rockets found the explosives that Christian had set years ago. The dam burst in its entirety, releasing billions of gallons of water that rushed into the valley. The power of the water was unmatched; the noise it made was louder than anything Christian had ever heard. The rushing water washed away all in its path from the face of the earth.

Christian turned his gaze momentarily to the crowd around them; every man, woman, and child in the crowd was now running frantically away, giving every last effort to escape the destruction that would be upon them in seconds.

"No!" Mabus yelled. He took flight to try and stop the water. So many had already died, and he could feel his power draining.

Christian could think of nothing better to do, so he settled for flipping Mabus off. He knew he had survived earlier that day through some form of miracle, but had no idea if he would again. The water rushed ever closer, and he closed his eyes, trying to make peace with what was to come. If nothing else, Mabus would be dealt a blow he may not recover from. His family, his friends would be safe.

"This is gonna be close, get ready." His coms were working again, and Mary's voice was screaming in his ear. He looked around frantically and saw the lights from a speeder blasting towards him from the other side of the valley.

"Too close, babe; peel off; you won't make it," he answered her calmly.

"No," she answered.

"Think of your daughter, our daughter. She will need you after this."

"No!" Mary yelled louder. "She will need both of us, damn it. Now, maybe you could use those super-powered muscles of yours and jump towards me, to cut the distance down."

Christian smiled. She was determined, and he thought it best to at least try. Christian stepped back slightly and took a run at it, pushing off from the edge of the bank.

He soared through the air. To the untrained eye, he appeared to take flight. His timing was perfect; his hands grasped the weapons rack on the side of the vehicle a split second before the tidal wave crashed over the area.

Christian clung to the side of the speeder, trying to take in the scope of what he had done, justifying his mind. He could see the writing on his skin like tattoos, reminding him that there was a greater power, perhaps a greater purpose at work here. He had faith that it was all for the greater good, and he could take solace in that.

The speeder was being splashed from the spray of a wave, the vehicle compensated and rose above and carried on towards the other bank of the now raging river beneath them. Mary looked at Christian and smiled through her tears.

"I told you," she said, helping Christian climb aboard.

"Yes, dear."

"Now isn't that easier; no arguing, just yes dear," Mary said playfully, as her relief overcame her. She giggled uncontrollably as Christian rubbed her back to try to soothe her.

"Yes, dear," he answered quietly, then leaned in and held her tightly around her waist. "The best part was when you said, "super powered muscles." Christian used Charlette's line playfully.

***   ***   ***

The wave washed away tens of millions of souls that day. The power that they offered Mabus was taken with them, leaving the enemy weak.

The craft slowed as they approached the far bank. They could see Mabus fall from the sky and begin to crawl; his best effort in his weakened state, to get away. Just past him, he could see Rafeo and Balthazar carrying each other, but still able to intercept Mabus at the end of their swords. Gabriel landed and trained his gun on the former immortal, while Charlette watched from the cockpit.

Mary and Christian hopped from the speeder before it stopped moving, guns drawn. Mary kicked Mabus as he crawled, knocking him onto his back. Christian rushed just past Mabus and took Rafeo by his other arm, propping both men up. He and Balthazar exchanged an awkward glance.

"It's okay, Christian; he is my burden," Rafeo explained. Christian could hear the resolve in his voice, weak though it was.

"What's wrong with you?" Christian asked.

"Our mission is over; the book has been delivered to the Guardian. Our bodies won't last," Rafeo explained.

"But it didn't work," Christian said bluntly. "Shouldn't I be able to ascend or whatever? You can't go, Rafeo; I'm not ready to be alone. I don't know what to do."

"Why don't you start by ringing the last bit of your power from this asshole's neck?" Gabriel said, slamming Mabus back to the ground after he tried to stand and get away.

"It doesn't work that way." Another weak voice came from behind them. Constantine had dropped through another portal, still weak from his earlier efforts.

"We still both hold residual energy from all those years ago. Even if you kill us, the energy will die with our mortal form. You would never recover all your energy, and therefore, never ascend."

Christian thought for a moment, and drew his sword, holding the tip of the blade to Mabus' throat. "That doesn't mean I *can't* kill him, though, right?"

Mabus squirmed slightly; he could hear the conflict in Christian's voice. He knew the young man was trying very hard to maintain control of his own emotions.

Constantine tilted his head and nodded in response to Christian's question.

The group fell silent. Charlette came out from the ship to take her parents' hands, this simple act reassured Christian despite the circumstances. They all looked amongst themselves, hoping the other would have an idea, an answer. But this could not be fixed now.

"It cannot be done," Mary said, frustrated.

"No, it cannot be done here." To everyone's surprise, it was Balthazar who spoke. "If they could be prevented from stealing the power in the first place." His voice broke, and he violently coughed up blood.

"Yes," Constantine whispered. "Yes. You must go back to the beginning." Constantine perked up slightly, having connected the dots in his mind. Maybe there was a way to fix all of this.

"If I couldn't stop them the first time, why would it be different now?" Christian asked.

"It will," Rafeo said, then dropped to his knees,

coughing as well.

Christian shivered; it was all too much all at once. He looked with concern at Rafeo, his oldest and dearest friend. Rafeo was at death's door, and Christian was not sure if he could deal with that.

His attention then turned to Mary, they made eye contact. She had the look of a woman about to lose everything.

Finally, Christian looked down into the eyes of his daughter. She returned his gaze with a clear and absolute innocence. For a moment, the little girl's smile was able to envelope Christian in the warm glow. For a moment, the rest of the world fell away. For a moment, Christian could smile.

"No," he whispered in answer to a question not asked.

Mary could not contain herself and wept audibly, covering her mouth to hide her relief. It was selfish of her. If he stayed, Christian was condemning the human race to this fate, to this madness. At the same time, in this moment, she didn't care. Christian had chosen her and their daughter. Rafeo, Gabriel, and even Balthazar seemed to understand his decision.

"What?" Constantine's tone was unmistakable. Christian turned slowly to face Constantine, his expression hardening in the time it took him to turn his head.

"I said no," he smiled sarcastically. "There is no way I am leaving her," Christian nodded to Charlette. I don't care what kind of portal you open or where you want to send me, my place is here. I'm a father and a husband." He smiled at Mary, who nodded. "I'm a friend and a leader. I am needed here."

Everyone in the assembly slumped slightly with the realization that this doomed them, but at the same time, none of them could expect or demand anything different. How could they ask this man to give up everything?

Mabus attempted to capitalize on the fact that the entire group was focused on Christian and his daughter. He used all his strength to kick Gabriel in the face, rolling with the momentum of the attack to gain his footing again. He burst into a mad dash, forming a portal while he ran. If he could make it through, then he would be able to manipulate the events of the past; he could steal all the Guardians' power alone and keep it all for himself.

Christian reacted with lightning reflexes, drew his gun, and fired. The rounds found their target, striking Mabus directly in the head; the large-calibre projectiles did not leave much intact. Mabus' headless body dropped and slid to a stop.

"The best part was when his head exploded," Christian said in jest. He looked at Charlette and smiled. She squeezed his hand and smiled back very excitedly.

Before the sound of his voice died from the air, before the smile in his daughter's eyes faded. Christian felt the weight of his decision. He knew if he didn't leave, if he didn't go back and try to set this straight, he might never regain his true form.

Christian dropped to his knees and hugged Charlette tightly. He pulled away after a moment and looked into her beautiful brown eyes. "I just want you to know that no matter what I have ever done, or will ever do." He paused for a moment to collect himself. "The greatest thing I'll ever be is to be your father."

The moment was shattered as Mabus' body stood and carried on its way, attempting to escape. In the shadows, his head returned to his shoulders, seeming to regrow out of nothing. Before anyone could react this time, he opened a portal and disappeared into the folds of time.

The remaining members of the fellowship exchanged a terrified look. Rafeo, though extremely weak, tried to offer a smile to reassure Christian. Though the effort was appreciated, unfortunately, it did not help.

"We can only hope that our counterparts in the past can persevere...this time," Rafeo's words dug into Christian's soul. Perhaps in the same way, the Guardian could not bring himself to destroy the human race even when ordered to by the council of Quies, he could not bring himself to leave his existing family. He would rather die.

Mary moved and took hold of Christian and Charlette. The hug was intense, and Christian longed to be able to stay in this warm, safe, and happy moment forever. He looked down at Charlette, smiled, and then locked eyes with Mary. His smile was warm, his eyes deep with emotions, but as though in slow motion, his expression changed. Slowly at first, but it soon felt as though Christian was ripping open an old wound. Later, his hands slipped from Mary's and Charlette's grasp as he was thrown several feet backwards before his brain could catch up to the reality of the situation.

Constantine had grabbed him and torn him away from his family. As he passed through the opening of the portal, his surroundings changed instantly. The dark skies, overcast with clouds and smoke from the battle, were replaced with a bright blue sky. The rushing water in the river, the desert of the abandoned wastes beyond, were replaced with lush meadows and flowing grass stretching to the calm blue ocean beyond.

Through the portal, he could see Mary and Charlette watching in horror as Christian fell away from them. Their outstretched arms were far too short to reach him. As he fell, he saw a white flash from Constantine's hand that spread out in all directions, covering the entire sky for only a split second.

"You bastard!" Christian yelled to Constantine. The Demi-god turned; his task completed. He disappeared into another portal before the other one had closed. Christian could only watch as he fell away from those he had loved.

He landed with a thump on the ground after falling some fifty feet. He had hit his head and watched through blurring vision as the portal closed, and darkness overtook him.

***   ***   ***

Christian lay in the middle of a green field on

a bed of clover. He didn't know it, yet, but he had arrived at his destination in time, nearly twenty-four hundred years in the past. It was 436 AD, and the world was much different from the world he left behind.

It would be some time before he would regain consciousness.

While he lay there, his consciousness floated from his physical form, and before he knew it, he could see the white cliffs of Dover, then, in a flash, he was blasted across the water and over France. He floated on and on, slowing as he approached an enormous forest. He floated through the trees, watching the light of the sun break through the canopy. He could hear the songbirds and smell the flowers around him like French lavender bushes, Pyrenean scabious flowers, and wild pansies, even the freshness of the grass was a welcome change to the wastelands of the future he had just left.

Eventually, in a clearing, his thoughts floated towards a small village. The huts, mostly made of tree limbs and animal skins, surrounded a central longhouse. Smoke from the communal fires bellowed through multiple openings in the roof of the long house.

The people of the village peacefully went about their day. Some were working the fields, some hunting in the woods nearby, others still, mending the roof on one of the village huts.

His consciousness wandered close by a small group practicing meditative combat forms, something similar to tai chi, maybe; he was uncertain. As his consciousness floated by the group, he noticed a star-like birthmark on the necks of those performing the forms. He was drawn to the only stone structure in the village, just past the group, in the center of the village.

The building had several markings and pictograms adorning the walls. It depicted what resembled rituals or ceremonies, which were nothing he was familiar with. Through the images, he could see interactions between people and someone or something of great power. The powerful being appeared to be female, and her form was bathed in light. The villagers gathered around her, offering items in tribute.

He rose above the building to the top of the dome roof. At its center, there was an opening, which let in almost the only light into the structure. Christian floated down towards a simple altar at the center of the structure.

The only thing he could make out in the low light was a book. The book appeared ancient, leather-bound, sitting on a large single candle. He struggled to get closer, close enough to see the cover.

Christian's consciousness could make out written characters on the cover in a language he did not recognize. He didn't know what the words said, but as he studied the characters for anything familiar, the writing on the cover changed before his eyes. The letters turned to a black liquid and began to move around the cover, as though it were alive. The black liquid grew as more words liquified, then pooled into a large black mass just before they repositioned themselves to form a single word on the cover; that simply read: "Mary."

About the author:

Michael Richardson is intelligent and knowledgeable, with a deep passion for storytelling and a keen interest in world history. His love for research has led him to explore diverse cultures, historic events, and legendary narratives, inspiring him to craft engaging and insightful stories.

With a talent for weaving historical accuracy into compelling narratives, Michael brings a unique blend of intelligence and creativity to his work. His writing captures readers' attention and sparks curiosity about the rich tapestry of our world's past.

His earlier work, The Fall From Grace, will be joined by Rain, Rain Go Away. These are the first two volumes of the Tickers trilogy. The third and final volume will be out in early 2026.

Michael is also the host of the "Love the North" Podcast.